Soul Objective

By

Steve Johnson

Grosvenor House
Publishing Limited

This book is published by
Grosvenor House Publishing Ltd
Link House
140 The Broadway, Tolworth, Surrey, KT6 7HT.
www.grosvenorhousepublishing.co.uk

This book is a work of fiction. Any resemblance to
people or events, past or present, is purely coincidental.

A CIP record for this book
is available from the British Library

Paperback ISBN 978-1-83615-253-8
eBook ISBN 978-1-83615-254-5

stevejohnsonwriting@gmail.com

ACKNOWLEDGEMENTS

"Thanks to my son Robert, for the technical help and the supply of Bounty bars!

To Jasmine at GHP for her patience and guidance.

To everyone who shared their memories of that golden time.

And special thanks to Aretha, Marvin, Diana, Stevie, Martha, Otis and all the other artists whose music fed my teenage soul."

Steve Johnson xx

CHAPTER ONE

UNFINISHED BUSINESS

Wednesday, June 18th. For the third time, Joe stirred the coffee that he was too nervous to drink. He could feel a bead of perspiration form on his top lip and his heart was racing. In all his twenty-one years he'd never felt so tense. But then, in all his twenty-one years, he'd never mentally prepared himself to kill someone. That the person in question was his father undoubtedly added to his heightened state of anxiety. His left hand wiped his mouth whilst his right hand reached into his jacket pocket and reassuringly caressed the grip of the small firearm nestling inside.

A female voice startled him, 'Just can't stay away, eh?'

It was Donna, the waitress who had served him on his two previous visits. Damn. She had seemed really nice, so he'd been hoping that she wouldn't be here working a shift when he returned.

'So, what's your verdict on our city?' she continued, automatically brushing some stray tabletop crumbs into her hand.

'Different,' was his economical reply, not wanting to get distracted by small talk.

'It's certainly that. Are you eating tonight?'

'Not tonight, no.'

'No problem. If you change your mind or want a refill, just holler.'

'I will.'

As Donna took another customer's order, Joe's focus returned to watching the steady stream of human traffic on the other side of the plate glass window. Would he instinctively recognise James Northbridge? Did he share any of his facial features? Maybe he looked just like him. Or maybe he looked nothing like him at all. Soon, he would find out. He glanced up to check the wall clock was showing the same time as his wristwatch. It was: 6.30 pm. Half an hour to go. Presuming Northbridge was a punctual man, Joe figured it would all be over by 7.15 at the latest. And by 7.30, one of two scenarios would have played out: he'd either be handcuffed in the back of a police car, or he too would be dead, shot by some trigger-happy cop. He could see the headline on the evening news: TWO ENGLISHMEN KILLED IN SHOOTOUT AT DINER.

It was the name of the diner that had inspired Joe to pick this establishment for his rendezvous with the man who had torn his world apart. He'd spotted it in the guidebook on New York he'd picked up in England and thought it was the most American sounding thing he'd ever heard. '*Big Dino's Diner, West 56th St and 7th Ave.*' The red neon almost flashed at you off the page. It sounded like something out of the 1950's, and it turned out to look like it too, it's exterior constructed in silver steel to outwardly resemble a railway carriage with the wheels removed. Inside, it was a rock n' roll shrine built of chrome, red leatherette and Formica, with the brightly lit Wurlitzer jukebox acting as the altar. Right on cue, the voice of one of the genre's high priests, Chuck Berry, emanated from the record machine, asking Maybelline why she couldn't be true.

Joe stirred his coffee for the fourth time and checked his watch: 6.33. His t-shirt felt clammy on his lower back as his eyes scanned the moderately busy eatery. It housed the same type of patrons who were there yesterday; an early evening mix of colleagues out for a quick bite after work, the regulars (he recognised three of them) sitting at the counter, and a few loners, desperate for some human contact - *any* human contact.

Thankfully, there were no children present. He'd have hated being responsible for the scarring of any young, developing minds. His attention returned to trying to read the face of every man who entered the diner, or even walked past, and once again he wondered if he'd be able to pinpoint the piece of garbage who had violated an innocent girl of just seventeen. It was the repulsive crime that had resulted in Joe, nine months later. A sardonic grin found its way to the surface as he considered the absolute purity of what was shortly to unfold. The man who had given him life through an act of violence was going to forfeit his own life through an act of violence. It was karma at its finest. Perfect poetic justice.

The British judiciary system had failed Joe's mother, but *he* wouldn't. This oxygen thief, this rapist scumbag, was going to pay the ultimate price for the damage he'd done. The clock now read 6.38. Twenty-two minutes to go until father and son set eyes on each other for the first (and last) time. It would be close to midnight back home. Only he wasn't back home, was he? And he never would be again. He got to thinking how the year that had started so positively had, at its mid-point, turned on him so savagely and placed him here – in a '50's time capsule', three and a half thousand miles from everything and everyone he held dear, with a gun in his pocket and murder in his heart.

CHAPTER TWO

MOVE ON UP

Early indications were that 1975 was shaping up to be Joe Holland's year. In February he'd passed his driving test, at the second attempt. His previous effort had seen him fail on a couple of minor faults, which his instructor suggested the examiner might have overlooked had he been in a better mood. This time, though, when a supermarket trolley rolled in front of the car and he executed a textbook emergency stop, he knew he was going to pass. And so it proved. He was a driver now, with all the opportunities that went with it. For example, it was a well-known fact that girls found lads more attractive if they came with four tyres and a steering wheel. Having his own transport would also be useful for ferrying tools and materials from job to job.

One of the first things Joe planned to do when he could access his late grandfather's inheritance was to treat himself to a decent second-hand motor. That day would be May 17th, on his much-anticipated twenty-first birthday. His party, in the function room of the local leisure centre, had been booked for almost six months. The invites were out, and eighty guests had already confirmed. As had DJ 'The Soul Trader', whose real name was Dougie Pratt, a warehouseman from West Watford. Dougie's knowledge of American soul music was almost as extensive as Joe's, and he knew which tracks would fill the dancefloor. He always started proceedings with Sly Stone's "Dance to the Music", and it built from there.

April saw the second major event of the year for Joe Holland. On the 29th he went to bed as an electrical apprentice and the following morning he woke up as a fully qualified electrician, with a City & Guilds certificate to prove it. Overnight, his wages leapt from twenty to sixty pounds per week. It seemed like a fortune, even after giving his mum a third for his keep. Joe guessed it was how a caterpillar must feel when it becomes a butterfly. And there was more to be earned if he wanted to do a few private jobs at the weekends.

Way back in 1970, when he was two weeks away from his sixteenth birthday and as green as the Incredible Hulk's balls, his mentor, Lenny Coleman, had told him that if he stuck with the apprenticeship and got his ticket, he'd be laughing. That the modern world couldn't function without electricity and demand was only going to increase. Wise man was Lenny.

As April reached its end, Joe's lucky streak continued when word reached him that Linda Palmer, junior wages clerk at Edwards & Sons Electrical, had made it known that she would be receptive to meeting up with him outside of work, should he ask her. Now, this was a major feather in the Holland boy's cap. Linda was the unattainable dream girl for every young (and not so young) bloke who gazed upon her. And she knew it. Long blonde hair. Curvy. She was sex on legs. Very long, very shapely legs. Every Friday afternoon, all the sparks and their apprentices would gather at the firm's head office to receive their pay packets. At 4pm the idle chatter would stop as all eyes turned to the door at the top of the stairs. At 4.01, said door would open and Linda would appear carrying a wire tray full of the small manilla envelopes that contained the employees hard-earned cash.

During the warmer months, she'd wear miniskirts and, when she descended the eighteen steps of that cast iron staircase, for many present it was akin to a religious experience. In fact, one of Joe's fellow apprentices had once confided to him that, if reincarnation was real, he wanted to come back as Linda's office chair. Clearly, he hadn't grasped the concept. It was certainly a strange coincidence that Miss Palmer's newfound interest in Joe coincided with word getting out that his bank account would be ten grand fatter on his upcoming twenty-first. Stranger still (at least to the men of Edwards & Sons) was that Joe chose *not* to ask Linda out. To them, this could only mean one of three things. He must either be blind, gay, or insane.

The smart money was on gay, but in fact he was none of the above. There was no denying Linda's attractiveness but to Joe she came across as a bit of an airhead. Vacuous even. Plus, and this was the deal breaker, during one of their early conversations, they got onto the subject of music, and she'd revealed that her favourite group was The Bay City Rollers. Trying to disguise his horror, he hoped she might redeem herself and asked her what she thought of Aretha Franklin. Her puzzled look told Joe all he needed to know. She'd never heard of the queen of soul. His heart sank like a torpedoed boat as he realised at that moment that they could never be together. Of course, that was his opinion whilst sober; at his party he most definitely would not be sober so, as the drinks start to go down and his brain is relegated to being his *second* most important organ, there was a real possibility that his stance might change. Meantime, he revelled in the jealousy her flirtatious smiles towards him caused.

What neither the lovely Linda, nor many others knew was that Joe already had plans for his windfall. He'd spend up to a thousand on a car and most of the rest was earmarked as a down payment on a flat, or perhaps even a modest house. It was his chance to get his foot on the property ladder. On his skilled man's wages, he could afford the mortgage repayments and Paolo, his best friend, had shown an interest in becoming his lodger.

CHAPTER THREE

RESPECT YOURSELF

Joe Holland and Paolo Massetti had been best friends for almost ten years, ever since they met on their first day at Francis Combe secondary modern school, on September 7th, 1965. At that time, only twenty years had elapsed since the end of WW2 and a deep mistrust of any country who'd backed the wrong horse still pulsed through British society. Being half Italian made Paolo a prime target. In the playground on that warm, late summer day, Tony Henderson, the biggest, and meanest boy in their class cornered the much slighter Paolo and sneered, 'Hey, Massetti, what did your dad do in the war?' His group of hangers on dutifully sniggered.

Paolo shrugged his shoulders and calmly replied, 'I don't know. Your mum probably.'

A large circle of students formed, as it became clear that a fight was now imminent. Joe believed it would be a fight in name only and hoped a teacher would notice what was happening and come out to stop it before Paolo got seriously hurt. But no such luck.

'I'm going to enjoy this, you mouthy little wop,' smirked Henderson, drawing back his large right fist. To everyone's amazement, Paolo hit him three times in lightening quick succession before he could strike. Left-right-left. As his eye blackened, his lip fattened and a trickle of blood vacated his nose, Henderson blinked in disbelief. Then the tears came. No-one present could believe it. Certainly not Henderson. Definitely not Joe. Only the unruffled Paolo seemed unsurprised. When two of the weeping bully's cohorts moved threateningly towards the victor, Joe stepped into the circle to indicate that he would even up the odds if need be. The would-be assailants backed off, and from that moment on a bond formed between Paolo and Joe. Unspoken, unarticulated, but rock solid.

Word spread like wildfire that the new Italian kid was a bit tasty with his fists. Over that first term it soon became apparent that Paolo Massetti was the antithesis of the *'cowardly Italian'* stereotype that the Brits loved to make jokes about. If some boy wanted a scrap with him, he was always happy to oblige, regardless of his opponent's size or age. A recurring theme through their school years were various lads wanting to test themselves against him. And Paolo never backed down. Most times he came out on top, occasionally honours were even, but Joe never saw him beaten. Cut and bruised, yes, but never defeated. The boxing club he'd attended twice a week since his father's death had obviously had a big impact on him. As had the words of his trainer.

'Respect yourself. Respect others. But don't take any shit off them.'

Paolo had no ambition to become a serious boxer, but he enjoyed the discipline and strength building of the 'noble art'. Getting to know each other over the ensuing weeks, the boys discovered that they shared a lot of similar interests. Football (Joe – Liverpool, Paolo – Arsenal) and the madcap, surreal humour of Spike Milligan being just two. Also, the fact that both their dads were deceased was another common denominator that cemented their friendship. Each as a result of a road accident too. Paolo's father was knocked down on a zebra crossing and died two days later. Young Paolo had been holding his hand at the time but escaped with just minor bruising, though the nightmares would continue long after the abrasions had healed. Regarding his own dad, all Joe had been told was that his mum had been pregnant with him when his father's motorcycle skidded and hit a lamppost, killing him instantly. Whenever he asked about his dad, his mother would get upset and agitated, so he kept off the subject. She'd remarried when he was four, but Joe and his stepdad didn't get on.

Clearly though, it was the Massetti family who had endured the toughest time. Giovanni had been a POW in a camp near Comrie in Perthshire. There were around four thousand prisoners, Germans and Italians. And they absolutely despised each other.

Ellen Robertson had lived in Comrie all her life and met Gio at the village dance just a week after the war ended. He was twenty four and she was nineteen. Much to her parents' dismay, she started dating the handsome Italian and soon they were engaged. Her folks' main objection to their daughter's choice wasn't that he was a foreigner (Although that was bad enough). Nor that he was a former prisoner of war (At a push, that could be tolerated). It was that Giovanni was raised a catholic and the Robertsons were a protestant family. There was no getting around *that* obstacle, and they refused to give the union their blessing. So, Ellen was forced to choose between her family and the man she loved. The marriage ceremony consisted of bride, groom, two witnesses and the registrar. Given the family animosity they faced, the decision to move south of the border was an easy one, and they eventually settled in Watford, after short stays in Carlisle and Northampton.

Giovanni was a skilled baker and soon secured a job in a local bakery. Though desperate to start a family, they'd just about given up hope when Ellen fell pregnant in 1953, and Paolo made his bow in February '54. Three years later, the Massettis' happiness was complete with the arrival of Lilah. For Gio, it was love at first sight. He dubbed her Lilah the smiler, as she was such a contented baby. But, as everyone learns sooner or later, happiness is a fragile gift and theirs was shattered in the bleak winter of 1963, when a van driver tried to beat the traffic lights and robbed a family of a loving husband and father. His untimely death made his nine-year-old son even more sensitive to any slurs or insults regarding his roots. As Tony Henderson would one day learn.

But at school, it wasn't just a few fellow students who took exception to Paolo Massetti's ethnicity. His history teacher in his third year had lost a brother fighting the Italians in Egypt and made no secret of his disdain at having to educate the offspring of one of 'the enemy'. It was with undisguised spite that he set the class an assignment to write an account of what they imagined life in WW2 to be like. They were given carte blanche to place themselves in any scenario.

Predictably, most of the boys envisaged themselves as Spitfire pilots, battleship captains or tank commanders. To be fair, Henderson showed a little more imagination and wrote of himself as the soldier who recognised and arrested SS chief Heinrich Himmler and 'gave him a swift kick in the goolies for all the aggro he'd caused'.

Paolo didn't shirk the task and bravely wrote his tale through his father's eyes. He used Gio's own words, taken from a diary his wife had found whilst going through his possessions after he'd died. It was written in Italian, but she had it translated and read it aloud to her heartbroken children, to give them an insight into the kind of man their father was.

My name is Giovanni Eduardo Massetti, and I was born and raised in Positano, on the south-west coast of Italy. Childhood was not a happy time for me. My father was a cruel man, especially when the drink was in him and often beat my dear mother, as well as me and my older sisters, Rosa and Maria. They both married young to escape and I moved into lodgings as soon as I started earning. When Italy entered the war, I was learning to be a master baker. Baking was my passion, and I had no desire to do anything else. My calling was to feed people, not to kill them.

My friends and me never cared for Mussolini, with his arrogant posturing, but when we were conscripted, we had to go. To refuse meant jail or, in some cases, execution. So, like many others, I reluctantly put on the uniform and took the rifle I was handed. My dream of owning my own baker's shop, selling fancy cakes of my own design would have to wait. After three months at a training camp my unit was sent to fight the British in Libya. To my relief I was captured before even firing a shot and eventually shipped off to a POW camp in Scotland. This was to be my home for the next four years. I never dreamed that summers could be so cold, and the winters were torture for those of us brought up in warm climates. But at least I was allowed to bake again. Only basic stuff like bread and rolls but, at Christmas, mince pies made from blackberries picked in the summer and preserved. Also, the guards would give me extra cigarettes for making birthday cakes for their families. In May 1945, the war finally ended. At a dance I met a beautiful Scottish girl who captured my heart, and my life truly began. With Italy in chaos, we decided to make our lives in England.

His English tutor chided Paolo for how brief his story was, but its contents must have hit home because after that he was a lot less abrasive towards him, and eventually, they struck up a decent teacher/pupil relationship. Proof that it wasn't just the physical fights that Paolo had the determination to win. Since his father's untimely death, he'd taken up the mantle of 'man of the house', seeing it as his duty to look out for his widowed mother and younger sister, Lilah. Ah yes, Lilah, Lilah, Lilah.

CHAPTER FOUR

YESTER-ME, YESTER-YOU, YESTERDAY

The first time Joe had set eyes on Paolo's sister she had been eight years old. One Saturday morning he'd turned up at the Massetti house for a pre-arranged kick about at the nearby recreation ground. Although only a fifteen-minute bus ride away, it was plain to Joe that his friend's neighbourhood was a notch down the social scale from his. The houses were mostly terraced, whereas in his area they were semi-detached, with large front gardens, not small, concreted spaces. The cars parked around there were fewer in number and older, and there were no trees planted at intervals along the pavements. A group of teens milling outside the parade of shops eyed him warily as he got off the bus. He thought for a second that they might follow him, but they didn't. Even so, he was pleased that Paolo's house was in the next street.

The door was opened by a strange little creature. It wore an eyepatch, a red bandana on its head and had an Errol Flynn moustache drawn in felt pen under its nose. After leading the visitor up to Paolo's bedroom, it offered a quick, 'Your friend's here,' and was gone. Joe's bemused expression brought forth the explanation, 'That's Lilah, my little sister. She has to wear the patch in the mornings because of a lazy eye and I thought the bandana and the tash would make good accessories. I don't suppose you have a stuffed parrot on you, do you?'

'Damn, I knew I'd forgotten something.'

Paolo pulled on his trainers, grabbed a plastic football from under the stairs and the duo set off for the rec. As they chatted and casually passed the ball to each other, Joe became aware of the four-foot-tall pirate following them at a distance. Inside the parkland were half a dozen of the lads who'd given Joe the once over at the bus stop and a couple of other boys, who were shouting lewd suggestions to some girls walking a dog. They were soon silenced when one of the girls replied, 'Shut your trap, Daniel Morton, or I'll tell your mum. Anyway, your brother told me your winky is like a tadpole.'

'A baby tadpole,' corrected one of the other girls and they all giggled.

Daniel's protestations were drowned out by the all-round laughter as he sulkily followed his friend to join the main group. Once the locals knew Joe was Paolo's mate he was accepted immediately, and they picked teams. When Lilah pleaded to join in, they decided on a five versus five, with her in goal. This caused a lot of amusement as, with her good eye covered, she had to rely on her lazy eye, which basically resulted in her throwing herself where she guessed the ball might be but rarely was. When one of the players started to make fun of her, Paolo warned him to stop. It was okay for *him* to tease her, but he wouldn't tolerate it from others. It was plain to Joe that she hero-worshipped her big brother, and she was never happier than when her idol allowed her to hang out with him and his friends.

Joe soon became a frequent visitor and was always made to feel welcome. Mrs Massetti had a dry, Scottish humour and he liked her a lot. And Lilah was... well, Lilah. The archetypal tomboy. Thick, raven hair always tied back in a ponytail. Permanently grazed elbows and knees where she'd climbed (and occasionally fallen from) trees. She lived in T-shirts and denim dungarees or jeans. Except on schooldays when her mother would bully or bribe her into wearing a skirt.

It was two years later that Joe first realised that Lilah had begun staring at him. A lot. She had developed a deep crush, which Paolo found amusing but the object of her affection found awkward. After all, he was a grown man of thirteen, and she was just a ten-year-old kid. One time, they were all playing football at the rec and it was Joe's turn in goal. An opponent missed the ball and kicked Joe in the head. It was a pure accident but, before the boy could apologise, Lilah was on him, running up and punching him on the nose. Her brother had to physically pick her up and pull her away, her little fists still flailing. Joe wasn't sure which hurt most, the kick or the embarrassment.

CHAPTER FIVE

BE YOUNG, BE FOOLISH, BE HAPPY

In the winter of 1969, Joe and Paolo entered A1 barbers in an alley off Watford High St. When they left, ten minutes later, it was without three quarters of their hair. The two fifteen-year-olds couldn't help but laugh when they looked at each other. All that remained on their craniums was a quarter inch of hair, all over. They'd done it. They were skinheads. In at junior level of the latest working-class youth culture to sweep Britain. Had they been born five years earlier they'd have been mods. But they weren't. This was *their* time, and this was *their* thing. As usual, regarding the younger generation, the tabloid press got it all wrong. Even the term 'skinhead' was a misnomer, designed to scare elderly ladies and outrage retired colonels. The hair was cut very short but not shaved off entirely. Why would anyone do that? It's not a good look.

The media decreed that the whole movement was based on racism and violence. Maybe, for a few, it *was*. But those individuals would have held those views whatever the current fashion. In truth, like most youth movements, for the vast majority it was all about the look and the music. Belonging to something bigger than you were. A new phenomenon was taking off and you were in, or you were out. Simple as that. The press was only interested in scaremongering – highlighting 'skins' from different towns and cities fighting each other at football grounds. Which, in that most tribal of games, would have happened if they'd had hair down to their knees and wore beads and sandals. And would a white supremist movement's music of choice really be Jamaican reggae and ska? It was lazy journalism. But mud sticks.

In most households, though, ex-military fathers approved of the look. Smarter than that hippie lot. Mothers, on the other hand, were puzzled why their sons chose to resemble Victorian convicts. Joe's mum was perceptive enough to realise that it was just a fad and would pass, just like the teddy boys and the mods and rockers before it. Her only comment was, 'Your hair, your choice.'

Truth be known, it didn't matter what parents, or indeed, any of the older generation thought. At fifteen, the only thing you have in common with adults is that you breathe the same air. They live in their world, and you live in yours. Theirs is black and white, and yours is technicolour.

His stepdad showed his usual lack of interest in anything Joe related and said nothing, which suited Joe fine. He'd now given up all hope of any meaningful relationship between them. Ever since he could remember, he'd tried everything to please Nigel Holland. But nothing he did was ever right. Nigel didn't treat him with contempt, just indifference, which, to a small child, is just as bad. Aged ten, he'd even joined a colts rugby union team as he knew that was his stepdad's favourite sport. Nigel did come to watch once, but all Joe got from him was criticism over his ball handling and running style, when all he wanted was a few words of encouragement. He longed for just a crumb of approval, but his plate remained empty, so he quit halfway through the season, despite his mum insisting that he was doing great.

All Nigel's focus was on his biological son, Joe's half-brother, David. Granted, he was Nigel's blood, so he'd naturally favour him, but was it necessary to completely freeze his adopted son out? Even so, Joe got on well with David, though he couldn't help feeling some resentment. Now, in his mid-teens, the older Holland brother had resigned himself to the situation. He and his stepfather tolerated each other but that was all. It didn't make for a happy home, despite his mum's best efforts. Poor mum, it couldn't have been easy, stuck in the middle. It was only to please her that her first born referred to her husband as 'Dad' when he was younger, but that had long since stopped. Since Joe started secondary school he called him Nigel, on the rare occasions that they spoke.

Consequently, Joe found himself spending more and more time at the Massetti house. It was a welcome escape from the constant underlying tension of his own abode. It had become his bolthole. His sanctuary. The place where he was first introduced to spaghetti. It may have looked like a tangle of earthworms, but it tasted delicious. Paolo's mum's take on the boys' new look wasn't as diplomatic as Mary Holland's. Joe was there for his tea the day after their haircuts, and Ellen still hadn't come to terms with it. As she buttered the bread, she tutted and declared in her no-nonsense Scottish burr, 'The pair of you look like you've escaped from Devil's Island.'

Lilah's opinion? Her brother looked 'alright', but Joe looked 'really handsome'.

'Now there's a surprise,' mocked Paolo, stealing a Jaffa cake from her plate, and earning himself a playful clip around the ear from his mother.

Every army has it's uniform and, in the Watford area, the quartermaster was *'Charlie, down the market'*.

Charlie was a shortish, sad-eyed feller who could sell a fridge to an Eskimo. His stall was always stacked with the latest streetwear. You want Levi jeans or Sta-Prest? A Ben Sherman or Brutus button-collared shirt? A Harrington jacket? Red braces? A Crombie overcoat? Charlie was your man. He was never short of customers because the clothes were of good quality and cheaper than the shops were charging. If he saw you so much as glance at his wares, he'd be on you like a hawk on a sparrow.

'Look at that stitching. That's quality mate. You won't find better. Not at these prices.'

There was only one thing that Charlie couldn't tolerate – seeing a potential sale get away. If a browser walked off empty handed, he took it as a personal insult. Joe soon learned that if say, a Ben Sherman shirt was priced at thirty shillings, and you explained that you only had twenty-eight shillings, the trader's response would go along these lines. 'I can't sell it for that. What am I, a schmuck? I'll make nothing. You're taking the bread from my kids' mouths.'

If you looked disappointed, held your nerve and turned to walk off, you'd inevitably hear, 'Alright, just this once. But don't tell anybody!'

Naturally, Joe told *everybody*, and soon all the kids were employing the same tactic, with the same result.

For your Doc Marten air cushion soled boots, though, you'd need a trip to a shoe shop. As for the girls, they'd buy some gear from Charlie, but acquire their miniskirts, patterned tights, short jumpers and accessories from Chelsea Girl – or Martin Fords, if they were on a tight budget.

For the youngest Massetti child, this was a period of deep frustration. She was desperate to get in on this new trend but, at barely twelve years old, even the smallest sizes were too big for her. And when she begged her mum to let her wear her hair in the new short, feather cut style, her request was met by a flat refusal. Even a bout of forced crying didn't work. So, Lilah took the only course of action left open to her. Literally taking matters into her own hands, in the shape of her mum's dressmaking scissors, she cut her own hair. *Hacked* is probably a better word. When she'd finished, her fringe was an inch higher at one end than the other, the sides were of unequal length and density, and the back looked like she'd been attacked from behind by Jack the Ripper.

Ellen arrived home from work just as the last, uneven clump of hair was hitting the bathroom lino. After surveying the tonsorial carnage she wailed, 'Your lovely hair! What have you done?'

Wedging a woolly hat on her daughter's head she marched her off to the hairdressers. With a look of horror, the stylist said, 'I'll do what I can, but I only have scissors, not a wand.'

In fact, what she did was remarkable. Lilah walked out of the salon with a very cute pixie crop. Mission accomplished. She had to go the long way round but got there in the end.

Paolo's sister was nothing if not persistent, and as the last year of the 60's progressed, her mum finally gave in and let her attend the local youth club – with the proviso that Paolo was there to keep an eye on her. This didn't sit well with her brother, afraid that having a younger sibling tagging along would cramp his style; his presumption being that he had any in the first place. But, after much pleading, he relented. So, on Friday evenings, Lilah would clip her red braces onto her denim jeans and accompany Paolo and Joe to the North Watford 7th group scout hut, where, between 7 and 9pm, dozens of young teens would congregate to pose, drink warm Pepsi and dance.

In a corner of the hut, a table was bedecked with blinking yellow fairy lights borrowed from the scouts' box of Christmas decorations. Behind the lights sat a very impressive stereo with twin turntables and large speakers either side. On the decks, and looking even more impressive than the sound system, stood nineteen-year-old Alan Curtis, or Acey as he was universally known.

Physically, Acey was everything the younger boys aspired to be. Tall, slim, stylish, with something that Joe & co could only dream of; sideburns, trimmed to the same length as his cropped hair. His threads hung perfectly on him. Black and white gingham check Ben Sherman – tucked into his turned up white Sta-Prest trousers – which were held up by the obligatory red braces. On his feet, high cut, cherry red (not black, which were for mere mortals) Doc Martens.

During the cooler months he donned his black Crombie coat, with the red silk in the breast pocket. He looked the business. The boys wanted to *be* Acey, and the girls wanted to be *with* Acey. Many of them danced without once taking their eyes off him, hoping to attract his attention. No-one really cared that he rarely smiled. Or questioned why he never introduced his selected tracks or talked in between them. He just played the music, and that was good enough. The first time Joe heard him utter a word was when he spotted one of the boys had smuggled a bottle of beer in and was showing off by swigging from it as he danced. Acey beckoned the miscreant over, and Joe was in earshot of the conversation.

Acey (sternly): 'Underage drinking will mean the end of Friday nights in here. Do you want that?'

The shame-faced boy shook his head, 'No.'

Acey: 'Right then. Get rid of it. Now.'

Boy: 'Where?'

Acey: 'Think.'

The lad racked what passed as his brain but had to admit defeat. 'I don't know. You tell me.'

Acey leaned in menacingly and repeated, 'Think.'

The frightened kid stood frozen, not knowing what to do or say and looking like he was going to burst into tears, until the exasperated DJ pointed toward the hut's tiny kitchenette. 'Think! Pour it down the fucking think.'

So *that's* why Acey rarely spoke. Not to enhance his 'mean, moody and magnificent' image. He had a lisp. Unfortunate for anyone, but especially for someone with aspirations to be a disc jockey. Shamefully, Joe couldn't help finding a guilty pleasure in Acey's speech impediment, reasoning that it wouldn't have been fair if God had given him *everything*. Joe and Paolo truly admired Alan Curtis though. He owned a car, worked for his dad's scaffolding firm; hell, he probably even had his own bank account. Acey was firmly ensconced in the adult world. But they hadn't *got* him. He was 100% a 'skin'. Still one of their own. And they appreciated the fact that he gave up his time for them and introduced them to floor-fillers like Elizabethan Reggae; Liquidator; Red, Red Wine; Wonderful World, Beautiful People; and The Israelites. The last song always made the pair laugh, as when Desmond Dekker sang the title, it sounded like he was saying, 'Me ears are alight.'

Members of the youth club were white, black, mixed race and at least six of Italian extraction. And when Acey spun the anthemic Skinhead Moonstomp, that wooden hut seemed to jump to the beat, as rows of kids obeyed the West Indian singer's instructions.

Front and centre in the throng was Lilah, her arms swinging and her feet stamping for all she was worth, basking in the joy of this glimpse into the realm that the older kids inhabited. From her first visit, she loved her Friday nights, as did her brother and his best mate.

Little did any of them know that the Christmas '69 disco would be the last they'd enjoy at the scout hut. On New Years Day 1970, persons unknown decided to burn it down. Lilah, Paolo and Joe were just three of the many kids who mourned it's passing. As Lilah observed through misty eyes, 'Why would anyone do that? Why are they even born?'

CHAPTER SIX

SWEET SOUL MUSIC

With just a couple of months to go until he was old enough to walk out of the school gates for the very last time, Joe still didn't know what he wanted to do for a job. Then, as it so often did, providence stepped in. One of the organisers at Paolo's boxing club, an electrician by trade, mentioned that his company were taking on apprentices in late April. He could put in a good word if Paolo fancied it. The offer was declined because the car crazy teenager had already bagged himself a start as a trainee mechanic at the Vauxhall dealership, within walking distance of his house. He did however mention that his best friend might be interested.

With nothing else on the horizon, Joe leapt at the opportunity, as he would have done had it involved plumbing, bricklaying or carpentry. The important thing was that it was an apprenticeship. If you weren't going on to further education, getting yourself a trade was the way to go. Yes, a factory or warehouse job would pay better in the short term, but in the long term, if you were a skilled man, you'd be quids in. And fate had decreed that Joe Holland's skill would be electrics.

Of course, you couldn't just say 'Yes please' and be handed a five-year apprenticeship. The company was investing in you, and there were requirements to be met. Joe would need O level passes in English and Maths. He'd have to sit an aptitude test. And provide written confirmation from a doctor that he wasn't colour blind. When he explained to his head of house what was on offer, he kindly arranged for Joe to take his exams early. Academics didn't come naturally to him, but through dedication and lots of revision he gained passes in not only the two subjects required, but also Geography. The aptitude test consisted of one hundred questions. Most answers were basic common sense, and Joe scored an impressive ninety-six. And he cleared the last hurdle when his GP quickly ascertained that he had no trouble distinguishing red from green and blue from yellow. By the time the Easter eggs hit the shops, he was good to go.

Which is how, on Monday 27th April, a nervous, fifteen year old turned up at the head office of Edwards & Sons Electrical for his first day as a working man. There, he was introduced to the electrician who would mentor him for the next five years – Lenny Coleman.

Lenny was a real character. A big man with a big heart. He was forty-eight years old, a staunch trade unionist, married, with two grown daughters. Joe soon discovered that, as well as being a great teacher, he also enjoyed a joke, and a few beers on a Saturday night at the British Legion. Lenny walked with a slight limp, and sometimes his apprentice would hear him wince if the job entailed him kneeling for too long. Joe was too polite to mention it, but a few weeks in, they were doing a first fix on a house in Hemel Hempstead when Lenny said, 'I suppose you're curious about the limp. Would you like to know how I got it?'

'Only if you want to tell me, Len.'

Lenny went on to reveal how he'd been a corporal in the 3rd Infantry division, the first British troops to land on Sword beach on D-Day. During the intense fighting he'd taken a German bullet to the leg. He asked the surgeon who removed the bullet it if he could have it as a souvenir. Ever since that day he'd worn it on a chain around his neck to remind himself how lucky he was. Reaching inside his shirt collar, he showed the awe-struck teenager the evidence.

Two weeks later, Lenny was off with a stomach bug, so Joe was temporarily placed with another sparks. When the youngster mentioned Lenny's heroic tale, the older man laughed, leaving Joe baffled, then went on to explain. 'Len *was* one of the first soldiers to land on D-Day. And he *was* under heavy fire. But he came through unscathed.'

'But what about his limp?' queried Joe.

'He had a barney with his Mrs one night, got pissed and fell over a dustbin on his way home from the pub. Broke his tibia in two places.'

Feeling a little foolish, Joe still appreciated it was a good wind-up, even if it was at his expense. When Lenny returned to work, the apprentice bided his time before revealing he was on to him. As they ate their sandwiches he confided, 'Len, I can totally understand why you wear that bullet on your neck chain.'

'Can you really son?' came the doubtful reply. 'I mean, *can* you?'

'Absolutely. Cos wearing a dustbin on it would give you a hunched back.'

The pair of them laughed for a full five minutes. The truth was no less impressive though. A German bullet had imbedded itself in Lenny's belt buckle, and he did indeed wear it to remind himself how lucky he was that day. On another memorable occasion in May, they were working on a shop refit in Croxley Green and decided to make the most of the spring sunshine by taking a lunchtime stroll along the Grand Union Canal. Walking towards them were two young lovelies wearing hot pants and tight t-shirts. Lenny noticed one of them smile at Joe as they sauntered past.

'You jammy buggers have got it made,' sighed the older man.

'What are you on about?'

'The girls these days. All on the pill. Walking around wearing next to nothing.'

'Are you jealous, Leonard?' grinned Joe.

'Of course I'm bloody jealous! When I was your age, they were all scared of getting pregnant. Even if you did find a willing party, by the time you got through all the layers, you were too knackered to do anything.'

The days were never dull with ex-Corporal Lenny Coleman. He liked a laugh, but he took the work seriously. 'You can't take liberties with electrics. If you do, you can end up killing yourself or others.'

Len's outlook meant he was a superb instructor. Meticulous, patient, but demanding. If Joe's tray work, trunking or conduit bending wasn't up to scratch, he'd find it scrapped and told to do it again.

'Never forget the tradesman's golden rule. Measure twice, cut once.'

Joe knew he couldn't be in better hands, and the first time Lenny commented on the neatness of his work, he felt ten feet tall. The big man didn't dish out a lot of praise, which made it even more special.

'Good work. I think we'll make a sparky of you yet, young 'un.'

Naturally, now that their schooldays were behind them, Joe and Paolo were seeing a lot less of each other. There was no danger of them losing touch, though – their friendship was too strong for that. They still met up at least one evening a week and every weekend. One Friday afternoon, whilst waiting to collect their wages, a fellow apprentice told Joe that a fun place to go on a Saturday morning was the youth disco at Top Rank, Watford's premier night spot. It was for kids under drinking age, so no alcohol, and you had to dress smart, so no boots. Joe had heard of it but was underwhelmed until he was told, 'There's loads of girls, and when they dance, if the spotlight shines on them, their tops become see through.'

'You can see their actual bras?' he gasped.

'Yeah. Sometimes even their knickers, if they've got white skirts or trousers on.'

This was heady stuff. That evening, with great enthusiasm, Joe relayed this momentous information to Paolo by telephone, and they made an immediate decision to check it out the very next day. The adolescent female anatomy was a mysterious, unexplored, foreign land. And whilst the lit-up outline of a girl's brassiere wouldn't gain them entry, it was a start.

Saturday morning found Joe checking himself one last time in the hallway mirror. Left profile, right profile, front on. An hour earlier he'd run the razor over his top lip, although it wasn't strictly necessary as he'd only done it two weeks before. The weather was dry and warm, so clothes wise, he'd settled on his black Sta-Prest and the lime green Ben Sherman he'd recently purchased from an exasperated Charlie – 'Don't you ever have the right amount of money, son?'

Slipping on his blue denim Levi jacket, he left the house. It felt so good to be able to buy his own clothes and not have his mum dipping in her purse. Her wages as a school nurse weren't huge, and even though his stepdad was a deputy headmaster, on decent money, Joe would rather wear rags than ask *him* for anything.

As he sat on the bus to Paolo's, Joe had no idea how momentous this trip to Top Rank would be for him. How could he know that this was to be the day that he'd fall in love? Let alone how enduring and deep that love would prove to be. Walking up the High St from the bus stop, they were surprised to see the number of kids waiting for the doors of the club to open. There must have been well over a hundred congregating around the pond area. A mixture of ages from ten to sixteen. The duo checked out the ones who looked around their age. Most of them were girls – result. And a fair number of those girls were in light-coloured clothes – double result.

At 9.45 am, the doors swung open and in they all trooped. The queue diminished surprisingly quickly and, in no time, they were ascending the plush carpeted stairs, entrance money in hand. Inside, the large, swanky club was dimly lit, but they could make out a figure on the wide stage – obviously the DJ, finishing setting up. He had longish bouffant hair and a Mexican moustache. For a split second, Joe pined for Acey. You'd never catch *him* with a moustache, Mexican or otherwise.

As their eyes adjusted to the light, the boys could see it was an impressive place. The large dancefloor in front of the stage was flanked by orange plastic chairs. To the left was a long bar with a good selection of soft drinks, crisps and peanuts. There was even a machine that churned out flavoured crushed ice concoctions commonly known as slushies. Talk about exotic. It was kids being allowed to play grown-ups, but the atmosphere was friendly. Ensuring it stayed that way were two stocky individuals wearing penguin suits. It appeared that there was an invisible barrier between the sexes. Like two separate tribes, boys and girls eyed each other with a wary fascination. All trying to appear aloof and cool.

Paolo handed his friend the Pepsi he'd asked for, impressed at how chilled it was. Much more refreshing than the lukewarm ones at the ill-fated scout hut. Joe noticed the D J give the thumbs up to the unseen lighting operator, hidden somewhere up in the gods. Immediately, red and blue diamond shapes crept along the floor and up the walls. The chatter subsided and the regulars, aware that proceedings were about to begin, excitedly rushed onto the dancefloor in front of the stage. A single white spotlight patrolled the crowd, just like a searchlight in those old war films. The boys' eyes eagerly followed it, waiting for it to land on a white-shirted mademoiselle. The amplified voice of their host, speaking in double quick time, as most DJ's felt obliged to do, addressed the throng. 'Okay, welcome one and all to the Saturday club at Top Rank suite, Watford.' (Loud cheers and whistles.) 'We're gonna kick things off with a Motown section, starting with Mr Marvin Gaye and "I Heard It Through the Grapevine".'

The following three minutes and twenty seconds would change Joe forever. It totally blew him away. The unique sound, the words, that voice. As it faded out, he looked at Paolo and saw his own entrancement reflected in his eyes. Before either could say a word, the next song kicked in – "Dancing in the Street" by Martha Reeves & The Vandellas. The joy and the energy didn't let up from first note to last and the two newcomers were as animated as everyone else; once this music had a hold of you, it didn't let you go. Neither Joe nor Paolo would ever forget their first encounter with the Tamla Motown sound. It captivated them. It was love at first sound. They had found a portal to a whole new world. A place where happiness and heartache were infused with the same infectious beat. There were still a few good reggae songs mixed in – "Double Barrel" by Dave & Ansel Collins and the catchy "Young, Gifted and Black" by Bob & Marcia, to name just two. But there was a definite change in the air. Reggae was for your feet, but soul was for your feet *and* your brain.

Over the next two hours, interspersed with 'the poppy stuff', Masters Holland and Massetti became acquainted with The Four Tops, The Isley Brothers, The Supremes, Stevie Wonder and The Temptations. It seemed as if everything on this Motown label was amazing. Joe and Paolo were instant converts, and like all converts, everything that came before had to be swept aside. As far as they were concerned, reggae moonstomped off into the wings that day, leaving the stage free for American soul.

Upon leaving 'the Rank', the duo headed straight to Musicland, the record shop further up the High St. They methodically went through the alphabetically arranged album sleeves until Joe found the treasure he sought – Marvin Gaye. The LP was titled, "In the Groove", and there, track four, was "I Heard it Through the Grapevine". Paolo chose The Four Tops – "Yesterday's Dreams", primarily because he'd liked the lead singer's voice on "I'm in a Different World". The red-haired assistant took the empty sleeve from Joe.

'Can't beat a bit of Marvin, eh?'

She looked in her early twenties. Confident. Bubbly. Joe's answer was a reserved smile. 'May I ask,' she continued, 'are you buying this because of the single that's on it?'

Noting Joe's blank look, she explained, 'Because, to be honest, there's a better album that it's on. If you look in the rack, you'll find Motown Chartbusters Volume Three. It's in the silver sleeve. It has "Grapevine" and fifteen other hits by various artists. It's fantastic.'

She glanced at the sleeve Paolo was holding and revealed, 'Same goes for this one.'

The boys did as she suggested and immediately put their original choices back in the rack. The LP she'd guided them to must have been the one that the DJ had taken the Motown medley from because all the songs they'd heard were on it. Even the silver reflective album sleeve was unlike anything else on display. Reading the track list, excitement levels increased, and Paolo joined Joe in purchasing a copy. The redhead informed them that Volume Four was due out in October and was supposed to be just as good. Seeing how impressed the boys were by her knowledge, she divulged that Motown wasn't the only label making great soul music. 'Check out Stax and Atlantic.'

Over the next few months, Elaine, their new musical guru, was good enough to pass her vast knowledge of the soul genre onto her two eager acolytes.

CHAPTER SEVEN

IT'S ALL IN THE GAME

Sunday: 14th June 1970. To borrow President Franklin D. Roosevelt's line, 'A day that will live in infamy.'

Of course, he was referring to the Japanese bombing of Pearl Harbour, which admittedly, was more seismic than this day's event in Mexico. But only marginally. For this was the day that the England football team were two nil ahead in the World Cup quarter final against West Germany – and lost. No Englishman thought it possible that the holders, the country that gave birth to the game, could surrender a two-goal lead, and a stunned nation went into shock. Such was the silence across the land that, legend has it, the laughter from Scotland could be heard as far south as Coventry.

A dejected apprentice electrician skulked off to his room and took solace in his recently acquired Motown Chartbusters Volume Two, particularly Diana Ross & The Supremes track – "Some Things You Never Get Used To".

Since Elaine had pointed the way with Volume Three, he'd bought its two predecessors. The quality of all three albums amazed him. A lot of the tracks concerned love lost and angst, but each presented these ideas to the listener in an original and interesting way – with a great beat and fantastic singing. Every song was a three-minute novel, with characters you knew and cared about. When Diana Ross sang "I'm Gonna Make You

Love Me", you had no doubt she could do it. You really felt sad for Smokey Robinson hiding his heartbreak in "The Tracks of My Tears". And if Jimmy Mack didn't hurry back, he *was* going to lose that girl. Joe was learning that it wasn't called soul music for nothing. At its finest, it really did touch your soul.

The sporting disaster he'd just witnessed was the final slap in the face from a weekend that had promised so much. For yesterday, at Saturday morning club, he had experienced his first *proper* slow dance. And it was everything he hoped it would be. The girl was with three friends, had wavy fair hair, and was dancing nearby to "Spirit in the Sky". Joe had noticed her regular glances but wasn't sure if they were directed at him or Paolo. Only when his friend disappeared to the toilet, and the glances continued, did he have his answer. He would never forget what she was wearing. Light blue top with navy blue Sta-Prest and white shoes. She looked around his age, maybe a year younger, and had a nice face – smiley.

The Norman Greenbaum song faded out and the room was filled by the intro to the much slower "All in the Game". After treating him to one last smile, she turned to leave the dancefloor. Joe realised he should seize the moment and ask her to dance. But what if he'd misread the signals? What if she said no? He'd be left to do the dreaded walk of shame. He'd witnessed it happen to other lads, and it was painful to see. Where five feet six inch teenage boys visibly shrank to one foot six by the time they'd slunk back to their mates. Some shrank to nothing, evaporated into the carpet and were never seen again. He had to decide whether to take the risk. His mind was in turmoil.

What are you waiting for, a written invitation? Ask her!

Why would she want to dance with a dodo like you? Don't ask her!

What the hell... nothing ventured, nothing gained. Taking a deep breath, he walked across and gently touched her elbow. 'I was wondering if you'd like to dance?' She treated him to that nice smile. Pretty green eyes too. They found a space, and to his disbelief, were holding each other at arm's length and slowly rotating.

Joe thought asking her name would be a safe, if predictable, icebreaker. That's what they always did in the films. Before he could speak, she beat him to the punch. 'I'm Alison, what's your name?'

'Joe.'

Good, a nice easy one to start.

'I've seen you and your friend here before,' she continued.

'Have you? I didn't see you. I'd have remembered.'

Excellent. Well done. You're hitting your stride now. Keep going.

'Where do you live then?' he asked.

'In a house,' she replied, causing him to laugh far too hard at such a feeble joke.

'Me too,' he replied, 'Small world.'

Alison smiled, moved in closer and placed her head on his shoulder. *His* shoulder. The shoulder that belonged to *him*. What a great feeling. But something strange was happening. Oh, God no, not now. The stirring in Joe's loins indicated that the unpredictable entity living rent free in his y-fronts was waking up. What to do? It had a will of its own, so it was pointless trying to reason with it. His only chance was to turn his

37

thoughts to something other than the attractive girl in his arms and hope it would lose interest and go back to its slumber. As he concentrated, the anti-stimulants arrived thick and fast.

Granny from The Beverley Hillbillies. *Olive from* On the Buses. *Hilda Baker. Margaret Rutherford. Barbara Cartland. The elderly lady from three doors down with no teeth and a whiskery chin.*

His plan was working. The curious creature below went back to sleep – for the time being. But Joe had learned it couldn't be trusted so continued the thought process until the last note of the song faded away.

He'd made it. Embarrassment averted. But what now?

Ask her if she'd like a drink.

That was it. They always did that in the films too. Linking her arm into his, Alison said she'd love a pineapple slushy and they set off for the bar. A pineapple slushy! Not only was his new girlfriend cute, she was sophisticated too. Joe wished Paolo would hurry back, to see the prize on his arm. Alison added that she didn't want to sound cheeky, but could she also have a bag of crisps, as she'd had no breakfast. Of course she could. If he'd owned the moon, he'd have given her that too. He prayed he had enough cash on him. He'd bought some tools for work that week, leaving himself low on funds. Luckily, he had just enough money.

Receiving his gifts graciously, she took them over to where her friends were sitting without a backward look. After five minutes, Joe got a sinking feeling in the pit of his stomach. After ten minutes the sinking feeling was somewhere just above his knees. At this point Paolo returned, which was more than Alison ever did.

'Bloody hell, you've got a face like a smacked arse. Cheer up, it might never happen.'

'I think it already has.'

Paolo followed Joe's line of vision. 'Not the girl in the blue top? Did you buy her that slushy?'

Joe nodded affirmatively, 'And a bag of crisps.'

'You've been taken mate,' confirmed his friend. 'She pulls the same stunt every Saturday.'

'Well, you could have warned me,' said the wounded victim.

'I wasn't here, was I? And don't get narky with me cos you got turned over.'

In truth, Joe was disappointed, annoyed and embarrassed in equal measure. Disappointed because he liked Alison. It felt good holding her. Annoyed because if Paolo had previously spotted her game, why hadn't *he*? And embarrassed at being her latest mug.

On Monday morning, as Lenny drove them to work, all talk was about England getting knocked out of the World Cup. And it was Len doing most of the talking. 'It's the Mexican humidity, see? Our boys aren't used to it.'

His passenger thought it best not to point out that neither were the Germans.

'If Banks had been in goal instead of that clown Bonetti we'd have won. Bloody Bonetti. What idiot nicknamed him "The Cat?" Should be "The Sealion", the way he fucking flaps.'

'Perhaps he drinks milk from a saucer,' ventured Joe.

By the afternoon, just to change the subject, Joe recounted his Saturday morning episode at Top Rank. The whole sorry story. As he emptied the last of the tea from his flask, Lenny took on a philosophical look. 'Well, there's a lesson right there.'

'Oh yeah? Enlighten me, oh wise one.'

'You get nothing for nothing in this life.'

'Well, *she* did. A pineapple slushy and a packet of ready salted.'

The older man shook his head. 'No, no, my young friend. She *traded* you a dance for them. To her it was a business transaction.'

Joe was incredulous. 'Oh really? Well, nice as that dance was, it didn't cost *her* any money, did it? I'm the only one out of pocket.'

'Exactly. I'm telling you, that girl will go far.'

'The farther the better. Devious cow.'

'Don't be bitter now. You can't put a price on your first proper smooch.'

'*I* can. Twenty pence. It was all I had. My mate had to lend me my bus fare home.'

As he sloped to the van to fetch a reel of cable, Joe noticed Lenny was red in the face, had tears in his eyes, his shoulders were heaving, and he was biting his bottom lip.

CHAPTER EIGHT

A CHANGE IS GONNA COME

The following twelve months were significant, both for Joe and Britain as a whole. On a personal level he'd recovered from his wobbly start down the road to romance. He wasn't yet Tour de France standard but at least the stabilisers were off. By Christmas he'd clocked up a fair few dance partners who *hadn't* conned him into buying them drinks, and he was learning all the time. By observation alone, he noticed that the best-looking boys who took themselves too seriously didn't have as much success with the young ladies as the average looking boys who made them laugh. It was a revelation. His assumption that the prettiest girls only go for the handsomest boys wasn't strictly true. If you had a bit of charisma and didn't look like a train crash, you were in with a chance. He'd even dipped his toe into the dating pool and found the water warm and welcoming.

For the most part, he'd take his dates to the cinema, then participate in some awkward snogging and nocturnal fumblings afterwards. He wondered what sadist invented bra clasps? Or, come to think of it, the bra? Paolo and he were on the same mission and often compared notes and tactics concerning, 'Operation Lose Your Cherry'. The hormones were raging but the two walking, talking testosterone bombs would meet with limited success for quite some time.

As ever, fashion too was moving on. The skinheads had morphed into something less intimidating, and therefore, more socially acceptable. Throughout the realm, scared elderly ladies and outraged retired colonels slept easy again. Utilising their obsession with labels, the morons in the media dubbed it the 'Suedehead' look. A ridiculous name, that neither Joe, Paolo nor any of their number would ever use to describe themselves. They simply grew their cropped hair out. Not by much, just enough to get a comb through.

The Doc Martens were soon relegated to workwear if you did a manual job or consigned to the back of the wardrobe if you didn't. The much less threatening black loafers with twin tassels took their place. Levi jeans and Sta-Prest were gradually phased out in favour of two-tone (or tonic) trousers and suits. As the name suggests, the fabric incorporated two interwoven colours, blue and gold being the most popular combination. The 'Benny' and Brutus shirts stayed, as did the Crombie coats, but the braces were discarded. New accessories included Fred Perry shirts, chunky cardigans and sleeveless V neck jumpers. It was an altogether smarter look, and a period Joe would always look back on with affection. Girls also embraced the two-tone fabric, both as jackets, skirts and trousers. Some also wore loafers. Regarding street fashion, the sexes had never been more in sync.

To Joe's delight, more and more youngsters were getting into American soul. Well, the ones who liked to think as well as dance. His record collection was constantly growing, as he discovered Otis Redding, Sam Cooke, Aretha Franklin and a host of others. He knew, before he was seventeen, that whatever happened in his life, this would always be his go-to music. The sounds that sustained him. As the 1970's established itself, Motown was evolving too. The songs up to then had been, mostly, high standard boy/girl fare. Now, they increasingly contained political and social commentary and were all the better for it. Marvin Gaye was no longer too busy thinking about his baby, he was condemning the way governments were treating the planet in "Mercy, Mercy Me (The Ecology)". And Stevie Wonder, The Temptations and countless others were marching right alongside him. Oh, and Elaine at Musicland was right – Motown Chartbusters Volume Four, *was* as good as Volume Three.

One of the youngest soul devotees was thirteen-year-old Lilah. It would have been more of a surprise if she hadn't been smitten, considering her brother had it playing in the house on a daily basis. She was too young to fully appreciate the nuances of the lyrics; she just loved the infectious vibe of it. Soon she was immersed enough to join in the game that Joe and Paolo had devised. They called it 'The Chartbuster Quiz', and it was quite simple to play. It involved the four Motown Chartbuster albums (sixty-four tracks in all). Each player, in turn, would ask, for example, 'Chartbusters Vol Two: Side two. Track six?'

The first one to correctly answer, '"If I Were A Carpenter" – The Four Tops,' would earn two points, one for the song, one for the artist. First person to ten, wins. It was as much a test of memory as anything, but always fun, as the song in the question was then played, before the next player's turn. Super fan Joe usually came out on top, but not always. The first time Lilah won she cracked them up by whooping joyously and dancing around the living room. All she lacked was a tomahawk and warpaint.

February 15th, 1971 was not only Paolo's seventeenth birthday but also the day that Great Britain officially changed from pounds, shillings & pence to the decimal system. For a couple of years, the fifty, ten and five pence coins had been integrated, but from this day on, you couldn't use 'old money' only 'new money'. In general, younger people saw this as a progressive move, if only for the fact that having one hundred pence to the pound instead of two hundred and forty would make the maths a lot easier. Some older folks, though, saw it as the latest nail in the Empire's coffin. Naturally, some unscrupulous businesses exploited the confusion of the elderly to ease up their prices during the crossover period. To Joe it didn't matter much. He was young, fit and healthy and had almost completed the first year of his apprenticeship, which he was enjoying immensely. His wages provided him with enough money to enjoy himself and buy clothes and records. Life was good.

Early March saw Lilah turn fourteen, the age at which her brother said she could come along to Top Rank on Saturday mornings. She'd been pestering him for almost a year and now he had to make good on his promise. The trouble was that he and Joe had outgrown it. It was predominantly for sixteens and under. Most teens above that age had climbed the next rung of the ladder and were frequenting pubs, including Messrs Holland and Massetti.

In 1970's Britain, neither the publicans, nor the police, were too bothered about enforcing the underage drinking laws. If you could pay, and you didn't get too loud or lairy, most bar staff weren't interested in the date on your birth certificate. It wasn't even the booze that made it so appealing. It was simply a rite of passage. That, plus the thrill of doing something mildly illegal.

The weekend after her birthday, Paolo and Joe took a very excited Lilah to Top Rank's Saturday club. Her first visit would be their last. Ellen Massetti had reluctantly agreed to let her daughter go, as long as the boys didn't leave her, and got her home safe and sound. As it turned out, it was *her* who left *them*. When Joe got back to the table after a slow dance with a girl, he asked Paolo where she was, to be told that she said it was boring being with them and next week she'd return with a couple of school friends. Apparently, she then left to make the short walk to Clements, the department store where her mum worked, telling her brother he could pick her up from there. She'd nagged and nagged them to bring her and when they did, she left after half an hour. How could any male possibly understand the workings of the female mind?

CHAPTER NINE

YOU CAN'T HIDE FROM YOURSELF

The May weekend of Joe's Seventeenth was eventful, to say the least. He and Paolo made their return to the Top Rank suite, but this time for a *night* out. Entry was gained without being challenged about their age but, once inside, they began to feel like fish out of water. The layout was familiar, but the clientele most definitely was not. Obviously, they'd expected *that*, but they hadn't anticipated feeling so out of place. Their impression was the same one you get when you leave junior school and start senior school. You've just reached the top of one hill only to find yourself at the bottom of the next. The club goers all looked in their twenties to early thirties, making Joe and Paolo feel like comparative infants. Plenty of the other punters wore tonic suits and slim ties, just like them. But unlike them, the men exuded confidence and the women were... well, women – not girls. They looked sophisticated and unattainable. Which they were, for two lads for whom shaving was still a novelty.

There were groups of females scattered around but the notion of talking to them, let alone dancing with them, was laughable. They'd probably ask why the duo were out past their bedtimes. So, unwilling to risk the humiliation, the boys contented themselves with downing a few lagers, having a little shimmy in the shadows and observing the real grown-ups. Slowly, buoyed by the alcohol, they relaxed into the evening. Everyone in the nightclub seemed to be having a good time until, just after midnight, the atmosphere changed.

Angry shouts could be heard and then the sound of breaking glass and screaming. Beer mugs and ashtrays were being hurled from the upper balcony onto the packed dancefloor below. Whether it was at specific targets or lobbed haphazardly was impossible to tell. Only the throwers knew. The main lights came on, the music stopped, and the DJ appealed for calm. A dazed young man holding a rapidly reddening white handkerchief to his head was being helped away from the chaos as a sobbing female clung to his arm. A man on the dancefloor shouted something up at the balcony and more glasses rained down. The whole scene was deeply unpleasant.

A team of four doormen sped past Joe and Paolo and raced up the stairs. Shouting, swearing and thuds could be heard as they laid into the troublemakers. It only took the bouncers about five minutes to restore order, but it seemed longer. The burly club employees manhandled six men down the carpeted stairway, shoving them towards the exit – a protesting blur of dishevelled blood-spattered clothes. The lights dimmed, the music resumed but the dancefloor remained half empty, as a cleaner swept up the shattered glass and mopped up the spilt beer and blood.

'Happy birthday mate,' said Paolo, in a tone that dripped sarcasm.

The duo had seen enough and they drank up and left. They'd been expecting something like an adult version of the Saturday club. What they'd got was more akin to a Wild West saloon. All that was missing were the swing doors and the piano player. It would be almost a year before they went back.

Next morning, as on most Sundays, Joe slept late. Somewhere, in the outer limits of his consciousness, he heard a church clock chime eleven times. His dry mouth sent a message to his brain to supply rehydration. In turn, his brain ordered his hands to peel back the covers and his backside to get itself into gear.

His mum was in the kitchen, washing the dishes, Radio Four playing quietly in the background – some bloke with a plummy accent waffling on about the lost treasures of the Incas. Mary didn't hear Joe enter but, sensing a presence, she turned, smiled and chirped, 'Morning, love. I'll just finish rinsing these and I'll do you a fry up.'

'Cheers,' he replied, seating himself at the small table under the serving hatch. Joe preferred eating in the kitchen, it was less formal. Casually, he flicked through the sports pages of The Guardian that Nigel had left on the table. He'd always thought the title of Nigel's favourite newspaper was ironic, since he wasn't much of a guardian himself. Perhaps that was a bit unfair; he was ultra protective of little saint David.

A brief scan of the sports section was enough. Eight days after the event and they were still banging on about Arsenal winning the league and cup double. And who had they luckily beaten in the FA cup final on May 8th? Joe's team – Liverpool. Paolo hadn't stopped smirking, like a dog with two dicks. At an early age, Joe had chosen Liverpool as his team because it was the city his mum came from. Plus, he liked their all-red kit.

Fortunately, the sound of sizzling sausages drowned out the monotone drone of the Radio 4 presenter. If the BBC seriously wanted listeners to care where the Incas riches had vanished to, then surely they could have found someone with a more interesting voice.

Breakfast arrived with a steaming mug of hot tea. Just the job. Mary pulled up a chair and sat down. Her husband had taken David to Garston park so it was just Joe and his mum in the house. It felt nice. A rare chance for them to talk. There was something that had been nagging at him for some time, and he needed to get it off his chest. However, it was Mary who spoke first. 'How was your night at Top Rank then?'

'Smashing,' answered Tom with a knowing grin, seeing no reason to worry her with the violent details. He couldn't think of an easy way to introduce what was bugging him, so decided to wade straight in. 'Mum, I want to talk to you about dad.'

'Look, I know you two don't get along,' she sighed.

'Not Nigel,' he interrupted, 'my proper dad. John Hudson. I know so little about him.'

Her eyes took on a sad, faraway look, left his, and stared ruefully into her teacup (she always drank tea from a cup, never a mug). It was an expression he'd seen before, whenever he'd tried to broach this subject, and he could see it pained her. Instinctively, his right hand found hers. 'I realise talking about it makes you sad, mum. But I'm seventeen now. I want to know.'

'Your breakfast will go cold.'

'Then I'll heat it up.'

Joe pushed his plate to the side, got up, turned the radio off and retook his seat. He'd waited so long for this chat, and there could be no distractions. This time he held both her hands and squeezed gently. After a few seconds reflection, she lamented. 'It was such a long time ago and we were so young.'

'I know. Just tell me everything. Please. There are so many gaps.'

Raising her eyes to meet his, she began. 'As you're aware, your grandfather was very protective of me.'

Not protective, a tyrant, thought Joe.

'I was all he had after mum died giving birth to me. I didn't have many friends. Had to go straight home from school. He wouldn't let me go out to play, not even in the summer. I used to watch the neighbourhood kids from my bedroom window and longed to join in their games.'

Grampy, you cruel bastard.

'I read voraciously. Anything I could get my hands on. Each page was a rung on my escape ladder. *The Secret Garden* was my absolute favourite. I loved it. I *lived* it. I wasn't Mary Parsons anymore. I was Mary Lennox, an orphan learning how to survive. The one place I could go to without boundaries was my imagination.'

This was more than Joe had dared hope for. He thought she might just give him an insight into his real dad, but he was getting glimpses of who *she* was too. Filling in those gaps. His mum had never been anything other than loving to him, but he never felt he really *knew* her. And he wanted to. She'd never spoken of her childhood, so he'd guessed it wasn't a happy time. Now here she was, confirming it.

He was only four when Grampy died, so he had few memories of him. But the ones he did have were all negative. There was always an aura of sternness and unapproachability about him. Joe couldn't recall ever seeing the man smile. Not once. The overriding memory was the smell of tobacco on him. And a cigarette, like an extra appendage, wedged between his yellow nicotine-stained fingers. As soon as he'd smoked one, he'd immediately light another one. Did he think having 'Dr' in front of his name would protect him from lung cancer? It was awful but true that when he died, Joe had felt that a cloud, both metaphorically and physically, had lifted. Young as he was back then, he had sensed it, clear as day, and remembered it.

'At sixteen I left school and started training as a student nurse,' she continued. 'It was wonderful. I existed outside my house. I had thoughts and opinions, and I could express them. I made a good friend there, Evelyn. She loved jazz and used to go to a jazz club every Thursday evening. The Blue Note, it was called. One week she asked me if I'd like to go with her. I really wanted to, but your grandad said it was stupid American music, with no value.

'For the first time in my life, I stood up to him. I told him I wanted to go, and I was going. His face was like thunder, but what could he do? I wasn't a child anymore; I was almost seventeen. Reluctantly, he relented but told me that at the stroke of 10pm he'd be locking the front door.'

'So, you went?'

She nodded affirmatively, allowing herself a wry, triumphant smile. 'I did.'

He squeezed her hands. 'Yes! Well done, Mum.'

'It became a regular Thursday night outing. It wasn't just the music that drew me. It was being with people my own age, who listened when I spoke.'

'Was it at the Blue Note that you met John Hudson?'

'Yes. He was with a friend, and I was with Evelyn. The four of us got chatting and we all went for a coffee afterwards.'

'What was he like?' urged Joe 'Do I take after him?'

'He was shy, like me. I thought he was very handsome. I couldn't work out why he was talking to *me*. He had kind eyes and a lovely smile. So yes, you do get those from him. Same small ears too.'

'We started seeing each other every Thursday with the other two, and then whenever we could, on our own. He used to pick me up on his motorbike.'

Joe chuckled. 'I can't imagine Grampy being too thrilled about you going out with a jazz loving biker.'

'I didn't tell him. Not at first. It was our secret. I'd leave the house and John would be waiting around the corner. We'd leave the city and explore the surrounding countryside. And he had his own flat. Well, more of a bedsit.'

'Free at last, eh?' beamed Joe. He'd always thought of his mum as being a naturally timid, reserved woman. But she wasn't, she had simply been held back; beaten down. 'When did you know you loved him?'

'I don't know exactly,' she replied coyly, 'a couple of months in, I suppose.'

'You said you were seventeen when I was born. How old was he?'

'Twenty one. Very mature though. Dependable.'

'Did you marry in church or a registry office?'

Mary was hesitant, as if uncertain how he'd react to what she was about to share. 'I fell pregnant with you around three months after I met your dad. We were never married.'

Seeing the shock on her son's face she elaborated. 'We planned to. It would have happened if...' her voice trailed off and an immense sadness engulfed her.

This revelation was unexpected. His mum had always referred to Nigel Holland as her second husband. But, come to think of it, only when he wasn't around. Mary's eyes took on a faraway look. 'He was on his way to my house when it happened. The overnight rain had turned to ice. He skidded, lost control of the bike and hit a concrete lamppost. It was the day I was going to tell him about you.'

She swallowed hard, fighting to keep the tears at bay. Joe too felt a wave of sadness ripple through him. He rubbed the top of her hand with his fingertips. 'It's alright, Mum. I'm sorry.'

'Don't you ever say that, Joseph. I'm the one who's sorry. The three of us would have been so happy. I'm certain of it,' she sniffled, dabbing at her eyes with the hanky she always kept up her sleeve. This was just what he *didn't* want to happen.

'You've talked enough for now. Save the rest for another day, eh?'

Shaking her head, she composed herself. 'No, you've a right to know. It was a terrible time for me. I was devastated at losing John, and I still hadn't told my father I was expecting. At four months even the baggiest of jumpers couldn't hide my growing tummy. He went ballistic. I'd never seen him so angry. It was different in the nineteen fifties, not like now, where people are more understanding. Single mothers were ostracised back then; the lowest of the low. And don't forget, Grampy was a well-respected man. Not just a GP, but vice-chairman of the Parish council, *and* a mason. For his daughter to have a baby out of wedlock would have been quite the scandal.'

Joe's heart ached at the thought of that scared young girl, not only losing the man she loved but also being reviled by the self-righteous prude who called himself her father.

You were one horrible, vindictive bastard, Grampy. I'm glad you're dead, thought Joe.

'You don't need to say any more, Mum.'

'There's not much more to tell. Dad sold up and we moved south, where he opened another practice and bought this place. To save my reputation, he suggested we tell people that I'd been married, but my husband had died young in a road accident. He even bought me a wedding ring.'

'Save *his* reputation, more like,' seethed Joe.

'I can't say too much. After all, I went along with it.'

'What else could you do?' he offered, guilty that he'd instigated her dragging up such painful memories. 'You were just a girl.'

Now it was her squeezing *his* hand as she beamed, 'But a few months later, it was all worth it, when you arrived. Right here, in this house. Your father wasn't there to share my joy, but at least I had *something* of him.'

While the lid was off her box of secrets, Joe wanted to ask why on earth she married Nigel Holland within six months of her father's passing. No sooner had one emotionally stunted man departed her life than she replaced him with another. But that conversation could wait. He was aware that he'd put her through the emotional wringer, and it was time to stop turning the handle. Joe now knew a lot more about his biological father, and that had been the object of the exercise. The things he'd also learned about his mother were a welcome bonus.

Right on cue, the back door flew open and in bounded David, like an excited puppy. He was more innocent than Joe was at eleven; a sensitive but happy go lucky boy who was still, just about, at the age where everything was an adventure.

'Hi Mum. Hi Joe.'

'Hello love. Where's Dad?' asked Mary, without much enthusiasm.

'He dropped me off then said he was going to visit his sister. Guess what, Mum? Some older kids let me join in their game of rounders in the park.'

'Did they now? That sounds like fun.'

'It was. And I saw a dead fox. Its mouth was open and its tongue was hanging out. Like this.' David then treated them to his best dead fox impression.

'Lovely,' grimaced his mum.

Joe chuckled and said, 'How about I finish my breakfast and we have a kick around in the back garden?'

'Great! I'll be Arsenal.'

'Arsenal?' puzzled Joe. 'I thought you were a Liverpool fan, like me.'

'I was,' explained the boy, ''til they lost in the cup final. I'm Arsenal now.' Then he raced off into the garden shouting, 'You're in goal first.'

'Kids,' muttered Joe, cutting his barely warm poached egg, 'they're so fickle.'

CHAPTER TEN

LOVE CHILD

Joe soon made peace with the disclosure that he was born out of wedlock. This was the late 20th century; what did it matter if his parents had a piece of paper from the State or not? He was a product of their love and that was the important thing. All the same, he chose not to tell anybody. Not even Paolo. Why would he? It was nobody's business but his. And Mary's.

He did feel desperately sad for his mum, though. Tortured for years by the thought of the life she might have had, if the rain hadn't turned to ice on that long ago winter's day. One positive though was that Joe felt closer to Mary since their heart to heart. He understood her more. And having John Hudson's blood flowing through his veins clearly made him very precious to her. One day, though, he vowed that he *would* find out what had possessed her to take up with Nigel Holland. Perhaps she was one of those people who believes they don't deserve happiness. They're out there.

There certainly didn't appear to be any real affection from either party in her marital union. It was more like a business arrangement; Nigel brought in the bulk of the money and paid the bills while Mary cooked, kept house and raised their son. As for Joe, he only spoke to the man when it was unavoidable, or vice versa. Polite apathy best summed it up. He looked upon his mum and stepdad's relationship as a lesson in what a marriage should *not* be, and vowed he'd rather stay single his whole life than be trapped in something similar. Maybe it had been different at the beginning. No doubt plenty of couples grow bored with each other. If you don't water a flower, it will shrivel and die.

What showed no sign of dying was Joe's love affair with soul music. Ellen Massetti had taken to playing bingo on Tuesday evenings with a couple of colleagues from Clements. So, most weeks, Joe would get home from work, have his dinner and a quick bath and spend the evening at Paolo's. On the way he'd pop into an accommodating off licence and pick up a four pack of lager for him and his friend. Lilah was allowed a small glass if they were feeling generous.

Inevitably the evening would include a few rounds of The Chartbuster Quiz, which meant listening to their favourite artists. One visit, Lilah was very pleased with herself when she told the boys about a new soul song she'd heard on the radio called, "I'm Gonna Run Away From You" by Tami Lynn. Neither of them was familiar with either the song or the singer. To her delight it rose to number four on the singles charts. It wasn't often she stole a march on them musically, so she savoured the moment.

Joe was now in the second year of his electrical apprenticeship and still enjoying it, partly because he had an aptitude for it but mainly because of Lenny Coleman. His even temper made learning fun and he was a great raconteur. Some of his anecdotes from the war were pure gold. Joe's favourite entailed Lenny and a few mates out on patrol in occupied France after the Normandy landings. Suddenly, they came under heavy artillery fire. They took cover behind a farmhouse and within minutes the whole building was reduced to rubble. Len said he was certain that if he stayed there, he'd be killed, so he took off back to his own lines like a bat out of hell. On a blind bend on a country road, he ran straight into a British officer, knocking him to the ground. Mortified, he helped him up, dusted him off, saluted and said, 'I'm really sorry, Major.'

The angry officer said, 'I am not a Major, I'm a General.'

Lenny replied, 'A General? Christ, I didn't think I'd run *that* far back!'

As with his 'bullet in the leg' on D-Day, you didn't know how much (if any) of Lenny's stories were true. But it didn't matter because they were always entertaining. For all his joking around, Len gave off an air of calm authority. A worldly-wiseness.

That perhaps explains why, on a tea break, Joe decided to open up about the family matter his mum had recently divulged. Lenny listened intently, quietly weighing up what he was being told. 'That's a sad tale, young 'un. Sounds like your poor mum's been through a lot. So, what is it about the situation that bothers you?'

'I'm not sure,' admitted Joe. 'I was just led to believe that my mum and my real dad were married.'

From what you've said, they would have been, if fate hadn't put the boot in. And if being born the wrong side of the blanket isn't sitting well with you, right off the top of my head, I can give you three examples of well-known names that didn't let similar beginnings hold *them* back.'

He counted them on his fingers. 'One; William the Conqueror. Two; Marilyn Monroe. Three; Yours Truly.'

'You?' exclaimed Joe, disregarding the more famous two.

'Me,' confirmed the older man. 'The penny dropped when I was eleven and my parents were planning a party for their *tenth* wedding anniversary. Like you, I was a bit taken aback but is it really such a big deal? It's not where you start, it's where you finish. Now, it's doubtful that you'll ever successfully invade another country, like Willy did. Or even stand on a subway grating with your dress blowing up, like Marilyn, though I'm not discounting it. But, you have been given the opportunity to introduce people to the modern miracle called electricity, like moi.'

Not for the first time, Lenny's ability to find the right words resonated with the young man in his charge. Without either of them planning it, he'd become Joe's father figure. Screwing the top back on his flask, the great sage concluded the exchange. 'Now, stop fucking yapping and get the generator set up. We've got a house to wire.'

CHAPTER ELEVEN

HELP ME MAKE IT THROUGH THE NIGHT

As the calendars for 1971 were being replaced by those for 1972, Joe and Paolo still hadn't accomplished 'Operation: Lose Your Cherry'. Though there *had* been a few near misses. In Paolo's case, he had been just about to enter the home straight (aka Diane) on his lounge sofa, when his mum had to go downstairs in the early hours for a glass of water. Game over. Better luck next time.

The previous night, Joe, in the less comfortable setting of a furniture shop doorway, was getting to know a young lady extremely well, whilst waiting for her last bus home. Along with Joe, the shop window was starting to steam up when disaster struck. The bus came. And he didn't. Just ten more minutes and the bragging rights would have been his.

Socially, they were casting their nets a little wider in pursuit of their quest. As well as local pubs, they'd tentatively given Top Rank another try. They'd also started to frequent the New Penny, a disco club at the other end of the High St.

Now, a little bit about Joe Holland's hometown. Until the mid-1800's, Watford was just a small settlement, until the opening of the London-Birmingham railway. The nearby Grand Union Canal, with barges from the Midlands filled with all manner of goods, also made it a good location. However, the foundations of the town were built on the brewing and print industries. A nice pint and something to read; what more could anyone want?

Watford became known as a print town, which in the 1920's, thanks to the Sun Printers and Odhams Press, made little old Watford a contender for the biggest printing centre in Europe. With its prospect of well paid employment and close proximity to the capital, the town started to thrive. In time, other important employers would include companies like Croxley Paper Mill, Fishburn Printing Ink and the Rolls Royce engine plant at Leavesden Aerodrome. In the one hundred years up to 1971, the population grew from just over 12,000 to around 75,000. Watford was booming, so, by the law of averages, you had to stand a better chance of losing your virginity in a busy town than if you lived out in the sticks. Didn't you?

The main difference between Top Rank and The New Penny was that you could fit 'the Penny' into a corner of 'the Rank' and no-one would notice. But, in this case, size didn't matter. Yes, the smaller venue was dimly lit, sweaty and cramped. It was a claustrophobic's worst nightmare, but the atmosphere was terrific. It was next to empty until around 10pm, when the punters, primed with alcohol elsewhere, would pile in. Members to the left, non-members to the right.

To call it a nightclub would be like calling a window box a garden, but it was always a good night in there. The dancefloor wasn't much bigger than the average front room and the carpet was so sticky from spilt drinks that it felt like you were wearing deep sea diver's boots when you walked across it. No-one cared, though, because everyone was there to kick start the weekend. Even rival factions that wouldn't normally mix would tolerate each other, rather than risk getting banned. Naturally, there was the odd punch up, courtesy of alpha male chest beating, but most of the time it was under twenty-fives out for a few late-night drinks, a laugh, and a boogie. And, of course, to meet the opposite sex.

On a rainy Friday night in November, Joe and Paolo made their way upstairs to the bar. They were already merry and ready for the hunt when they were approached by two attractive girls. A tall brunette and her shorter blonde friend, who was, just about, wearing a very low-cut top. The taller girl, who seemed to know Paolo, spoke first. 'Here he is, the Italian stallion.'

'I can see that,' said her friend admiringly before turning her attention to Joe and commenting, 'And this must be his sidekick, the bony pony.'

The squiffy girls giggled. Joe didn't. 'I'm not bony, I'm wiry,' he pointed out tetchily.

'Touchy,' replied the blonde, 'It's just a joke. Buy me a Bacardi and I'll dance with you.'

'I've got a better idea. Buy your own Bacardi and dance by yourself.'

He'd come a long way since the pineapple slushy mugging. The dark-haired girl gave Paolo an, 'Oh well,' look and she and her friend retired to the Ladies' room.

'What the hell's the matter with you?' chastised Paolo. 'Do you *want* to die a virgin?'

'She's got too much mouth.'

'Maybe, but exactly the right number of boobs. And she's not shy about displaying them. I think I'm in with that brunette. I vaguely remember chatting to her last week, but I was a bit Brahms, and she was with a bloke. What's the harm of having a drink with them? See how it pans out.'

Joe mulled it over. 'Okay, Mr Stallion. Whatever you say, Mr Stallion.'

Paolo playfully ruffled his friend's hair. 'I think someone didn't like me being complimented.'

Joe's response was an amiable, 'Piss off.'

'I think someone is a teeny bit jealous.'

As Joe smoothed his hair down, the overworked barmaid urged, 'What can I get you?'

'Pint of lager please,' he requested, 'and a nosebag full of oats for my friend here.'

'Make that two pints,' corrected Paolo, 'with a bit of luck I'll be getting my oats later.'

Joe shook his head and sighed. 'If God loves a trier, He must bloody adore us two.'

Out of the corner of his eye, he noticed the girls returning. Still miffed, Joe pretended not to notice them, so Paolo bought them each a drink and the foursome found an empty table. Paolo and the taller girl, Kelly, were soon chatting away, making the silence between the other two even more noticeable. The blonde spoke first. 'Sorry if we got off on the wrong foot. It's my weird sense of humour. I get it off my mum.'

'Have your parents been divorced long?' enquired Joe.

'How did you know they're divorced?'

'Oh, just a wild guess.'

The remark made them both smile. The ice was melting. 'I'm Suzanne,' she revealed. 'Do you have a name or do I just call you smartarse?'

'Smartarse will do, but I'm Joe to my friends.'

'Am I your friend?'

'Do you want to be?'

'Maybe. I haven't decided yet,' she teased, sipping her Bacardi and coke.

After their shaky start, the conversation started to flow and it was soon apparent that Suzanne was right about her sense of humour. It was quirky, offbeat and cutting. To her credit, though, she could take it as well as dish it out and, as the night progressed, the pair swapped light-hearted banter, and the odd put down, without malice. She was irreverent, fun and confident. And though Joe shared the first two of those traits, he had to bluff the last one. Three hours and five drinks later, they were enjoying the last slow dance of the evening, when Suzanne whispered, 'Do you want to come back to my place?'

To a young, single man, no poet, in fact no writer in any genre, has ever come up with a line so full of anticipation and promise. In the early hours of the morning, in a disco, those nine words could only mean one thing. They are not open to misinterpretation. She's not asking you back to see her collection of novelty teapots. Joe had received an official invitation to the unveiling of those magnificent, creamy white orbs, and it would be bad manners to say no.

Earlier in the evening, Suzanne had already mentioned that she and Kelly were both twenty-one, panicking the boys into saying they were nineteen; and the girls *still* made a joke about being a couple of cradle snatchers. If Suzanne knew Joe was seventeen and a half, she'd probably make him a warm drink back at hers, tuck him in and read him a bedtime story. So, in answer to her question, with feigned nonchalance he replied, 'Do you live alone then?'

'No, but I've got the flat to myself tonight.'

Paolo had already divulged earlier that Kelly had offered to drive them home later. So, to recap: They were now mixing with young women who had their own transport *and* lived independently from their parents. It was like going from jumpers for goalposts in the local park to Wembley Stadium. Joe found it hard to play it cool when what he really wanted to do was sit up and beg like a dog, tongue out and panting. But he managed a blasé, 'Yeah, alright then.' As they shared the latest in a succession of long, passionate kisses, Joe steeled himself for what was ahead.

This is it, Joseph. Everything you've trained for. You're about to make your debut, son.

Kelly dropped them at her friend's home in Abbots Langley before setting off for Paolo's house. As he alighted the car, Joe saw his own excited apprehension mirrored in his best friend's face. Would they rise to the occasion, or was their inexperience about to be unmasked?

Suzanne's flat was one of a block of four. Modern looking. Two bedrooms, living room, kitchen and bathroom/toilet. Once inside, she guided him by the hand, straight to her bedroom. No instant Nescafe and small talk for this girl. Joe wondered if he looked as nervous as he felt. Being told to, 'Just relax,' gave him his answer. But Suzanne was a patient and capable teacher, and he was an eager and willing student. Nothing was said, but she knew it was his first time. And Joe *knew* that she knew. Thankfully, though, even after an encore a few hours after the main event, she didn't make any sarcastic remarks or negative comments, so he guessed he'd done alright.

At 9.15am, Joe Holland, former virgin, now sexual gladiator, needed to pee. As gently as he could, he eased Suzanne's outstretched arm from his chest and slid out of bed. He remembered her telling him that the bathroom was along the hall, last door on the left. Whilst emptying his bladder, his eyes casually scanned the room. The windowsill housed the usual Aladdin's cave of lotions and potions that women can't seem to live without. Before he lost interest, he listed zesty lemon shampoo, anti-frizz shampoo, moisturiser with coconut oil, moisturiser *without* coconut oil, blushers, toners, cleansers, hair grips, tweezers and wax strips. He smiled as he contrasted it with his own meagre collection of grooming products, a comb, a toothbrush, a cheap razor, some underarm deodorant and a small bottle of Brut aftershave. As he washed his hands, he studied his face in the mirror. He didn't *look* any different but the throbbing between his legs told him everything had changed. He was up and running. A man. Get in!

It was whilst drying his hands that he noticed the faces of Sooty and Sweep on the towel. Then he spotted the three yellow plastic ducks sitting between the bath taps. With distant alarm bells ringing and curiosity piqued, Joe decided to take a peek inside the second bedroom. The door was slightly ajar so he quietly pushed it open and peered in. The Winnie the Pooh wallpaper and the cuddly toys adorning the tiny bed led him to the conclusion that there were only two feasible possibilities. Either Suzanne shared the flat with a very immature dwarf or (and he was leaning heavily toward this one) she had a child.

Back in her bedroom, Suzanne was slowly stirring. 'Morning. Would you like a tea or coffee?' she yawned as Joe hastily pulled his clothes on.

'No thanks, I'd best be getting off,' he answered, trying to locate a missing sock.

Perceptively she responded, 'So you've seen my son's room then?' The realisation that he was out of his depth hit home. He had never been in a situation anywhere near as awkward as this one, and he didn't have the experience or the skills to handle it.

'I'm not looking for a surrogate daddy for him, if that's what you're thinking. He's got a dad who loves him. He's away at the moment, and I get lonely sometimes, that's the truth of it.'

Joe couldn't think of anything to say and just wanted to get out of there. Giving up the search for the elusive sock, he made for the door.

'That's right, off you go. Mummy will be worried,' was her parting shot. He felt deflated. In one sentence, Suzanne, she who had made him a man, had relegated him back to being a boy again. In silence, he slipped his shoes on, picked up his jacket and set off on the two mile walk home. With each step he cursed himself for not knowing what to do or say. If he ever bumped into Suzanne again, he vowed to apologise, although she'd have every right to blank him.

After lunch, Joe phoned Paolo to compare notes. Kelly had driven him home and gone in for 'coffee'. This time Mrs Massetti hadn't gone downstairs for a glass of water and the Italian stallion did indeed get his oats. So, 'Operation: Lose Your Cherry', had ended in an honourable draw. The difference being that Paolo and Kelly had arranged another date. Joe felt awful about the way he'd rudely walked out on Suzanne and asked his friend to prudently find out more about her situation. It transpired that Kelly was quite talkative.

As Joe had suspected, the baby's father being 'away at the moment', didn't entail him being at university or doing missionary work in Africa. His nickname, Mad Mick McCreadie hinted that calm discussion wasn't his forte and his temper had landed him with a two year stretch for GBH. His victim's crime? Chatting up Suzanne in a pub.

A cold shiver ran through Joe. He was several streets on from merely chatting her up. If Mad Mick found out some other bloke had been doing the horizontal tango with his girlfriend... well, he didn't sound the type to forgive and forget. McCreadie would have been out by now if he hadn't beaten up another prisoner for borrowing his toothpaste without permission. That gained him an extra six months inside, and Joe the satisfaction that he'd live to see another Christmas.

CHAPTER TWELVE

SHOP AROUND

Joe was pleased that Paolo had found a steady girlfriend. If that's what he wanted, good luck to him. Up until then, he'd thought it was what *he* wanted too. But now he realised that he didn't. Not yet. But it was what you were supposed to do when you were of working age, wasn't it? Meet a girl, get engaged, marry, have kids. It's what convention expected of you. Well, sod that. He wasn't even eighteen yet. Just starting out. Suzanne had shown him the ropes (not literally, but she probably had some) and not to share his newly acquired knowledge would be selfish. The world was a fairground and it was open for business. Of course, he hoped to settle down one day but trusted that he would instinctively know when the time, and the girl, was right. Meanwhile, it was time to have some fun.

Lenny Coleman's opinion was that every man should stay single until they were at least twenty-five. 'Travel. Experience life. Put it about a bit.'

When Joe related the story of Suzanne and her psychotic boyfriend, the older man urged caution. 'That's called playing with fire, young 'un. Never mind the psychos, even the most docile men don't take kindly to their women being test driven by other geezers. Blokes have been murdered for less. You'd better pray that she doesn't tell him.'

'Are you kidding? I've already worn out the knees on two pairs of trousers.'

'I was in the army with someone who caught his wife cheating on him.'

'I thought you might have been,' sighed Joe, rolling his eyes.

The three main protagonists of Len's stories loomed large, 'Was it Ivor Griffiths, Jug Ears Jackson, or Smudger Smythe?'

'It might not have been any of them,' retorted Lenny, 'but as it happens, it was Smudger. He got an unexpected twenty-four-hour pass and thought he'd surprise his missus. And boy, did he surprise her. He walked in and found her in bed with his best friend. Devastated he was. Crestfallen. Once he'd gathered himself, he told her straight, 'You've always been an old slapper, so this is no great surprise.'

Then, turning to his best friend he said, 'But I'm disappointed in you, Rover. You're a bad dog. Now get to your basket!'

Grimacing, Joe responded with, 'That's rough, Len. Ruff, ruff.' He was forced to duck as Lenny's pliers hit the wall behind him. As their laughter subsided, Len took on a more sombre tone.

'Just watch yourself. There are some nasty bastards out there and this McCreadie character sounds like one of them.'

With all the charms of a new girlfriend to occupy him, Paolo naturally spent less time with *his* best friend. They still went for the occasional beer, and Joe's Tuesday visits to the Massettis continued, but there had been a shift. Understandably, he'd been bumped down to number two and, gradually, the boys' nights out dwindled. This left a Paolo-sized hole in Joe's social life, and it needed filling. He required someone new to knock around with. Step forward, Christopher Cross. Yes, really: Chris Cross. When choosing names some parents just don't think it through, do they?

Chris was a fellow apprentice at Edwards & Sons. He was a decent enough looking lad, but his problem was his personality: he didn't have one. His crippling shyness probably owed something to being teased about his name since the age of five. A TV general knowledge show called Criss Cross Quiz just threw petrol on the fire. Young Mr Cross found it difficult to converse with fellow males, and next to impossible to speak to anyone born without a willy. His main interests were stamp collecting and his model railway. Nothing wrong with that. Joe was pretty sure that, by the law of averages, there must be young female philatelists out there, and perhaps even one or two young ladies who'd be only too happy to discuss 00-gauge locomotives. Unfortunately, these women didn't frequent the late-night drinking dens of Watford. But Chris not having a personality was cancelled out by the one thing he *did* have. His own car. That ace up the sleeve in the 70's dating game. In the cold, wet, early hours of the morning, the offer of a lift home was hard to resist. Even with what appeared to be an android behind the wheel.

Joe was convinced that the more Chris sampled the throbbing disco beat and flashing lights, the more at ease he'd become. It was a fair assumption. For most people, a couple of bevvies relaxed them and made them more talkative. For Chris, alcohol had the opposite effect. It actually made him shrink even further into his shell, which was some feat. On more than one occasion, Joe, in all seriousness, had been asked if his friend was a mute. Not quite, but he was proving to be a poor substitute for the sociable, outgoing Paolo. Thanks though to Chris's Ford Anglia, Joe did obtain a few phone numbers which led to future liaisons. Charisma-light Chris wasn't so lucky. One time, a girl in the front passenger seat jokingly held her compact mirror to his lips to check if he was alive. The verdict: undecided.

In the New Penny on New Years Eve, Joe froze when Suzanne walked in with a friend. He turned his back and kept his head down but in a club that small she couldn't fail to spot him. Confirmation came when a firm tap on his shoulder caused him to turn. A stony-faced Suzanne was delving in her handbag. For a second he feared she might be reaching for a sharpened steel comb, or one of Mad Mick's spare knuckledusters. Before he could react, her hand flashed toward him and dropped something in his beer glass, with a curt, 'I think this belongs to you.'

Floating on top of the froth was the sock he'd lost at her flat two months previously. What a relief. A sock in the beer was preferable to a sock on the jaw. Delivery completed; she made to walk away but his voice stopped her. 'I owe you an apology. Can I buy you a drink? Please?'

Suzanne relented and they stood at the bar. Joe handed her the Bacardi and coke and tentatively asked, 'Where was it then? The sock.'

'In the lampshade.'

He couldn't contain a reflective smile. She tried not to follow suit but failed.

'I didn't mean to rush off like that,' he continued. 'I'm really sorry. I don't want you to think I used you.'

With an honesty that disarmed him she replied, 'You *did* use me. Same as I used *you*. It's fine. We both wanted it to happen, and it did. You bailed because you found out I've got a kid.'

'Well, it was a bit of a shock.'

'No doubt Paolo's told you that my feller's doing time. He won't be out for at least another six months. I'm twenty-one, for Christ's sake. I just want to have some fun.'

'If he put someone in hospital just for talking to you, he'd most likely put me in the cemetery,' opined Joe, furtively tucking the beer-soaked sock behind a nearby radiator.

'I'm not likely to tell him, am I? And I'm not a slag. I liked you.'

'I liked you too – eventually,' he revealed, squeezing her hand. Suzanne's companion had soon given up on trying to talk to Chris and gone downstairs for a dance. Joe panicked as Suzanne looked Chris up and down, fearing that a sarcastic salvo from her would result in him never leaving the house again. Thankfully, the music drowned out her voice as she asked Joe, 'What time is he due back at Madame Tussauds?'

'He's alright. Just a bit shy. Hey, you haven't got any girlfriends who collect stamps or build model railways, have you?'

She looked at him as if he was speaking a foreign language. Getting back on track he concluded with, 'I'm really glad we've cleared the air.'

'Me too,' she smiled. 'I'll see you around.'

And she did. Around midnight to be precise. They'd been exchanging flirty looks all evening, even whilst talking to other potential partners. The sexual tension between them was palpable, and when they found themselves dancing next to each other as 1971 died and 1972 was born, they were snogging heavily. Cautiously, Joe proposed meeting back at her flat. She readily agreed, even when he said it was best not to leave the club together in case word reached HMP Wandsworth. You never knew who was watching. He was aware he was embarking on a very dangerous game, but danger is the twin sister of excitement.

Chris dropped Joe off at Suzanne's and she arrived fifteen minutes later in a taxi. The weather was freezing but once inside they soon warmed each other up. Talk about seeing the new year in with a bang. Afterwards, as she slept, he thought about what she'd said in 'the Penny'. They *were* using each other, but not in a deceitful way. And anyway, is it possible to be used if you're aware of it? Having no delusions that this might lead to some big, enduring romance was liberating. At the very most it had a shelf life of six months and they both accepted it. The illicit lovers agreed to keep it low key and casual. The moment either of them started to get possessive or too emotionally attached would be when they'd call a halt. It was *their* exclusive secret, and it worked perfectly for them.

In the early months of 1972, Joe glimpsed the flipside to Suzanne's abrasiveness. A softness and sensibility that was rarely shown but always there. He only visited when her son was staying at her mum's, but it was clear she adored the boy. She was fond of Mick too, when he was calm. It was on one of her fortnightly visits to Wandsworth that she gave him an ultimatum. When he got out, they would try and make a go of it, but they had a child to consider now and she'd had enough of his foul temper. If he couldn't control it or went back to prison, they were finished and he was out. Of the flat, *and* their lives. It took a lot of courage on her part and Joe admired her for it. And he hoped Mick could deliver. Suzanne was a good mum and a good person. She deserved her shot at happiness.

CHAPTER THIRTEEN

SOUL SISTER, BROWN SUGAR

In February, just before Paolo's birthday, Kelly called time on their relationship. He hadn't told her his real age, so when she discovered he was about to turn eighteen and not twenty, she told him she didn't like being lied to and finished with him. It was hard for Joe to see his friend so devastated but, on a selfish level, it was good to have his old partner back. He'd missed him. His job now was to help him back up onto the horse. Once he'd got Kelly out of his system, the dynamic duo would be back in business. But what about Chris Cross? Three's a crowd and all that; but how to let him down gently?

Thankfully, Joe didn't have to broach the subject because Chris had got himself a girlfriend. And no, he didn't have to inflate her. He'd gone to a model railway convention in Hendon to buy a new coal truck for his Flying Scotsman and was so taken by the girl helping out on the stall that he bought a signal box too. Their eyes met across her rolling stock and, when she mentioned that the tunnel was on special offer, he was smitten.

'Truly,' thought Joe, 'there *is* someone for everyone.'

The first time they played the Chartbuster quiz after Paolo's unceremonious dumping; it was unusually subdued. In hindsight, Joe conceded that buying the bottle of vodka at the offy wasn't such a great idea.

Alcohol was a depressant and Paolo didn't need any help in that department. His dearest friend and his sister did their best to cheer him up, but his face remained like a wet weekend in Clacton. His first test for the other two players reflected his state of mind. 'Chartbusters Volume One: Side one. Track seven.'

To her delight, Lilah just beat Joe to the answer: 'Jimmy Ruffin – "What Becomes of the Broken Hearted".'

As the song played, Paolo stared into the middle distance, sighed and sipped his vodka and coke. When his turn came around again, he mumbled, 'Volume One: Side one. Track three.'

This time Joe was quickest, 'Four Tops – "Standing in the Shadows of Love".'

Joe and Lilah exchanged concerned looks. There was a pattern emerging. They both deliberately chose upbeat numbers like "Dancing in the Street" and "The Happening", but nothing could shake him from his malaise. Paolo had an acute case of lovesickness and there was no quick cure. His third choice of the evening, "I Want You Back" by The Jackson Five, confirmed their worst fears. As young Michael Jackson's voice faded away, Joe glanced at his watch and muttered, 'Time to feed next door's cat.'

'I forgot they're away. Do you want me to do it?' offered Lilah.

'No, you're alright. I'll go,' her brother replied, lethargically hauling himself out of his chair. Joe's attempts to get his friend back in the dating game hadn't borne fruit so far. They'd avoided the Watford hotspots in case they chanced upon Kelly. If Paolo saw her with another bloke, he likely wouldn't be able to contain himself, and his boxing skills would mean a bad outcome for the poor sod she was with. To his credit, he didn't want that to happen, so for a night out, the boys would bus it to nearby St Albans. An altogether more genteel place than Watford, but with no shortage of single young ladies. But even when they got chatting to girls in youngsters' pubs, like The Boot, The Fleur de Lys or Ye Olde Fighting Cocks, Paolo's lack of enthusiasm sabotaged each mission. The night of his eighteenth birthday was only marginally more fun than having a boil lanced.

As the front door closed, Joe observed, 'He's still got it bad, hasn't he?'

Lilah nodded, 'Sometimes, I hear him sobbing at night. It's horrible.'

Changing the subject, she said, 'My turn to choose. Chartbusters Volume Four: Side two. Track seven.'

Quick as a flash, Joe answered, 'Junior Walker and The All Stars – "What Does It Take to Win Your Love for Me?".'

'Correct,' she confirmed, sliding the vinyl out of its red and blue sleeve.

Paolo wasn't the only one who'd changed. Lilah had turned fifteen the previous week, and, seemingly overnight, had blossomed. She'd lost her gawkiness and was unrecognisable as the tomboy with the lazy eye from six years ago. Her jet-black hair was now shoulder length with a centre parting. She was developing fast, and not just physically. Recently, she'd started as a Saturday girl at the local hairdressers and dealing with people seemed to have given her a maturity beyond her years. It was only doing the mundane jobs – sweeping up, making hot drinks, sterilising the equipment etc – but it was all good experience. The nearest she got to the clients' hair was washing it, then handing the combs, rollers and hairgrips to the stylists. But she absorbed everything, knowing that one day she'd be the one holding the scissors and asking, 'Have you booked your holiday yet?'

The stylus dropped and the sweet sound of Junior Walker's tenor saxophone dripped from the speakers like warm honey. Instead of retaking her seat opposite him, Lilah held out her hand to him. 'Come on, let's dance.'

Caught off guard, he blurted out, 'You and me?'

'No, me and the hoover. Of course, you and me, you dummy.'

Earlier, he couldn't help noticing her shapely legs, from her slim ankles up to her smooth thighs, accentuated by the cut off denim shorts she was wearing. Placing his glass down, he rose and took two paces to meet her. He slid his right hand around her waist and, with his other hand holding hers, they swayed to the rhythm. Joe wondered if it was possible for something to feel both strange and natural at the same time. She rested her head on his shoulder, and he noted her hair smelt like flowers. He was also keenly aware that her breasts were pushing into his chest. And it was plain she was braless under her T-shirt. After about thirty seconds of being lost in the music, she lifted her head and aimed her wide brown eyes at him. And before he knew it, they were kissing.

By now he'd kissed quite a few girls. After all, he was only six weeks off being eighteen. A veritable man about town. But invariably it was always an alcohol fuelled smashing together of mouths, tongues revolving like ships propellers. This was different. It was slow. Sensual. Gently, he probed her lips apart with his tongue, to be welcomed by hers. The softness of her, the closeness of their bodies and the hypnotic music was intoxicating. All of the above, plus the vodka, had rallied his hormones and they were on full alert. With some consternation he felt himself getting hard. She too must have felt it on her upper thigh but made no attempt to move. Neither did he.

What the hell was happening here? This was his best friend's little sister. Except she wasn't little anymore. Somehow, the endearingly irritating tomboy had grown into a very attractive young woman. *But,* whispered the unwelcome voice of reason, *she's fifteen. Fifteen mate!*

The sound of the front door closing took her out of his arms as they scurried back to their respective seats. Just before Paolo re-entered the room, Joe picked up an LP from the rack and rested it on his lap to disguise his slowly fading erection. Fittingly, the album was by "The Temptations". Never again could he look at Lilah as merely Paolo's little sister. Nor trust himself to be alone with her. Where did she learn to kiss like that? If it came naturally, it was a rare gift indeed.

Just stop it, reprimanded his conscience, *this isn't some girl you've met on a night out; it's your best friend's sister.* And then it screamed, *And she's fifteeeeeeeeen!*

CHAPTER FOURTEEN

BEHIND A PAINTED SMILE

The next time Joe was at the Massetti's, there was a feeling of, not embarrassment, but awkwardness between him and Lilah. A line had been crossed, and they were both aware of it. Joe learned from Paolo that, on his last visit, Lilah had sneaked some of the vodka into her glass of coke. Did that play a part in what ensued? It was confusing. But whatever was evolving between them was powerful. Joe knew that, if he acted upon it, it could also be damaging, not to mention illegal. It might lead to him losing his best friend, and possibly his surrogate family. The trouble was, he wasn't certain he was strong enough to fight the feeling. But as long as they weren't left alone together, nothing could happen.

Joe and Suzanne still had their clandestine liaisons, but he got the feeling they'd almost run their course. It was whilst sitting up in bed, drinking tea on a Sunday morning that she confirmed how intuitive she was.

'Who is she then?' she asked, amiably.

'What do you mean?'

'You've obviously met someone you're keen on. It's okay. No strings, remember?'

'Is it that obvious?'

'Your body was here last night but your mind was definitely elsewhere.'

'It's a tricky one,' he conceded.

'Well, if you don't tell me, I can't give you the female perspective, can I?'

Joe came close to confiding in her but thought better of it, reasoning that he had to figure his own way out of this particular maze. It was on this occasion that Suzanne revealed that she was aware of his real age. He'd once mentioned that he and Paolo had gone through school together, so when Kelly discovered her boyfriend wasn't about to turn twenty, it became obvious that Joe had lied too. Unlike Kelly, though, Suzanne wasn't unduly concerned. Why should she be? Theirs was only a short-term arrangement with no future.

Try as he might, Joe couldn't stop thinking about Lilah. Her smooth, olive skin; the slow dance and sensual kiss they'd shared. Undoubtedly, he had feelings for her, but the near three year age gap seemed insurmountable. If he was twenty-five and she was twenty-two it wouldn't matter a jot. But eighteen and fifteen? That was different. Did he love her? Yes. But was he *in* love with her? He couldn't say as he'd never experienced it. How did you even recognise romantic love? Did it arrive fully formed or did it grow organically?

The physical attraction was intense, but it was more than that; he truly cared about her. Was that real, adult love? Thousands of articulate writers had tried and failed to define it, so what chance did an apprentice electrician have? Maybe love transcended mere words. It was all so baffling. All he knew for certain was that she was on his mind an awful lot. He wanted to discuss it with her, explain things, and get her take on it, but that would mean them being alone and he didn't trust himself. Maybe he could write her a letter? No, her mum or brother might find it. Telephone her? Even that wouldn't guarantee a private conversation. He wasn't even sure what he wanted to say, let alone how to say it, but he couldn't bear the thought of her thinking he was ignoring her. And it *was* just a kiss. So far.

In the end he decided to 'accidentally' bump into her when she finished work the following Saturday. It was drizzling when the salon lights went out and the chattering staff left the shop. From his shadowy vantage point across the road, he watched as a middle-aged lady locked up while the three younger females said their goodbyes and dispersed. Lilah turned the corner and disappeared from view but Joe quickly caught her up.

'Going my way?'

'Oh, you made me jump.'

'Sorry. I've just been into town. Can I walk you home?'

'Unless I get a better offer,' she teased, linking her arm with his. It was a nice fit.

'I wanted to talk to you about the other week, you know, when Paolo went next door.'

'Nice, wasn't it?' she giggled.

'No... I mean, yes, it was nice. Very nice. But it shouldn't have happened.'

'Why not?'

'Because you're barely fifteen, Lilah.'

'So?' she bristled, 'this time next year I'll be sixteen, shall I hide in my wardrobe until then?'

'Don't be like that. I'm just saying.'

As she retracted her arm from his, she shot back, 'Just saying what? That I'm a silly little girl who doesn't know her own mind?'

'No. You're putting words in my mouth.'

'Well, you put your tongue in mine. Or did I imagine it?'

Oh dear, this isn't going well at all, he thought.

'Sorry I'm not twenty-one like Kelly's friend.' She almost spat the words out.

How does she know about Suzanne? Fall back. Take up a defensive position!

'Sorry if I've upset you. I didn't mean to.'

'I'm not upset,' she corrected, 'I'm angry.'

'That wasn't my intention. I haven't explained myself very well.'

'Oh, message received, loud and clear.'

The remainder of the ten-minute walk home was shrouded in a deafening silence until they reached their destination. Lilah's parting words, her voice simmering with resentment, were, 'The world doesn't revolve around *you*, Joe Holland.'

Then she went inside, leaving him standing in the rain, which mirrored their conversation by turning from light to heavy. Not even a 'thanks for walking me home', or a 'come in and warm up with a cup of tea.'

Dejectedly, he sloped off to the bus stop. If he got pneumonia, it would be her fault. Then she'd be sorry.

If her last sentence was intended to hurt him then she got her wish. The inference that he was selfish really stung, especially as he had *her* best interests at heart. The unavoidable fact was that, at this juncture, Lilah *was* too young for him. The problem being, as he'd just found out, there was no easy way to say it. All he could hope was that, when she analysed their conversation, she would see it from his point of view. Truthfully, though, Joe couldn't help feeling that his failure to predict Lilah's reaction was on a par with the Titanic's failure to spot the iceberg – with the same result. Watching his bus pull away from the stop just fast enough to prevent him catching it didn't improve his mood. Thunder rumbled ominously in the distance. Perhaps he'd get struck by lightning. *Then* she'd wish she'd invited him in. Blowing a raindrop from the end of his nose he became aware that his left shoe was letting in water. All things considered; he'd had better Saturday evenings.

Thinking it best to let Lilah cool down, it was ten days before he showed his face at the Massetti's again, popping around on a Tuesday evening for a drink and a few rounds of the Chartbuster quiz. As usual, Ellen was at her Bingo night but Joe noticed there were only two glasses on the coffee table when there had always been three. As nonchalantly as he could, he asked Paolo, 'Where's little sis then?'

'Oh, she's not playing tonight. Going on a date.'

'A date?' repeated Joe, 'With a boy?'

'Yeah, some kid from her school. They're going to see *Love Story* at the Odeon.'

'On a school night? Anyway, that came out last year. Why are they showing it again?'

'I don't know. Maybe cos people still want to see it?'

'Don't you think she's a bit young for boys?'

'Not really, she's fifteen now, remember? And very mature for her age. You know that.'

'Me?' replied Joe defensively, 'How would I know?'

'Er, because you've watched her grow up. What the hell's the matter with you tonight?'

'Nothing. Let's play.'

He poured them both a large vodka and coke. Since Christmas '71 they'd incorporated the latest two Motown chartbuster compilations (Volumes Five and Six) into the game, making, in total, ninety six song titles to remember. Before they could start, the living room door opened and Lilah stepped in. She looked sensational. Long black hair framing her heart-shaped face and just enough make-up to accentuate her eyes and lips. She wore a black box jacket over a red top with a Prince of Wales check skirt. It was not quite a mini skirt but short enough for Joe to hope the boy didn't show up. Only her unfamiliarity at wearing heels stopped her scoring top marks for elegance.

'Oh, hi Joe,' she beamed, with an air that said, '*Look what you're missing.*'

'Hello Lilah, you look nice,' he replied, as casually as he could.

'Thankyou.'

She tottered unsteadily over to the window and peered through the net curtain.

'Don't forget what mum said,' warned Paolo. 'His dad is to drop you back here by half ten, at the latest.'

Half ten? thought Joe, *On a school night?*

'I know,' she sighed, before turning to the visitor, 'They still think I'm a child, Joe.'

'Well, you can't be too careful these days,' he warned, 'there are some strange people out there.'

'There's one or two in here,' she grinned. 'Anyway, Russell will take care of me.'

Russell. What a wanky name.

A car horn sounded outside. 'That'll be them,' she chirped.

'Enjoy the film,' smiled Joe, fighting not to add, 'but nothing else.'

'I will,' she assured, 'my friends are *so* jealous. Russell's the class heart throb.'

Her schoolfriends weren't the only ones to endure a visit from the green-eyed monster. Inside, it was devouring Joe. Lilah left the room, then poked her head back in. 'Let me kick things off. Volume Four: Side two. Track three.'

Within ten seconds the visitor was on it. 'Jimmy Ruffin – "Farewell is a Lonely Sound".'

'Spot on,' she confirmed smiling sweetly. 'Farewell, then.'

The sound of the front door closing was closely followed by a car door slamming and a vehicle driving away. Joe couldn't concentrate at all on the game that night and Paolo absolutely thrashed him. His mind was elsewhere and working overtime.

She knew I was coming to the house, which is why she chose tonight to go to the pictures with heart throb Russell wanky name. It was all to try and make me jealous. Well, you only try and make somebody jealous if you care about them. Right? But equally, you only get jealous if you care about the person trying to make you jealous. Oh God, why couldn't Paolo have had a little brother instead?

CHAPTER FIFTEEN

LET THE GOOD TIMES ROLL

The evening of Joe's eighteenth birthday was spent in The Copper Kettle, a quaint little restaurant in Watford High St. His mum had insisted on a family meal to mark the occasion. Despite the cordial setting, for at least two of the four people present, it was more of an ordeal than a pleasure. It was clear that his stepdad would rather have been anywhere else, a feeling shared by the birthday boy. The indifference they shared had progressed to an active mutual dislike, but they kept the peace for Mary and David's sakes. Consequently, the atmosphere was more fitting for a funeral tea than a birthday dinner, and Joe was pleased when the bill came; not least because Nigel reluctantly paid it, which must have hurt. If Joe had known who would be picking up the tab, he'd have ordered the most expensive items on the menu. Out of politeness he thanked Nigel whilst wondering for the umpteenth time why his mum had ever hitched up with the charmless, sour-faced git.

A much more enjoyable outing had come two nights earlier at the California ballroom in Dunstable, when Joe and Paolo had crossed the county line from Hertfordshire into Bedfordshire to see Bob & Earl, of Harlem Shuffle fame. It was a double celebration; Joe's upcoming eighteenth and Paolo recently passing his driving test, first time. He loved cars but, for now, he'd have to wait for the Aston Martin DB5 he dreamed of and make do with the seven-year-old, accident damaged Vauxhall Viva he'd acquired through his work. Intending it to be scrapped, the owner sold it for peanuts, but Paolo and one of the top mechanics repaired the chassis, gave it a paint job and overhauled the engine. After the Kelly setback, the project was something to focus on, and its completion had given him a real sense of achievement. Crucially, it had also given the boys mobility.

The show was good, although everybody was just waiting to hear "Harlem Shuffle", which of course came right near the end of set. For Joe, simply seeing two bona fide American soul stars was enough. The mood was amicable and friendly, and they even got chatting to a group of locals. They were careful, though, not to mention where they were from. Because of the intense Luton/Watford football rivalry, there were neanderthals who would glass you just for having a WD postcode. The fact that neither Joe nor Paolo supported Watford FC wouldn't have made the slightest difference. To be fair, it would have been the same if two Luton lads had come to Watford for a night out. There were lunatics in every town that couldn't be reasoned with. As Lenny said, 'Never argue with an idiot. Bystanders won't be able to tell the difference.'

Regarding the Lilah situation, after much thought, Joe's course of action was very simple: let her get on with it. He still maintained that not taking advantage of her tender years was the right thing to do. Noble even. If she wanted to go on dates with a whole posse of heart throbs with wanky names, then let her.

No fifteen-year-old girl was going to control *him*. Not even one with Mediterranean good looks and dreamy brown eyes, who was into soul music.

Just stop. Now! Go and have a cold shower.

Messrs Holland and Massetti had been kindred spirits since the day they met, with one fundamental difference. Paolo had always liked the idea of a traditional, steady relationship, which was anathema to Joe. Perhaps Paolo was simply more mature than he was? Actually, there was no *perhaps* about it. Witnessing the father he loved get fatally injured, and regarding himself as the man of the house at nine years of age, had made him grow up faster than most. He'd only mentioned what happened on the zebra crossing once, when he'd confided to Joe that the sound of the car slamming into his dad was something he'd never forget. The impact had knocked Gio eight feet into the air. The horror of it was impossible for Joe to even imagine. In comparison, his own upbringing didn't seem too bad, and getting better all the time. He was learning a trade and learning about life. The road stretching out ahead of him was filled with endless possibilities.

There was one more tryst with Suzanne. Mad Mick was to be released in early July, so it was agreed that this would be their last encounter. Joe presented her with a bottle of Bacardi as a goodbye gift and together they polished it off.

'I really hope things work out for you,' he announced, raising his glass.

'Thankyou. And I hope you find what you're looking for.'

'I'm not looking for anything,' he insisted.

'Joe, everyone is looking for *something*, it's just that some people don't know it. Be sure to recognise it when you see it, before it slips away.'

Where *did* females get their homespun wisdom from? The pair sat up drinking and talking until after 1am. That night would be the only time they shared a bed without having sex. He awoke on his side with his arm draped protectively across her stomach. Over tea and toast they laughed about various shared memories. One being his sock ending up in the lampshade during his rush to get undressed.

'I was scared you'd change your mind,' he confessed. Suzanne recalled how bolshie he'd got in 'the Penny' when she referred to him as the bony pony.

'I'm not bony, I'm wiry,' she giggled, trying to mimic the irritation in his voice. Then, more solemnly, 'You realise that if I see you when I'm out with Mick, I'll have to ignore you?'

'Please do. I don't want to end up with a face like a Picasso painting.'

'He's promised to keep a lid on his temper from now on. I really think he means it this time.'

'Good.'

The final curtain dropped on their time together with a brief last kiss in the hallway of her flat, before Joe stepped out into an agreeably warm Sunday morning. He breathed in the bracing morning air and felt as free as a bird, ready and eager to spread his wings.

CHAPTER SIXTEEN

IF IT FEELS GOOD, DO IT

Everything was evolving. Life experiences were coming thick and fast. The boys were no longer desperate virgins. Now they were desperate *former* virgins, which is slightly worse, because they knew what they were missing. The St Albans girls they'd met were a friendly bunch, up to a point. They would quite happily let you see them home, snog the face off you and allow access to the hilly areas, but try to sneak south of the border and you'd find it too heavily guarded. If they were feeling charitable, you may get a five-knuckle shuffle, which is better than nothing, but only just. It was time to return to the happy hunting grounds of Watford. If they chanced upon Kelly or Suzanne, it would be uncomfortable, but they could deal with it. And if they couldn't, they would leave and go somewhere else.

The normally subdued canvas of male fashion was now being splashed with sweeping brushstrokes of dandyism and colour. The tonic suits were being discarded in favour of wide-bottomed jeans, Oxford bags, loon pants and penny collar shirts, worn under knitted tank tops. Neat, short hair was allowed to grow long, with side partings moved to the centre. It was the age of the peacock.

Bright colours were in vogue, the more garish the better. 'Purple satin jacket sir? How about a tie-dye t-shirt and some maroon trousers to go with it?'

And it wasn't just the clothes. Wallpaper and furnishings came with complimentary sunglasses; avocado green, burnt orange and purple being particular favourites. The decade that taste forgot was in full swing. Joe and Paolo were swept along with it all, except in one area. Most mid-to-older UK teens were now devotees of T-Rex, Slade, David Bowie and other sparkly, sequinned performers. And whilst Joe could quite happily listen to, even appreciate, some of their music, it didn't speak to him or grab him like soul and funk did. His hair and clothes might alter, but his devotion to those black American artists would not.

Still feeling the sting of Kelly's rebuttal, Paolo decided to take a leaf out of Joe's book and play the field a little. There was no shortage of available candidates and the restored Vauxhall Viva was proving to be a godsend. Not once was the offer of a lift refused. Most girls still hadn't left home, so Paolo would park up somewhere nearby (not too well lit) to say goodnight. With one girl in the front passenger seat and the other in the back with Joe, saying goodnight could take anything from five minutes to half an hour. The backseat of a Viva wasn't the height of comfort, but it beat the hell out of shop doorways. Sometimes, if the four really hit it off, a further date would be arranged, normally for midweek. Joe was always honest, though, making it clear he wasn't looking for anything serious.

Through contacts they'd made in the pubs and clubs, the boys were also starting to get invites to house parties. These almost exclusively occurred when the host's parents were away. How their sons and daughters hoped to get away with it was a mystery. Unless by chance the carpets already had vomit, cigarette burns and wine stains when the parents had left. But then, young people by tradition are better known for their impulsiveness than thinking things through. These rare events were always great fun until the inevitable obnoxious drunk gate crashers turned up, demanding to be let in. Cue fists flying, shouting, screaming, and (on one occasion) a garden gnome being hurled through the front window. Try explaining that one to mummy and daddy as you're picking shards of glass out of the Axminster. Joe and Paolo soon perfected the art of making themselves scarce before the police arrived.

It was a hedonistic, self-serving lifestyle, but they weren't hurting anyone, and if you can't go a little crazy when you're eighteen, then when can you? All that energy had to manifest itself somewhere and, after Christmas, Paolo announced that he'd joined a Sunday football team and encouraged his friend to get involved. They'd both played for their school first eleven, so Joe didn't need much persuasion. Plus, Sunday leagues weren't taken too seriously; it offered the chance to run off any Saturday night excess.

So, in January 1973, Joe turned up for his first training session and Paolo made the introductions. After some warmup exercises, squats, star jumps and fitness training, the new boy really started to loosen up. But it was during the five-a-side games that he realised how much he'd missed playing. The manager must have liked what he saw because the following weekend Joe made his debut on the wing in the Watford Sunday League, Division two. His team won 2-1 and he set up the winner with a pinpoint cross. After showering, they all adjourned to The Three Horseshoes pub to discuss the game over a few libations. Apparently, this was the norm after a match.

His teammates were a diverse bunch of blokes ranging in age from eighteen to thirty nine. The fifteen or so squad members represented a wide spectrum of jobs, including a carpet fitter, a cleaning products rep and a painter and decorator. All useful contacts should Joe or Paolo ever have an illicit house party. Sport didn't curtail their socialising, though, and more often than not, Joe would arrive on Sunday morning bleary-eyed (Or should that be 'beery-eyed?). But whatever he'd been up to the previous night, he *always* turned up and gave 100%. Paolo, unquestionably the more sensible of the two, never exceeded the drink/drive limit and looked all the fresher for it.

As much as the training and games themselves, Joe enjoyed the post-match lunchtimes in the bar. He found it fascinating listening to the conversations of the married guys, especially concerning their wives. Most talked about the incessant nagging, with one player always referring to his Mrs as '*the ball and chain*' and another '*the enemy*'. If it was getting near the 2pm closing time and the pub phone rang, before it could be answered, the married men would all chorus, 'I've just left!' It was plain to Joe that a lot of it was exaggeration and said in affectionate jest, but it reinforced his stance of not giving up the single life any time soon.

The boys still played their Chartbuster quiz game, but only infrequently, and Lilah rarely joined in. Her and Joe's relationship had turned decidedly distant since their surreptitious kiss and its aftereffects. There was, undoubtedly, *something* between them but it remained dormant, unallowed to develop or even be acknowledged. Paolo picked up on the strained atmosphere but put it down to his sister hitting puberty,

95

and her crush on Joe cooling. Perhaps it had. How many fifteen year olds are able to articulate what they're feeling? They're not even sure themselves. The hormones are raging and emotions change from one day to the next. People say it's hard growing old, well, it's just as tough transitioning from child to adult. For his part, Joe wasn't happy with the situation and wanted to broach the subject with Lilah, but he didn't know how to approach it. And after his clumsy previous effort, when he walked her home from the salon, he feared he might make matters worse.

On Joe's next visit to the record store, Elaine, who had done so much for the boys' musical education, announced that she was leaving Musicland. As a final gift, she informed Joe of a London based magazine called Blues & Soul. It was a publication dedicated to the music he loved. As well as reviewing new releases and featuring interviews with the established artists, it also shone a light on the lesser-known groups and singers on small, obscure record labels. For the serious soul buff, it was a bible. From under the counter, she presented Joe with a copy.

He thanked her and wished her well in her new job. On the bus home he eagerly read it cover to cover, and it was a revelation. He prided himself on being pretty clued up on the soul genre, but this booklet revealed that he'd barely scratched the surface. There were dozens of recording artists, record labels and song titles he'd never heard of. People like Jerry Butler, The Flirtations, and Bobby Womack. Thankfully, there was an interview with Al Green, whose *Let's Stay Together* album was a staple of Joe's collection; so, he wasn't a complete ignoramus.

Plainly, Tamla Motown in Detroit, Stax in Memphis and Atlantic in New York were just the icing on a very large cake. And Joe lapped it up. Of particular interest was the news that The Four Tops would be touring Britain in the autumn and early winter of 1973, the nearest venue being the Hammersmith Odeon. He couldn't wait to tell Paolo. And as soon as he got home, he cut out the subscription slip to send off to the mag. It was a fortnightly publication, so six months' worth (thirteen editions) for the princely sum of one pound ninety-five would be money well spent. The only downside was that his purchase was issue number 87, meaning he'd already missed out on *so* much valuable information.

CHAPTER SEVENTEEN

THIN LINE BETWEEN LOVE AND HATE

Things came to a head between Joe and his stepdad on the morning of Christmas Eve 1972. The tension between them had been building for months and this was the day that the dam burst. It was a Sunday and he'd slept late after a big night at Top Rank with Paolo and some of their footballing mates. Joe was awoken by raised voices downstairs, with the deeper voice doing most of the talking. It sounded too loud to be the radio. His head was throbbing, which was no surprise as he had gone on the red wine after demolishing seven pints of lager. Now he understood Lenny's advice not to mix the grape and the grain. Oh well, Christmas comes but once a year.

After pulling on some jeans and a t-shirt, he splashed his face with cold water and went down to see what was going on. There was a phone number written on his left arm with the name Gail above it. He'd decide whether to call it after asking the others if they could remember who Gail was. He certainly couldn't. He vaguely remembered dancing with a dark-haired girl from Harrow.

The voices were coming from the kitchen and, sitting on the stairs, he soon picked up the gist of the conversation by the snippets emanating through the door: 'Coming and going all hours,' and 'he's not a good role model for David.'

Every time Mary tried to get a word in to defend her first born, she was shouted down. As the kitchen door opened an uneasy silence fell. Nigel sat down and picked up the Guardian, using it as a barrier. Mary was stood at the sink. She seemed to spend half her waking hours there. She had her back to Joe so he couldn't see how upset she was, but he could tell by her posture. The time for tactful diplomacy was over, and her son went straight on the attack.

'If you've got something to say, Nigel, say it to my face.'

The older man lowered his printed shield and replied, 'Alright. This is a family home, but you treat it like a dosshouse. Do you think your behaviour on weekends is acceptable?'

'Yes,' fired back Joe, 'now let me ask *you* a question. Why would I want to spend one more minute around you than I have to? You've never shown any interest in me. And just for the record: I'm not here to be a role model for David, I'm here to live *my* life.'

'Please stop,' pleaded Mary, but her request was ignored.

'Some life,' sneered Nigel, 'boozing and chasing girls.'

'It's what normal teenage boys do, Nigel.'

'I didn't.'

'Exactly. I rest my case.'

'Enough,' urged his mother, in a slightly louder voice.

'No Mum, this has been building for months. Years even.'

He turned his attention back to the brooding, seated figure. 'And another thing, I don't want to hear you raising your voice to my mum anymore.'

'Your mum; *my* wife.'

'That doesn't give you the right to shout at her. Do it again and you and me are going to fall out, big time.'

'Is that a threat?'

'More of a promise.'

Mary could stand it no more. 'Shut up,' she hollered. 'Both of you. Just stop it.'

Seething, Nigel got up from his chair and headed for the door. Under his breath he muttered, 'Waster,' then louder, 'I'm going to pick David up from town.'

As the front door slammed, Mary burst into tears. Crying harder than Joe had ever seen her. Instinctively, he walked across and held her and she sobbed into his shoulder. It was awful to see her so upset, knowing that he was, at least partly, to blame.

'Sorry, Mum. I just couldn't hold it in any longer.'

Between sniffles she lamented, 'None of you know what it's like to be *me*. I can't take much more.'

She'd always had a fragility about her, a vulnerability just beneath the surface. In an attempt to placate her, he made a pot of tea and walked her over to the table, where they sat down.

'Right, Mum, it's time. Explain to me why you're with that man. Other than David, what keeps you with him?'

Wiping her eyes with her hanky she explained. 'He wasn't always so cold. In the beginning he was kind. Absolutely doted on you. I'd never have married him otherwise.'

In his mind's eye, Joe glimpsed a vague fragment of a memory. Dreamlike. A sunny day. He was being carried on Nigel's shoulders. So high up. A bit scary but exhilarating. Then, riding on a miniature train with him. He recognised the place as Cassiobury Park. Everything looked so huge and he felt so small. A long, long time ago.

'I wish things had turned out differently,' she continued, 'that you'd known your real father.'

A teardrop glided down her cheek. He patted her hand, 'Me too. But why do you put up with Nigel? Grampy left this house to you. If you split up, you're not the one who would have to leave.'

She gave him a weary, resigned look. 'I've made my bed, so now I've got to lie in it.'

Joe and Nigel embarked on a shaky Christmas Day truce. As usual there was a strict December 25th protocol to follow. By 9am the whole family had to be up, washed, dressed and downstairs for the opening of the presents. Each of them opened a gift in turn until all that remained under the tree was scrunched up wrapping paper among the pine needles. Fixed smiles and polite 'thank yous' over, Nigel turned on the radio for the annual BBC carol concert, this year from Kings College, Cambridge. It was a relief to have music filling the room, but why did those British church choirs always sound so solemn? Maybe one year have a gospel choir; now those people knew how to worship God *and* enjoy themselves. Plus, many of his favourite soul singers, including Aretha Franklin and Dionne Warwick, came from that background.

When David asked Joe if he'd join him out back to put his new Adidas Telstar football through its paces, his older brother readily agreed. His heart sank though when David asked, 'What about you, Dad?'

Thankfully, Nigel answered, 'Err… no, I'm going to help your mother clear up and prepare the vegetables for dinner.'

As always, the actual dinner was delicious but the atmosphere in which it was eaten was torturous. Mary's Johnny Mathis album got its annual outing, but the previous day's harsh words were still raw and neither of the two main protagonists were in a conciliatory mood. So there the four of them sat, in near silence, paper crowns on heads and knives and forks clicking in time to "Have Yourself a Merry Little Christmas".

Not much chance of that, Johnny.

As the last mouthful of Christmas pud headed south, Mr Mathis was put back in his sleeve for the next twelve months and at 3pm the TV was turned on for the Queen's speech. Somehow, Joe had survived this charade for six hours but now his resolve was wavering. As soon as Her Majesty finished speaking, he jumped up and announced to his mum, 'Right then, I'm off for a bath, then for a listen to the Otis Redding LP you so kindly bought me. I'll see you in a couple of hours.'

As he lay on his bed luxuriating in the smooth vocals of Mr Redding, Joe wished he could have spent the day at the Massettis', despite the delicate Lilah situation. He'd popped in briefly last year and had a taster of what a true family Christmas could be. Laughter, games, gentle mickey taking. All wrapped up in genuine love and affection. Ellen set a place at the table for Giovanni (As she had every year since his passing). His framed photo sat on a table mat facing them, and before a morsel was eaten, they'd drink a toast to

'Papa'. Joe thought it a lovely gesture. Everything flowed naturally between them. Nothing was forced. A complete contrast to his lot. Paolo's was a real family. Whereas his had become a *'shamily'*.

The album was really good. It was a 'Best Of' compilation with a whopping twenty-five tracks, including "Try a Little Tenderness" and Otis's biggie "(Sittin' On) The Dock of the Bay". Joe had seen it advertised in Blues & Soul, and his mum had bought it for him, as well as a new herringbone overcoat. She was such a giving woman. Why did she think she deserved such a drab, unfulfilling life? Hopefully, his present to her might bring some pleasure. She enjoyed theatre so he'd bought two tickets for the February production at the Watford Palace Theatre for a restoration comedy called *The Provoked Wife*. When Joe had seen the title, he couldn't resist. The plot concerned a put upon wife provoked into being unfaithful by her sour, bad-tempered husband. Maliciously, he hoped Nigel would go with her and squirm his way through it, but if he didn't, then Joe would accompany her himself.

His eyelids were getting heavy, and he felt himself nodding. As he was drifting off, he realised that he'd inadvertently washed the phone number off his arm without writing it down. So, he may never find out who the mysterious Gail was. But he was willing to bet she was having a better Christmas than he was.

CHAPTER EIGHTEEN

LOVE IS HERE AND NOW YOU'RE GONE

The year number had changed, but not much else, and the January frost wasn't confined to the outside. Joe's mum still continued with her charade of a marriage, her eldest son and her husband had as little to do with each other as possible and, regrettably, despite his mother's best efforts to shield him, David was collateral damage. Mary's assertion that she owed it to their youngest to stay with Nigel just didn't stand up. Surely it had to be healthier to be raised by one relaxed parent than two uptight ones, who didn't even seem to like each other? The continuation of the sorry saga meant that everyone was constantly walking on eggshells. But, for whatever reason, his mum wouldn't call time on it. So, for Joe Holland, 1973 started with him ploughing the same furrow. Pressing on with his apprenticeship, playing his football and letting off steam at the weekends. But it was all getting a bit... samey.

In February, Paolo found himself with nineteen candles on his cake and a new girl on his arm. Her name was Julie, and she was bright, attractive and good fun. As with Kelly, he'd met her at the New Penny but, crucially, she was a year younger than Paolo, so there was no lying about his age. It was in March – the 11th to be exact – that Joe's life also changed. And it wasn't a change he welcomed.

Ellen had arranged a sixteenth birthday meal for Lilah and, as an honorary member of the family, she invited Joe. If she'd known about their dalliance almost a year earlier, perhaps she wouldn't have. With a typical lack of pretention, airs or graces, Lilah chose to eat in the unfussy setting of the local Wimpy Bar. After subtly ascertaining from Paolo that it would just be the Massettis, him and Julie present, Joe accepted the invitation. Had there been any school heart throbs with wanky names on the guest list, he'd have politely declined. At the last minute, Julie had to cry off with a cold, so it was just the four of them.

After a lot of soul searching, Joe had decided the time was right to ask Lilah if she would like to go out with him. Proper boyfriend/girlfriend out. No more stolen kisses when no-one was watching. No more playing it cool. No more worrying what Ellen and Paolo thought. It was cards on the table time. He hadn't quite worked out how to word it, but when he got her alone he was going to do it. He'd done the honourable thing by waiting until she was sixteen, and more able to work out what *she* wanted. He now knew what *he* wanted: her. The novelty of being a teenage Casanova had worn thin, and he was pretty sure that he'd never feel as strongly about any other girl as he did about Lilah. If she was of the same mind, then he hoped her mother and brother would give their blessings.

The food was far tastier than it should have been from a place where ketchup was squirted out of a plastic tomato. Wimpy grills all round, except the birthday girl who ordered a Special Wimpy grill (it was the same as a regular but for six pence extra you got an egg). Four Knickerbocker Glories later and waistbands were starting to tighten. There was still space for birthday cake, though. As it was brought out, Lilah reddened slightly as everyone joined in the rendition of "Happy birthday to you".

To applause, she blew the candles out with ease – but then, sixteen isn't many. As the foursome sipped their drinks and chatted easily, Ellen declared proudly that she had an announcement to make. Lilah blushed again as she tried to head her off – 'Mum…'

Joe and Paolo exchanged puzzled looks and the latter shrugged his shoulders.

'They'll find out soon enough, so it might as well be now,' asserted her mum. Seeing protest was futile, Lilah sat back and let Ellen have the floor. Her mother went on to explain that since Giovanni's funeral she'd stayed in touch with his sisters, forming a special bond with Rosa, the eldest. They both put notes in each other's Christmas cards with updates on how their respective families were doing. Rosa was interested to learn that Lilah had designs on becoming a hair stylist as she was in the same line of work. Well, this morning, on Lilah's birthday, Aunt Rosa phoned, primarily to wish her niece many happy returns but also to make her an offer.

Rosa was co-owner of a large salon. As well as hairdressing, they covered all other areas of women's beauty, including manicures and body massage, which was becoming increasingly popular on the continent. If Lilah wanted to, once she'd finished her exams, she could go to Sorrento and get an all-round, hands-on education in the beauty business. Rosa would even pay her air fare. Ellen finished off with a cheery, 'How about that, boys?'

Joe felt like someone had punched him in the stomach but managed, 'Sounds fantastic. How long would you be out there, Lilah?'

'Initially, two months.'

Two months. That's not so bad, he thought.

'And if that works out – two years,' chirped Ellen.

Two years wailed his inner voice, and he felt despondent at the thought of not seeing her for that long.

'Two years of peace and quiet,' teased her brother.

'Oh shut up you,' she giggled.

What Joe longed to say was, 'Please don't go. I'll miss you too much. If you go, I've lost you. Please, please don't go,' but the words that came out were, 'You can't pass up an opportunity like that. Sorrento. Wow.'

'I know. It's not as if there's anything keeping me here,' she replied. Was she looking for a reaction from him?

Now's your chance. Tell her how you feel. Go on, you coward!

He ignored the voice in his head and said nothing.

'What has Sorrento got that Watford hasn't?' joked Paolo, 'Apart from blue sea and sunshine?'

Well, in a couple of months it would have one more thing that Watford didn't – Lilah Massetti. That night in his bed, Joe cursed himself for not voicing his true feelings. The thought of her being so far away was unbearable. A girl like that would have those Italian boys, not to mention male tourists, beating a path to her door. Pictures formed in his head of her sitting on the back of some good-looking local's Lambretta, heading for the beach, with her sunglasses on and her thick, raven hair blowing in the wind.

Serves you right. You should have told her.
Oh, fuck off, you.

But even if he had opened up to her and she had decided to stay in England, was it fair to ask her to turn down such a fantastic opportunity? In time, she would come to resent him if she missed out. In all probability, two years working at her aunt's salon would be the making of her. Teach her all about the beauty game and open doors that would remain closed in England. It would be super selfish of him to try and deny her all that, so he decided to pretend he was fine with it. Anyway, after two months she might not like it and come home.

Yeah, and she might love it and never come home.
I thought I told you to fuck off!

It was hours before sleep finally arrived, and he woke up with a tension headache. The following day, on his way home from work, he asked Lenny to stop off at Thomas Cook and picked up a travel brochure for Southern Italy. He was curious to see what this Sorrento place looked like. Perhaps it wasn't all it was cracked up to be. But as he looked at the photos, that possibility evaporated. It was paradise. He didn't need to read the blurb but did anyway: *Sorrento is a rainbow of colour. The sapphire waters of the Mediterranean Sea crash against white rocks, while it's cliff top setting offers spectacular views of Mount Vesuvius, across the glittering Bay of Naples.*

Even the breathtakingly beautiful view of the sun setting over the gasometer at the Dome roundabout couldn't compete with that. Napoli 1 Watford 0.

Hang on to that sense of humour, boy. You're going to need it.

The news concerning Lilah had left Joe dazed. He was in a blue funk, lacking in motivation and concentration. Things came to a head on the Thursday when Lenny allowed him to wire his first fuseboard unsupervised. When he'd finished, Len checked it over. Within seconds, his face hardened and he asked Joe, 'So, what have you done wrong?'

It didn't take Joe much longer to spot his error. 'Oh shit.' Somehow, he had got the live and the neutral wires mixed up.

'The next person who touched that could have got a nasty shock,' admonished Len, 'and what would that make you?'

'Responsible.'

'Close. The correct answer is "Irresponsible." Sort it out, and while you're at it, sort *yourself* out. You've had your head up your arse all week. What's the matter with you?'

'I'd rather not talk about it.'

'Fine. What happens in your personal life is your business, but when it affects your work, it becomes *my* business. It reflects on me. How many times have I told you, you can't take liberties with electrics?'

'Sorry Lenny,' replied his dejected apprentice.

'Alright then.' His tone softened. 'You've got the makings of a good sparks, Joe. One day it will all be second nature to you. But until then, *concentrate.*'

Joe nodded before setting about rectifying his error. His first big test and he'd fluffed it, plunging him even further into the doldrums.

Oh Lilah, what have you done to me?

The internal wrestling match went on for weeks, trivialising every other aspect of his life. Caught on the horns of a dilemma, he couldn't free himself: he was desperate for Lilah not to go to Italy but didn't want her to miss out on the chance of a lifetime. Selfishness versus selflessness. In the end, no matter the cost to himself, he knew he couldn't stand in her way. If you truly love someone you always want what's best for them. Even if it's not best for you.

Most times when he popped into Paolo's, she was in her bedroom, studying hard for her upcoming O levels. When they did cross paths, he wore a brave face, as he suspected, did she. It's easy to fake a smile but impossible to disguise a sadness behind the eyes. The conversation flowed easily enough between them, but it was all small talk with no mention of her impending departure. Neither needed reminding that their roads would soon be separating and may never merge again. Joe found it incredibly difficult to sustain this smokescreen when all he wanted to do was hold her, cup her lovely face in his hands, kiss her and tell how much she meant to him. But he never did.

The week before she left, Lilah suggested that the three originals have a game of the Chartbuster quiz, for 'old times sake'. Ellen was pottering around downstairs, which meant that, even if Paolo left the room, Joe and Lilah wouldn't be alone. He felt relief and disappointment in equal measure. Joe started them off. 'Chartbusters Volume Four: Side two. Track four.'

As he'd hoped, Lilah responded first, 'Four Tops – "Do What You Gotta Do".'

'Correct,' he confirmed, with a wistful smile, 'Do What You Gotta Do.'

From the stereo, Levi Stubbs sang the words that Joe wanted to say, telling her to follow her dream.

Her expression made it clear that she understood that he was giving her his blessing. Lilah's answer to him was: 'Volume Six: Side two. Track five.'

In unison Paolo and Joe said 'Diana Ross – "Remember Me".'

Joe was now certain that they were communicating through the music. He'd have rather she'd chosen "Someday We'll Be Together", but that was probably asking too much. In consequent rounds they deliberately chose songs that didn't fit their situation, just in case their game within the game was rumbled. If Paolo suspected anything, he didn't show it. Later, as Joe pulled on his jacket to go home, Lilah walked purposely across the room and kissed him softly on the cheek. To Ellen and Paolo, it had the appearance of a chaste kiss between friends, but they didn't hear her whisper, 'Thanks for understanding.'

On his birthday, Joe went out with the lads, drank too much and acted upbeat but only because it was expected of him. Behind the mask, he was counting down the days to her leaving like a condemned man awaiting execution. On Saturday June 23rd, Paolo had arranged to drive his sister to the airport and asked Joe if he wanted to come along for the ride. That was an easy decision: no, he did not. Watching her disappear into departures would be too much to take and he feared he might break down. Ellen wouldn't be there as she had to work but, even so, a bloke didn't break down in front of a mate. It just wasn't done. So, he lied that Lenny needed him on a job.

The evening before Lilah left, Joe dropped in unannounced on the Massettis, ostensibly to lend Paolo the latest edition of Blues & Soul , but really to say a last goodbye before she jetted off out of his life. Paolo was at Julie's but Ellen made the visitor a cup of tea and announced his arrival to her daughter, who was upstairs packing. Within seconds, she appeared and sat down next to him on the sofa. 'Hi,' she beamed.

'Hi. So, all set then?'

'Just about.'

'Excited?'

'Excited. Nervous. A little bit sad.'

He held her hand and felt her fingers intertwine with his. 'Goodbyes are never easy, are they?'

'Are you coming to see me off tomorrow?'

He shook his head, 'I have to work all weekend. Rewiring an office. I'll be thinking of you, though.'

'And I'll be thinking of you.'

'Be good if you dropped me the odd postcard once you've settled in. You know, just now and again, when you've got time.'

'I will. I promise.'

'Right then, I'd best be off and let you finish packing.'

He stood up and she followed suit, their hands still locked together. She walked him to the front door, where they stood in silence gazing into each other's eyes. He noticed a single teardrop form.

'Don't – you'll start me off,' he urged, his voice cracking. They embraced for a good minute, and he didn't want to let her go. But he had to.

'You take care of yourself,' were his final words.

'You too,' she responded, wiping the tear away before it started its downward trajectory.

His intention was to walk away but the urge to kiss her proved too strong. Actually, their lips met halfway, making it a truly shared kiss. A beautiful kiss, that he would relive many times. As he trudged, head down, to the bus stop, it felt like an invisible, malicious hand was squeezing his heart. And he wished it would rain, to disguise his own silent tears.

CHAPTER NINETEEN

I'M IN A DIFFERENT WORLD

On Saturday morning, when Joe knew his mum was out shopping and Nigel had taken David into town, he made himself tea and toast and took it up to his room. Cloaked in a fog of melancholia, he clock-watched the morning away.

9am – *they'll be leaving for the airport now.*

Noon – *her plane will be taking off.*

Aretha's *Greatest Hits* played in the background, but not even his favourite female singer could comfort him that day. At 3pm, there was a knock on his door and his mum entered, carrying a tray with a plate of ham sandwiches, a mug of tea and a selection of biscuits. She was surprised to see he was still in bed.

'Are you alright, Joseph? I haven't seen you all day.'

'I'm fine, Mum,' he lied. 'Just a bit fed up.'

'Well, we all get like that sometimes. It will pass. I'll leave this here then,' she said, placing the tray on his bedside cabinet.

'Thanks, Mum.'

'You're welcome. Right, I'll leave you in peace.'

She smiled and left the room, quietly closing the door behind her. The sandwiches and biscuits remained untouched. He didn't go downstairs for the rest of the day and declined dinner. It was the first Saturday night he'd stayed in for nearly two years. Sunday, he decided he couldn't carry on like that and took David to the local park for a kick around. The football season had finished and he found he was missing the banter and camaraderie as much as the matches themselves. The fresh air helped to clear his head, and he told himself that Lilah was gone and moping around wasn't going to bring her back. So, he decided he would put all his focus on work. Show Lenny that he was back on track and not make any more stupid mistakes.

It was a bit surprising not to hear a word from Lilah in the nearly three weeks since she'd left. Surely, she hadn't forgotten him already. Even more surprisingly, the Massettis hadn't heard from her either, other than a quick phone call to say she'd arrived safely. Joe was disappointed but buckled down and tried to put her to the back of his mind. Easier said than done, but very slowly he was starting to adapt. Which didn't mean he wasn't ecstatic on the Tuesday he got in from work and Mary said, 'A letter came for you today. Airmail. It's on your bed.'

He took the stairs two at a time to get to his room. On his pillow sat a white envelope with a red and green border. His heart quickened as he used his key to slice open the top. Carefully, he took out the contents. Joe had waited three long weeks for this, and he wanted to savour it. As well as a letter there were three postcards with views of Sorrento. Putting them to one side, he unfolded the scented notepaper and started to read. As he drank in Lilah's words, her excitement almost jumped off the page.

Dear Joe, I hope this letter finds you well. Sorry it's taken so long to write but it's been a whirlwind since I got here. I arrived on the Saturday and started work on

115

the Monday. The salon is huge, with six hair stylists, two manicurists, a massage room and three apprentices, including me. Everyone has been so kind to me, especially Aunt Rosa. You'd like her. She looks like Sophia Loren and zips around in a little red sports car. Her husband, Enzo, is an architect. He designed their house, which is on the clifftop, looking out to sea. It has five bedrooms and two big bathrooms with marble floors. My bedroom is about four times bigger than my one at Mum's. My window looks out on a small orchard with olive and lemon trees. There are also lots of red, white and yellow flowers that give off a lovely scent, but I don't know what they're called. Flowers are everywhere out here.

Aunt Rosa has three children, Frederico, Marco and Gina, all in their twenties. Sorrento is so beautiful. The postcards don't do it justice. At evening meal, I'm allowed a glass of red wine. Just one though. Then we all sit outside talking until bedtime, which is usually around eleven. I don't understand a lot of the conversation, but my Italian is getting better every day. In my blood, I suppose.

Last week, Rosa drove me to Positano to meet my Aunt Maria and Uncle Umberto. They have grown up twin girls called Luisa and Lucia. They are gorgeous. I wouldn't let you anywhere near them! That makes five cousins in all that I've met. My aunties showed me the house where they and Papa grew up. It is not a happy place for them. As you know, I was only five when he died so getting to know his sisters and hearing their stories makes me feel closer to him (if that makes sense).

I do miss Mum and Paolo, though, and of course, you. I think of you often, Joe, and the Motown

Chartbusters game we used to play. One night especially.
I think you know which night I mean. Soul music isn't
very big here, but I'm trying to spread the word. Lilah
Massetti – beauty therapist and missionary! Haha.
I hope you're still enjoying your job and your family is
okay. I know it's difficult regarding your stepdad but try
to get along for your mum and brother's sake, if not
your own. Well, it's nearly midnight and I have work
tomorrow so I'd better close this letter now and then
my eyes. I look forward to hearing from you. Take care.

Lots of love,

Lilah xxx

Joe folded the letter neatly and slipped it back into
its envelope, placing it under his pillow to read again
later. He studied the postcards, one at a time. The first
one was a cliff top esplanade view overlooking Naples.
In the foreground were large terracotta planters
overflowing with scarlet flowers. Below was the
coastline, snaking its way around the bay, with half a
dozen brightly painted fishing boats dotted on the clear
azure sea.

The second card showed an image of the town taken
from a boat. The hilly terrain housed clusters of
whitewashed, orange tiled dwellings, huddled around a
domed church, with the imposing, towering cliffs
behind standing guard over them. It likely looked the
same two hundred years ago.

The last image wasn't a photograph but a painted
scene, presumably by a local artist. It depicted the
exterior of a bistro on a high cliff top terrace. Again,
lots of flowers on show. Red and yellow umbrellas

shaded white-clothed tables where the al fresco diners would soon be sitting. Directly below were the crystal blue waters of the bay, the tiny houses dotted up the hillside and the misty blue mountains sleeping in the distance.

Lilah was right, Sorrento was beautiful. Joe chose the third one as his favourite and pinned it above his bed. It was wonderful to hear from her, but he felt conflicted. He couldn't help thinking that the writing wasn't just on the lavender notepaper, it was also on the wall. She was immersing herself in a different culture. Moving in a new stratosphere that must make Watford seem extremely dull in comparison. In six months, she'd barely remember his name. In a year, he would be a distant memory. His fears were proving founded. Lilah was slipping away.

That evening he thought long and hard about his reply. Struggled for something to say. What could he tell her that she didn't already know? Or that she'd find remotely interesting? Her life was a speedboat and his was a rowing boat, with only one oar in the water. Lilah was nearly three years his junior, but she was outgrowing him. Her bedroom window looked out onto lemon trees, his onto the coal shed. She was being chauffeured around the Amalfi coast in a sports car, he was still catching the 321 outside Garston bus garage. The clever money said that it wouldn't be long before some silver-tongued bastard would, literally, charm the pants off her. With that depressing thought he turned the light off, groaned and buried his face in his pillow.

The following evening his goal was to mentally prepare his reply to Lilah. Captivate her with the charm and wit that flowed so effortlessly through his pen onto the page. At 7pm he was an hour in and all he'd written was: *'Dear Lilah, thanks for your letter.'*

It was a solid enough start, if lacking in originality. But now what? There wasn't a lot to tell. *'The forecast is for rain tomorrow,'* or *'I hit my thumb with a hammer and the nail's gone black'* just wouldn't do. After another five fruitless minutes of waiting for inspiration to strike, he lost patience. He'd give coherent thought the evening off and just write down whatever entered his head, in whatever order. The finished product read:

Dear Lilah,

Thanks for your letter and postcards. Sorrento looks like a lovely place. It's great how your Italian relatives have taken you under their wing, especially your Aunt Rosa. Sounds like you're in safe hands there. Not a lot new going on this end, I'm afraid. Unless you count the latest James Bond film being released. I don't. Mind you, the cinema and the telly are the only places I get to see exotic, foreign locations, whereas you witness them firsthand every day. Jealous? Me? Yes!

I popped in to see your brother last Sunday. It still feels strange, you not being there. Oh, the tickets to see The Four Tops in October have arrived, so that's something to look forward to. Paolo and Julie seem to be getting along well. I hope she doesn't end up hurting him like Kelly did. I don't think she will, but you never know. Once you let someone into your heart it can happen, can't it? As for your aunts making you feel closer to your dad, that can only be a good thing, right? I wish I could've known my real dad, even if just for the five years you knew yours. It sounds daft to miss something that you never had, but that's how I feel sometimes. I also miss you, but it sounds like you're far too busy to miss us much!

I'm pleased for you, though. I really am. What an adventure you're on. Yes, I remember the night you mention in your letter. How could I forget? Anyway, while you're soaking up the rays, spare a thought for us sun-starved Brits on our chilly little island.

Love to you,

Joe xxx

P.S I'm expecting a free haircut when you're qualified. x

Reading it back, Joe was pretty pleased with it and didn't change a word. He was aware of his tendency to overthink everything, so it was refreshing to just jot down his thoughts as they came to him without analysing them. He'd managed to find enough things to say, which wasn't looking likely an hour ago.

Okay, so the person he wanted as a girlfriend was now his pen pal. That was the reality. Perhaps that's all she would ever be. There were only two possible outcomes: They'd either end up together or they wouldn't. Which saying was truer, 'absence makes the heart grow fonder' or 'out of sight, out of mind'?

He had an inkling that it would prove to be the second one, but it warmed him to know that, at least for the time it took her to read his letter, she would be thinking of him. The big question was, would a letter every four weeks (not guaranteed) be enough to sustain him? Or her? Paolo had informed him that one of their team-mates had just got engaged and was having a party at The Hertfordshire Arms next Saturday. Joe thought he might show his face. Just to be sociable.

CHAPTER TWENTY

LOVE THE ONE YOU'RE WITH

In the latest edition of Blues & Soul there was a feature on The Isley Brothers. The interviewer asked them about their 1971 cover of "Love the One You're With". Unsurprisingly, Joe had never heard it as it didn't trouble the British charts, but it reached number 18 on the Billboard 100. Apparently, it was a controversial message that suggested that if it was impossible to be with the one you truly love, then why not temporarily love the one you're with? Some interpreted the lyrics as an incitement to cheat on a partner, but Joe had his own take on it. In his situation, should he sit around lamenting what might have been with Lilah? What could still be, but probably wouldn't? Or should he get back in the game? Maybe Lilah had been a false alarm and 'the one' was still out there. If so, he wasn't going to meet her by sitting indoors waiting for the postman, was he?

Joe did go to the engagement party and among his fellow guests were the majority of the Sunday football team. As usual, the beer and the banter flowed. It was a real eye-opener seeing his teammates in a different social setting, though. Yes, they always had a few post-match drinks together, but this was different. After the game it was all blokes. Here, their partners were with them, and it was noticeable that some of the loudest characters on the pitch and in the dressing room were like church mice in the company of their significant others.

The funniest moment came when Paolo had to explain to Julie why the lads all referred to Robbo, the centre half, as 'Tackle'. Not unreasonably, she'd assumed it was because he relished the physical part of the game and never shirked a crunching challenge. Her boyfriend enlightened her by revealing that the nickname actually came about as Robbo was the proud owner of the largest 'wedding tackle' in the team, possibly even the league. The first time Joe saw Tackle in the showers, he had to do a double take, thinking he had three legs. Regular length shorts were of no use to him. Considering the human body only contained eight pints of blood, it must have taken around half that to get his missile primed and ready for action. No wonder his girlfriend was always smiling. She had plenty to smile about.

Joseph Holland was back on the scene and ready to party hard. Well, as hard as you can on an apprentice's wage. It did increase a bit per annum, but he wouldn't reap the full reward for almost another two years. Still, he was over halfway through his time and managed just fine. Especially as he was now confident and competent enough to do the small, private jobs that topped up his income. An outside light here, an extra double socket there.

Letters from Italy arrived approximately once a month, each one emphasising the growing gulf between Lilah's vibrant life and Joe's comparatively mundane one. She spoke of how her cousins were teaching her to water ski. Uncle Enzo letting her take the wheel of his speedboat. Catching a ferry across to Capri. Her visit to Pompeii.

In return he told her the latest news about her hometown. Lilah's letters were crammed with new and interesting experiences, whereas Joe felt his were increasingly dull and predictable. Almost interchangeable. His work, how the football team were doing, the latest thing Nigel had done to annoy him. The odd snippet from Blues & Soul that he thought worth mentioning. It was boring to write it so it must have been coma-inducing to read it. Naturally, he steered clear of mentioning certain aspects of his social life. He didn't suppose she'd want to hear about any liaisons he'd had with girls any more than he wanted to hear of any encounters she'd had with boys. It was highly unlikely that she was spending every evening sitting outside with her relatives listening to the crickets chirp and the waves lapping below, but Joe was quite happy to picture her doing just that.

Reverting to type when in a relationship, Paolo had gone off grid again, but this time Joe was better placed. He had the single lads from the football club to knock around with and, as a regular visitor to the town's popular pubs, clubs and bars, he could even go out alone in the knowledge that he'd pal up with somebody he knew. Such an occasion took place one Friday in late September. He was at the bar at The New Penny when a female tapped his shoulder. Joe turned but failed to recognise her.

'My friend's not very happy with you,' she admonished. Following her gaze his eyes landed on a lone, attractive girl with dark wavy hair, seated at a corner table. Her scowl cut right through him.

'I can see that,' he confirmed. 'What exactly have I done then?'

'It's what you *haven't* done. You said you'd phone her and you didn't.'

Accepting that it was out of character but not out of the question if he'd had a skinful, he probed, 'What's her name?'

'Gail.'

Joe racked his brain. Gail? He didn't know any.... Oh, *Gail*. The name he'd woken up with on his arm. Bloody hell, that was last Christmas at Top Rank – over nine months ago.

'I meant to phone; I lost her number. Tell her I'm sorry, will you?'

'Tell her yourself. And the least you could do is buy her a vodka and orange.'

'Fair enough.'

'I'm Anne, and I'll have the same, for delivering the message,' she added, walking away before he could object. As Joe approached their table with his peace offerings, it was plain to see he wasn't flavour of the month. Discreetly, Anne picked up her drink and left to go and talk to someone across the room. Gail was avoiding eye contact, so he spoke first, 'I think I owe you an apology. The truth is I mislaid your phone number.'

She gave him a withering look. 'Really? I wrote it on your arm so, unless you lost it in an industrial accident, I don't see how that's possible.'

Squeezing his left shirt sleeve she exclaimed in mock surprise, 'Oh no, look, there it is!'

Humbly, he began his explanation, 'You probably noticed I was rather drunk last time we met. I was hungover next day so I took a bath and your number washed off. I intended to write it down, but I'd had a row with my stepdad and I forgot.'

Unimpressed, her answer was, 'So your excuse is that you're not inconsiderate, just a moron?'

'Yes. A very clean moron, though.'

Despite herself, the flicker of a smile crossed her face and he was sure he heard the sound of ice cracking. As if by fate, the first bars of "Killing Me Softly" by Roberta Flack filled the club. Slow songs weren't normally played until the 'erection section' at the end of the night, so a gift like this couldn't be ignored. Joe held out his hand. 'Come on, let's dance.'

He'd already half turned, waiting to feel her hand in his when her reply fully registered.

'No thanks.'

'Pardon?'

'I said, "No thanks",' she affirmed. 'I don't want to dance with you. You had your chance and you blew it.'

'But I just bought you a drink.'

'Yes. Thanks very much.'

The cracks in the ice had definitely frozen back over. Another bloke approached and whispered something in Gail's ear. 'I'd love to,' she said and got to her feet to make for the dancefloor. As she passed Joe, she concluded their conversation with, 'Ta-ta then. Nice to see you.'

His ego insisted that she was temporarily punishing him and she'd soften up as the night progressed. But she didn't. He was invisible to her. At the time he wasn't best pleased, but when he looked back on it, he had to admire the classy way she'd got her own back. She had given him a lesson in humility. As Lenny once said,

'You learn more about yourself in defeat than you do in victory.'

He was referring to football when he said it, but it held just as true for the dating game as the beautiful game. Talking of Lenny, he absolutely roared when Joe told him what happened.

'Good on her. That's what you get when you don't phone a lass when you say you will. They get quite uppity about things like that. I had a mate in the army—'

'I don't want to know,' intercepted his apprentice, covering his ears.

Another encounter with a face from Joe's recent past took place three weeks later, in the exact same crowded nightspot, at the exact same bar. Once again, he was awaiting his turn to be served when he thought he recognised the back view of the blonde girl just in front of him. When she glanced to her left all doubt disappeared. It was Suzanne. Joe had seen Mad Mick's photo at her flat so furtively checked if he was anywhere to be seen. He wasn't. The space next to her became vacant so he filled it, waiting for her to notice him. 'Hello stranger,' she eventually beamed, 'how's things?'

'I'm fine. You?'

'Yes. Good.'

'How's your boy?'

'Growing up fast. He starts pre-school next January.'

'Blimey. And how's er… you know who?'

'Behaving himself. Mostly.'

'Mostly?'

'Well, he's working and he's brilliant with our son, but he's so possessive of me. I swear if he caught me talking to a ninety-year-old priest he'd think something was going on between us. He's meeting me here after the pubs shut.'

From behind them a male voice boomed. 'Who's this then?'

Automatically, Joe turned around to find himself staring into a chest that seemed as wide as the M1. Slowly his eyes moved upwards, past the bull neck, beyond the jutting jaw until he reached the two squinting, suspicious slits either side of the upper nose. It was McCreadie, all six feet, four inches of him.

'Hello Mick. You're early,' greeted Suzanne.

'Yeah. Who's this then?' repeated her boyfriend, his intimidating stare fixed on this unknown bloke his girl was conversing with. Joe was certain he was about to be mashed. His mouth was as dry as the bottom of a birdcage and his stomach was in knots. It was Suzanne's cool head and quick thinking that saved the day (and a trip to A & E). Turning to her former lover she asked, 'Sorry, what did you say your name was again?'

'Joe,' he replied, his voice as weak as his knees.

'That's it. I dropped my purse, Mick, and Joe here found it and handed it in behind the bar. Wasn't that kind of him?'

Mad Mick was like a composite of every nightclub bouncer who'd ever lived. Only bigger and meaner looking. A shaven-headed, man mountain. Joe was sure the huge predator could smell his fear as it assessed the nervous little creature in front of it, pondering what its fate should be. After what seemed like an age, McCreadie spoke: 'Yes, that was a very nice thing to do. Thankyou.'

The relief flooded through Joe and he wanted to laugh hysterically, but he controlled himself.

His heartbeat started to get back to somewhere near normal but spiked again when Suzanne said to her boyfriend, 'Well, offer him a drink then.'

Christ Almighty, Suzanne. Have you never heard of quitting while you're ahead?

'Sorry. Can I buy you a drink, friend?'

'No thanks, I'm fine,' assured Joe.

Mick leaned in closer. 'But I insist. To refuse would hurt my feelings.'

'Oh well, in that case, I'll have a lager please.'

Ignoring the customers waiting in front of him, McCreadie shouted, 'Oi, over here. Two pints of lager and a Bacardi and coke. With ice.'

Nobody chose to criticise his lack of manners, including the barman, who served him immediately. Handing over the pint, the giant wished Joe, 'Good health,' and guided Suzanne away from the bar area by her elbow. The only reason Joe's health remained good was entirely down to her, God bless her. He felt like a wounded zebra who had just crossed paths with a lion and lived to tell the tale. Joe Holland was certainly no coward and he'd been in a few scrapes, but you couldn't take on a man of McCreadie's size – not without a loaded bazooka.

He drank his pint and decided to call it a night, still shaken by his lucky escape. When he'd embarked on the affair with Suzanne, he remembered thinking that danger was the twin sister of excitement. That still rang true but now he realised it was also the first cousin of stupidity.

The Hammersmith trip in October to see The Four Tops was one to remember. Paolo offered to take the car, so Joe paid for the petrol, which still worked out cheaper, and more convenient, than going by train. Driving through the capital's urban sprawl made the boys thankful that their home was in the suburbs and not inner London. They found it overcrowded and impersonal. High-rise blocks were popping up everywhere. Surely living there must feel transitory, like you're just passing through. Or maybe it didn't. They were just glad that they lived further out, in a town, where you had enough open space to breathe.

The show itself was amazing. Yes, The Four Tops stage show was a little passé for 1973, with their matching stage suits and choreographed dance moves, but oh, those velvet voices. They sounded exactly like the records and just to be in the same building was special. By the time they ended with "Reach Out (I'll Be There)", the whole audience was on its feet, singing along with them. Money well spent.

The only downside was on the journey back to Watford, when Paolo let slip that Lilah was seeing a local boy in Sorrento. It wasn't a surprise, Joe had been expecting it, but it still felt like a knife through his heart. He wondered if she'd mention it in her next letter. She didn't. Nor in any subsequent letters. And he sure as hell wasn't going to ask. Anyway, why should she tell him? He didn't talk about the girls in *his* life, even though she'd undoubtedly have loved to hear about him being put in his place by Gail.

CHAPTER TWENTY ONE

MONEY
(THAT'S WHAT I WANT)

Britain in the winter of 1974 was a bleak time. January and February were cheerless months in any year; short days, freezing weather, Christmas in the rearview mirror and Easter a long way up the road. But this year was even more dismal than usual. The UK was going down the crapper. The trouble started at the tail end of '73 when the coal miners stopped all overtime to try to force a 35% wage increase. The Tory government wouldn't play ball, so coal stocks started to dwindle. This was a major problem as the nation relied heavily on burning coal to produce the vast majority of its electricity. And as Mr Lenny Coleman pointed out; the modern world can't function without electricity.

So, to save on coal reserves, shortened working hours were introduced on January 1st. This would come to be known as the three-day week, as factories and offices were only allowed to use electricity for three consecutive days. Most retailers either opened for morning trading or afternoons – not both. To further save on power, TV broadcasts closed down at ten thirty every night. It wasn't quite a return to the Stone Age, but it didn't bode well for the future.

With their wage demands unmet, the miners called a full strike on February 5th. Like many Brits, Joe thought the miners were being greedy and holding the country to ransom, but Lenny had a different perspective. They discussed it whilst second fixing a flat.

'Whatever they're asking for they should get.'

'But thirty five percent, Len. It's a bit steep.'

'Is it? Would you want to do their job? Grafting underground eight hours a day, breathing in the coal dust that'll shorten your life?'

'Why do it then?'

'Ah, the ignorance of youth. Where they live there's no other work. Not for their class. Which is your class too, by the way. They deserve every extra penny they can get but, for now, they're using the only bargaining tool they've got. The withdrawal of their labour.'

Joe still believed their demands were excessive but conceded that he'd probably have a different view if he was one of them. And no, he wouldn't want to do their job. The stalemate continued for three weeks before Prime Minister Edward Heath called a snap general election. His plan was for the electorate to send the strikers a message and his question to the nation was: 'Who is running this country, the government or the trade unions?'

His answer came just after the votes were counted and the removal van pulled up outside 10 Downing Street. Within days Labour leader Harold Wilson's slippers were under Ted's old bed.

Wilson gave the miners their pay rise and asked the unions, as fellow socialists, to help him steady the ship. Which they did. As usual, most members of the public were ignorant of these behind the scenes goings on and the political manoeuvrings that never cease. All they knew was that life was pretty grim. Being young, Joe and his ilk just accepted any changes and tried to get on with what was important, i.e. having fun.

On May 17th, Joe Holland left his teenage years behind and turned twenty. The best present he received was from his mum when she disclosed that when he was born his grandfather had set up a trust fund for him. This was a complete bolt from the blue. Her son had no idea. Grampy may have been a miserable, manipulative old sod but Mary had mentioned before that in financial matters he was a master. She went on to reveal that he'd invested wisely and every year the pot had grown steadily. When the money became available to Joe on his twenty-first it was estimated to be around the ten thousand pounds mark. Joe's jaw almost hit the carpet. An amount like that would set him up for life. It would be enough to put a hefty deposit on his own property, buy a decent second-hand car and go on his first foreign holiday. He was rich. Well, not for another twelve months he wasn't, but it was on the horizon.

What a year 1975 was promising to be. If all went to plan, before the summer, he'd be a qualified sparks, have celebrated his twenty-first birthday *and* have ten grand in his back pocket. By Christmas he could possibly have his own gaff. No more sharing a living space with Nigel bloody Holland. Parked outside his gaff would be his car. A Ford Capri – no, too common. A VW Scirocco – no, unpatriotic. Oh hell, Paolo had contacts in the motor trade, he'd sort him out.

Slow down, you're getting a bit ahead of yourself. You can't even drive.

No problem. I'll book lessons. Then I've got a year to pass my test. Trust you to piss on my cornflakes. Lighten up, worry guts; we're bloody loaded, son!

His first thought was to shout his good news from the rooftops, but after considering it he decided to only tell a select few. He didn't want to appear boastful and, anyway, as the final figure was investment related, the bottom might fall out of the market and he'd end up with a lot less than ten thousand. In the end, he only told the two people he trusted most to keep it to themselves: Paolo Massetti and Lenny Coleman.

His best friend was almost as shocked as Joe had been, and a tad surprised when asked not to tell Ellen or Lilah. When he asked, 'why not?' he was fed the little white lie that it was possible his friend could end up with nothing and didn't want to look silly. In reality, Joe had a half-baked idea of flying out to Italy to surprise Lilah, somewhere between his birthday next May and mid-June, when her two year stint was up. He hadn't worked out the details and it depended on many factors, not least, what was going on in their respective romantic lives. It was twelve months away and a lot could happen between now and then.

The ever-pragmatic Lenny urged caution. 'Ten thousand sounds a lot but just be careful,' he warned.

'You know why it sounds a lot, Len? Cos it *is* a lot,' declared Joe triumphantly, strutting around the room like a cockerel. Lenny laughed but he was adamant, 'Okay then, it's massive, you lucky little shit, but as I said, be careful. When word gets out, you'll find you've got friends you never knew you had. And they'll all have their hands out.'

Last thing at night, Joe would lie in bed picturing what ten thousand pounds looked like, in all its various denominations. He'd never seen a fifty-pound note, but he worked out that two hundred of them would fit into a Quality Street tin. In twenties it would be five hundred notes, so a shoe box would suffice. Mum's small vanity case was still large enough to accommodate a thousand tenners. The bread bin could house two thousand fivers (that's an awful lot of bread). And ten thousand crisp, green, one pound notes would nestle very neatly into his sports holdall. Of course, he was well aware that his inheritance wouldn't be in cash, but it made it more real to imagine it in readies. Never mind counting sheep to fall asleep, this was much more fun.

He tried to tell himself to put it to the back of his mind until at least the new year but it was impossible. *Ten thousand pounds*. It was like winning the football pools. Maybe money can't buy happiness, but it does offer you the chance to be miserable in extreme comfort. Before anything, he would treat his lovely mum. Buy her a whole new wardrobe of clothes, if she wanted. She could certainly do with a warm winter coat. He would provide his Sunday team with a brand-new kit, including tracksuits. The keeper could have some proper goalkeeping gloves, instead of him having to make do with his dad's gardening ones. And he'd pay for some bespoke shorts for Tackle. That would make the tailor question his tape measure.

CHAPTER TWENTY TWO

THE IN CROWD

Mary Holland had intended to wait until her son's twenty-first birthday to tell him about the trust fund, but when she received the solicitor's letter the week before his twentieth, she couldn't contain herself. It was such wonderful news and, although recently he seemed chirpy enough on the outside, she sensed a sadness in him. As she'd hoped, the news had a galvanising effect and put a spring in his step and an almost permanent smile on his face. Inevitably, word did get out. David told some kids at school, one of whom had an older brother who delivered to Edwards & Sons. Before long, it seemed like everyone and their dog knew about Joe Holland's imminent inheritance.

Three weeks after his twentieth birthday, Joe had his first driving lesson. There was a lot of talking and not much driving, but his instructor seemed a nice enough bloke. Paolo said he still had his 'L' plates in the shed, so they'd stick them on the Viva and take it to a private road. It would be a chance to get used to the pedals and gears. If he deemed Joe capable, he'd maybe let him have a short drive in traffic.

These days, it seemed that when Paolo wasn't working on cars, he was at the boxing gymnasium or out with Julie, so it would be good to spend some one on one time with him. Joe could not foresee a time when they wouldn't be good mates. His friend had even casually mentioned that if Joe bought a place he'd be interested in renting a room. His girlfriend stayed overnight occasionally, and he knew Ellen wasn't comfortable with it, so some privacy would be welcome.

Joe's chosen path had led him to the heart of Watford's weekend night-time scene. He'd become a familiar face in the popular watering holes of the town and made dozens of, not quite friends, but acquaintances. His affable, friendly demeanour meant he was welcomed wherever he went. If a bar had a lock in for an after-hours drink, he was invited. When there was a party, he was on the guest list. He was even on first name terms with the door staff at Top Rank, 'the Penny' and the lively pubs, meaning however busy they were, they'd always squeeze him in.

He met a fair number of girls, dated quite a few, but none of them made him contemplate giving up the single life. There was a lot to be said for going wherever you wanted, whenever you wanted, without having to answer to anyone. But, on the flip side, he'd witnessed friends, like Paolo, in loving one-to-one relationships and understood there was a lot to be said for that too. If it happened to *him*, though, it would have to be with someone extra special because there was no way he was going to compromise. Meantime, where's the party?

On the wider stage, the instability continued. In October, Harold Wilson called a second general election just eight months after the previous one. In February, his party had won but it was a minority government and he needed a working majority to get anything done. Preaching that Labour ended the miners' strike when the Tories couldn't, he was re-elected, earning forty two more seats than the Conservatives and some breathing space. Without doubt, though, the average man and woman in the street was sick to the back teeth of politics and politicians and just wanted their country back on an even keel, whoever was at the helm.

Five days before people went to the ballot box, the big news was of bomb attacks on two pubs in Guildford. Five people (four of them off duty British soldiers) were killed and over sixty-five injured. The Irish Republican Army claimed responsibility. Before 1974, the troubles in Northern Ireland had just been another story on *News at Ten* to most people, but now it had reached the mainland. On November 21st, it was Birmingham's turn when The Mulberry Bush and the Tavern in the Town were targeted, the explosions resulting in twenty one deaths and one hundred and eighty two casualties. Terrible as these events were, the darkest times produce the darkest humour, and there were even jokes doing the rounds about the IRA and their tactics. One such was, 'What's the fastest game in the world?' Most people guessed ice hockey or hurling. The answer: 'Pass the parcel in a Belfast pub.'

As a coping mechanism in hard times nothing can top humour. Not for the British anyway. Nobody Joe knew stopped socialising and the bars and clubs were as rammed as ever. However, the bombings did make the punters more vigilant. If a handbag was left unattended, a member of staff would be informed and it would be investigated immediately. And unfairly, but inevitably, any customer with an Irish accent would be treated with suspicion, and in some cases, open hostility.

Christmas Eve saw Joe perched on a bar stool in The Coachmakers Arms in the High St. It was only

6.45pm so the crowd hadn't piled in yet. Debbie, the barmaid, wearing tinsel in her hair and two red Christmas tree baubles as earrings, handed him his first pint of the evening. When he tried to pay, she refused, 'This one's on me. Merry Christmas.'

He leaned across the bar and kissed her on the cheek. 'Thanks. You too.'

Her perfume smelt nice. The pair had dated for a couple of weeks in the summer but soon realised they'd be better off as just friends.

'So, how's your year been?' she enquired. 'Other than failing to recognise me as the great love of your life, that is...'

Smiling, he replied, 'It's been okay, I suppose, but I've got a feeling that '75 will be incredible.'

'Had the crystal ball out, have you? Is that when you give all this up and become a monk?'

'Brother Joseph? I don't think so. I could handle the silence, but I'd struggle with the celibacy.'

'You're telling me,' she grinned and went off to serve a customer at the other end of the bar. His eyes followed her, noting how appealing her derriere looked in that pencil skirt. At 1am, after she'd finished clearing up, she went back to her flat with Joe. Yes, they were better off just as friends but, well, it was Christmas Day, wasn't it? A time to give and receive.

CHAPTER TWENTY THREE

FAMILY AFFAIR

What was to be Joe's seminal year started with a January setback when he failed his driving test. The examiner was well known for not passing any learner whose performance and knowledge of the highway code wasn't perfect. He didn't make any allowances for nerves or overlook minor faults. Joe's instructor told him it was rumoured that the crusty old curmudgeon had even failed people who had driven well if his piles were playing up. Well, obviously the Anusol wasn't working that day because Joe got the thumbs down. It diluted his disappointment when his tutor assured him that he was a good driver, ready for the road, and he should put in for a cancellation asap so he could retake the test.

In February, with a more amenable examiner, he passed with flying colours. From then on the year really took off. A week later Paolo turned twenty one and once more Joe was celebrating in the function room above The Hertfordshire Arms, along with seventy five others. He was secretly hoping that Lilah might make a surprise appearance, but she didn't. It was asking a lot. People of their class couldn't afford to just jet around Europe willy nilly. Mind you, after May 17th, *he* would be able to. That day couldn't come soon enough.

In the next three months Joe didn't put a foot wrong. Late April saw him complete his apprenticeship and be able to call himself an electrician. It was around about this time that he grew tired of the long-haired look and went back to a shorter style, though nowhere near as short as before. And it wasn't just his haircut that changed. As his horizons widened, his trouser legs narrowed, from twenty inch hems down to twelve. After a three-year hiatus he was returning to the cleaner-cut image that he felt was his true calling. It seems he'd unintentionally tapped into the zeitgeist as more and more of his contemporaries also ditched their flares and visited the barbers. After a dodgy start, 1975 was now unfolding into the year that Joe had hoped for. Life was good, and soon it would be the main event: his twenty-first birthday.

The one fly in the ointment continued to be his homelife. Since Nigel learned of Joe's upcoming inheritance the strained atmosphere in the Holland household had gone from bad to worse. His stepson's good fortune had stirred up feelings of envy and resentment in Nigel, which pleased Joe no end. Six days before his party, he was playing records in his bedroom when he went downstairs for a snack. As he passed the living room, he heard his mum and Nigel arguing, so he stopped and listened through the door.

'It's not right. When your dad was sick, we're the ones who looked after him. He didn't want to die in hospital, so who was it who carried him to the commode? Lifted him in and out of the bath? Helped dress and undress him? Muggins here, that's who. And what did he leave me? Sweet FA.'

'He left us this house,' protested Mary.

'No. He left *you* this house. I'm just a glorified bloody lodger.'

'Dad set up the trust fund for Joe when he was a baby. I hadn't even met you then. He *is* his grandson.'

'So is David, but ten grand isn't going to fall into *his* lap when he's twenty-one.'

'We never even had David when dad was alive. You're not making sense.'

'What makes no sense is giving that amount to someone who will probably piss most of it up against the wall.'

'Joeseph's more sensible than that. He's young and so what if he likes to go out and enjoy himself at the weekend? Good luck to him. I wish I'd had the chance.'

'Go on, say it. Instead of ending up with me. Well, the feeling's mutual. You should be grateful that I took you on. You and your precious boy.'

Joe opened the door and sauntered in. Nigel retreated to an armchair and pretended to pore over some school papers. Mary was seated at the table with her sewing machine, working on cushion covers.

'Everything alright?'

'Everything's fine,' replied Mary. As expected, her husband said nothing.

'Oh good. We don't want anything upsetting the harmony in our loving home, do we? Watford's version of The Waltons, that's us.'

He made to exit the room, stopped at the door and turned. 'Oh, Nige,' he said, knowing his nemesis hated his name being shortened, 'if you want to borrow a few quid when my inheritance comes through, you only need to ask.'

Joe couldn't be sure, but he thought he saw steam coming from his stepdad's ears. On May 17th the big day finally arrived. Followed by the much-anticipated night. If everyone who had confirmed turned up, there would be close to a hundred and fifty people in the leisure centre's function room. Until he wrote the invitations out, Joe wasn't even aware that he knew that many people, but the numbers don't lie. And there were probably another fifty that he had to leave out. Most of his work colleagues would be there, including Lenny and wife and the luscious Linda. All the lads from his Sunday football team and their plus ones were coming, as well as a good proportion of the night owls from Watford's pub and club scene. Some were, perhaps prematurely, billing it as the biggest party of the year.

Paolo and Julie had arranged to pick the birthday boy up at 7pm to get him to the venue early but, uncharacteristically, his lift was twenty minutes late. The guests were due from 8pm onwards, so it would still give him half an hour to check that the DJ and the buffet was set up. He'd waited so long for this evening and wanted it to go off without a hitch.

To wear, he'd chosen light grey trousers with a sky-blue shirt under a three-button black waistcoat. When he entered the large room he couldn't have been more pleased. Dougie already had his decks set up in the corner and the catering manager assured Joe that all was well, and the sandwiches and sausage rolls were being prepared as they spoke, ensuring they'd be fresh when the guests arrived. The bowls of crisps, peanuts and other assorted nibbles were already on the buffet table. Coloured balloons were pinned up all around the room and above the bar was a white linen sash saying HAPPY 21st BIRTHDAY JOE in red letters. Eight tables with chairs formed a semi-circle around the dancefloor and Dougie had set up some strobe lights. Next to the entrance doors was a smaller table for cards and presents. It was perfect. His mum had arranged all of this and spent three hours earlier that afternoon helping to set it up. At 7.55pm, the remaining food came out covered in aluminium foil, which would be removed at 9pm. Mary had planned it like a military operation. Paolo handed Joe a lager and, together with Julie, they clinked glasses. On the stroke of 8pm the music started and the trickle of people arriving became a stream, then a river. The host greeted everyone warmly and shared a few words with all of them. Except one. Nigel walked straight past him and headed for the bar, as his wife pulled an apologetic face. David simply looked excited. It was the first 'big do' he'd ever been to. Joe had half hoped his stepdad wouldn't show and was a little surprised that he had. After all, they hadn't spoken a word to each other in almost a week. That was okay, as long as he kept himself to himself and his gob shut.

By the time the buffet opened, any concerns Joe may have had about who would turn up were completely dispelled. The place was packed, as was the dancefloor. The 'Soul Trader' knew exactly what songs got people on their feet and the host started to relax into the evening. Just before 9.30pm, "Lady Marmalade" tore from the speakers and Linda grabbed Joe's hand and led him to the dancefloor. If she was a fan of Labelle, things might just work out between them after all. Conscious of, and revelling in, the testosterone-fuelled envy he was receiving, he got with the beat. As Linda gyrated in front of him, Joe wondered if she was aware that the French lyrics she was singing along to translated into English as, 'Do you want to sleep with me tonight?'

Or that every male in the room, with even a basic understanding of le Francais, was inwardly screaming, 'Oui, s'il vous plait!'

So, he was slightly annoyed when Paolo interrupted to tell him there were a couple of persistent gate crashers outside.

'Who is it?' asked Joe.

'I don't know them. But they're adamant they know you and won't go away until they've spoken to you.'

As Linda moved her hips from side to side and pushed her hair up, Joe sighed, 'Great timing. Come on then, let's go and sort it out.'

The night was shaping up well and the last thing he wanted was any unpleasantness so he decided that, providing he knew the uninvited guests, he'd allow them in. When he got outside, Joe couldn't see anyone. 'Where are they then?' he asked, impatient to get back to the dancefloor. From around the corner a familiar voice said, 'Buon compleanno.' Then into the light stepped… Lilah.

She looked amazing. The last time he'd seen her she was blossoming. Well now, at eighteen years of age, she was in full bloom. Italy had turned her into a confident, stylish young woman. She was four inches taller; her natural tan was now two shades darker and her long jet-black hair framed her lovely face and fell onto her bare, bronzed shoulders. She was wearing a black mini dress with chic gladiator sandals and looked like she'd stepped off the pages of a fashion magazine.

'That means, "happy birthday",' she beamed and moved in for a hug. It felt so good to hold her again after almost two long years and he only reluctantly let go.

'What a surprise. I thought you weren't back until next month.'

'I came early. Paolo picked me up from the airport about three hours ago.'

So that's why he was late.

She reached into her shoulder bag, took out a small gift wrapped in green crepe paper and handed it to Joe. He took it without once taking his eyes off her face. 'God, it's so good to see you.'

He turned to Paolo, who he'd temporarily forgotten was there, 'And, as for you, "gate crashers outside", eh?'

'Well, she is,' he laughed. 'I don't see an invite, do you?'

Joe put an arm around each of them and they went inside. Paolo joined Julie on the dancefloor and Joe sat down with Lilah. 'So, are you back for good?'

'I'm not sure. It depends. My aunt's offered me a permanent job in Sorrento.'

Trying to hide his disappointment, he replied, 'Well, it's great that you made it for tonight. I've kept all your letters. You write well. I really felt like I was doing all those things with you.'

'Maybe you were,' was her cryptic response.

'Watford must seem awfully dreary in comparison.'

'It's home,' she shrugged.

In the corner of his eye he spotted David, sitting alone and looking anxious. 'I suppose I'd better mingle. We'll have a proper catch up later, yeah?'

'Go,' she smiled. 'A good host looks after his guests.'

It was then he noticed something different about her eyes. They were still as expressive as ever, but they'd lost their innocence and gained a sort of... sophistication.

Joe asked David if he was alright and where their mother was.

'She's at the counter trying to persuade Dad to go home. He's drunk.'

The queue to be served was three deep and Joe couldn't see them. This was so out of character. Nigel was strictly a glass of sherry at Christmas and one G&T after a round of golf sort of bloke. 'A little bit drunk?' he asked his brother, who shook his head and revealed, 'Very, very drunk.'

While he was debating whether his intervention would help or make matters worse, the decision was taken out of his hands when the music stopped and the DJ's amplified voice called Joe up to say a few words. He was reluctant but when the handclapping and a chant of 'We want Joe,' grew in volume, he knew he had no choice. Someone had placed an upturned plastic beer crate in front of the disco so, to cheers, he hopped up on it and Dougie handed him his microphone. He waited for the noise to subside and then began. 'Firstly, thanks to all of you for coming tonight.' He turned his gaze in Lilah's direction. 'Especially the ones who have come a long way. I didn't know I was so popular.'

'We're only here cos you're rich,' came a good natured heckle, closely followed by 'Lend us a tenner.'

Joe let the laughter die down before responding. 'There's a special cardboard box for the begging letters on the gift table. I'll be burning it tomorrow morning. Seriously though...'

The sound of smashing glasses and a loud thud stopped him in his tracks. From his vantage point, Joe could see that Nigel had fallen off his stool, pulling a row of empty glasses on the bar down with him.

Mary and one of the footballers were trying to help him to his feet, but it was clear that he didn't appreciate their efforts.

'I think your dad's had enough, Joe,' shouted an unknown male voice.

Nigel managed to haul himself up and was using the bar counter for support. 'I'm not his dad,' he hollered, 'the thought of it makes me feel sick.'

A hush descended over the entire room as the tirade continued. 'I gave him my name, but I was never his dad.'

'I can vouch for that,' returned Joe.

'Just stop it, Nigel,' hissed Mary.

Ignoring her, he pointed an unsteady finger at his stepson. 'You don't even know who your dad is, do you?'

You really want to do this now, you fucker? thought Joe. *Come on then, let's do it.*

'Oh, I know. My real father was John Hudson. He died before I was born.'

'You know *nothing*,' sneered the swaying antagonist.

'Don't do this, Nigel. Not here. I'm begging you,' pleaded Mary.

As if she was invisible, he continued, 'You're not Joe Hudson. You're certainly not Joe Holland. You, dear boy, are the son of a convicted rapist.'

All eyes moved from Nigel to Joe and he felt very alone standing there on that beer crate, as everyone awaited his reaction. But his stepdad hadn't quite finished. 'You're...' He searched for the words and grinned sardonically when he found them, 'You're rape seed. Yes, that's who you are – Joe Rapeseed.'

He chuckled to himself as if he'd just come up with the funniest joke ever. Joe looked at his mother for confirmation that this drunken, malicious idiot was talking gibberish but what he saw was a broken woman, her expression one of sheer horror. Confusion reigned. Why wasn't she denying these blatant lies?

It was Lenny who acted first, striding up to the bar and confronting Nigel. 'Right mate, I think you've said enough. Now, get out or I'll put you out.'

'I'll leave when I'm good and ready,' came the slurred response. Joe had seen and heard enough. Looking out at the sea of faces, with their mixture of shock and embarrassment, he snapped. Years of simmering resentment came to the boil. In one movement, he tossed the mic back to Dougie, jumped down off the crate and ran towards Nigel, fists clenched. The crowd parted like the Red Sea in front of him. This bastard had ruined his party with his ridiculous outburst and now he was going to regret it.

Joe was almost upon his prey when Lenny and Paolo simultaneously grabbed him, tearing a button off his waistcoat. It took all of their considerable combined strength to hold him, but they succeeded and Nigel lurched out of the building while Mary comforted a visibly upset David.

'Let me go,' bellowed Joe, struggling to break free. 'I'll kill him.'

With his stepfather gone, Joe turned his focus to his mum. She looked absolutely mortified, her eyes filled with remorse and guilt, like a devout Christian who'd been caught stealing from the church collection plate. And that was the moment Joe knew, beyond any shadow of a doubt, that Nigel had told the truth. Paolo turned to the DJ and ran his finger across his throat in a cutting motion. The message was understood and solemnly Dougie announced 'Ladies and gentlemen, the party is over. If you'd like to finish your drinks and leave quietly, it would be greatly appreciated. Thank you.'

The guests started to file out immediately, some muttered muted 'goodnights' to Joe but most just slipped away, not knowing what to say. Lenny advised, 'You shouldn't go home tonight, Joe boy. Is there anywhere you can stay?'

Without hesitation Paolo insisted, 'He's staying at mine.'

'I am not staying at yours,' insisted Joe. 'I'm going to give that bastard what's coming to him.'

'Think about it,' urged his friend. 'He's off his head and you've had a good drink too. So, you beat the shit out of him. What happens then? You end up being arrested. What good will that do?'

'Sorting him out would be worth a night in the cells.'

'What about your poor mum?' interjected Lenny. Seeing his question didn't calm Joe at all he tried a different tack. 'And what about David? He doesn't deserve to witness his brother giving his dad a hammering, does he?'

It was the best thing Len could have said to calm the waters. David most certainly shouldn't bear witness to that. Slowly, Joe began to simmer down and, much to everyone's relief, nodded in agreement.

'I'll drive you home tomorrow morning and you can straighten it all out,' assured Paolo. Then he walked over to Mary and said something that Joe couldn't hear. Sombrely, she too nodded.

'We'll take her and the boy home,' offered Lenny.

Joe felt a soft hand he recognised as Lilah's slide into his still clenched fist. Dougie graciously volunteered to put all the gifts and cards in his van and drop them off when it was convenient. As Lenny and his wife ushered Mary and David out, she gave her eldest son a heart-rending look, as if she wanted to say something.

Paolo quietly apologised to the bar manager, who was very understanding and said his staff would take down the decorations. It was decent of him as, strictly speaking, it was the host's responsibility. But the last thing on this host's mind was balloons and banners. Underlining how sweet she was, Julie stated that she would order a cab home, so Paolo could take the shaken Joe straight back to his house. Matching her thoughtfulness, Lilah opted to share the cab, so her brother's girlfriend wouldn't be on her own.

When the boys arrived at the Massettis', Ellen already had the kettle on, and by her maternal look of concern for the lad she'd known since he was twelve, it was clear that the taxi company wasn't the only phone call the girls made. Lilah arrived home half an hour later to find the boys sat at the table in the living room. Her mother was finishing making up the sofa bed that Joe had slept in on numerous, happier occasions. There was little chance he'd be sleeping much that night, though.

It was the silence that hit Lilah first. Joe had gone beyond calming down and disappeared into himself. Ellen thought that maybe it was her presence that was preventing him from opening up, so she informed everyone that she was away to her bed. The carriage clock on the mantlepiece read 10.30pm. Before departing she kissed her son and daughter on the cheek and squeezed Joe's arm as she passed by.

After making herself a coffee, Lilah joined the other two at the table. Both men had mugs of tea in front of them, but Joe's remained untouched. As his sister took her seat, Paolo shot her a concerned look and mimed, 'What do we do?'

Neither of them had seen Joe like that before, primarily because he'd never been like that before. It didn't take a psychiatrist to see that he was traumatised. Lilah silently mouthed, 'Go to bed,' to her big brother, convinced that if anyone could get through to Joe, it was her. He acquiesced, telling his friend,

'I'll say goodnight, mate. Try to get some kip.'

Joe's answer was to stare unresponsively into his drink. As soon as the two of them were alone, Lilah moved onto the seat next to his and held his hand, repeatedly running her thumb over the top of it in a circular motion. After a minute or so, it seemed to have an effect and he raised his glassy eyes to meet hers.

'Are you okay?' she said softly, realising as the words left her lips it was a stupid question.

'No,' he confirmed.

With her other hand she stroked his face. His cheek felt damp. 'Even if what your stepdad said is true, it doesn't matter.'

'It matters to me.'

'What I mean is; it's not important which two people *make* you – it's what you make of yourself.'

'Lilah, I don't even know who I am anymore.'

Cupping his face with both hands, she locked eyes with him. 'I know who you are. I *see* you. You're thoughtful. And funny. And... I love you.'

Joe almost broke but held his tears. 'Please don't say that. Not now. Not tonight.'

'It's true. I've loved you for... well, forever.'

These were the words he'd dreamed of hearing for years. Longed to hear. Now, on his twenty-first birthday, this incredible, wonderful girl had declared her love for him. It should easily have been the happiest night of his life; but it was the worst. Everything positive was overshadowed, hijacked by the crippling revelation that he was the spawn of some faceless, vile scumbag. It was too much to bear. He should be honest with her, though; it was the least she deserved.

'I do have feelings for you. Deep, deep feelings. But tonight has shattered me.'

'Then we'll just have to glue you back together, won't we? You're the same person you were yesterday. The person that I flew home early to see.'

She leaned in and kissed him softly on the lips, but he was unresponsive.

'I'm sorry, my head's all over the place. Nothing's the same. Everything's changed.'

'Don't apologise. I understand. Really, I do. Just know this; you are *not* alone. Now get some rest and I'll see you in the morning.'

Happy that she'd made some progress in getting him to break his silence, she left him with his thoughts and walked away. As she reached the door his voice stopped her. 'Thankyou Lilah.'

His pitiful tone made her want to weep but she held out until she reached the top of the stairs. Joe stripped to his underwear and climbed under the covers. From the room above, Paolo's bedroom, he could hear muffled voices and knew they were discussing him.

The sad case downstairs. He was under no illusions that he'd get any sleep. How could he when his entire life had been turned upside down? And in front of just about everyone he knew. Instead, he made mental notes of all the questions he needed answering. So many questions. He was drowning in a sea of uncertainty, but of one thing he was sure. Whatever happened, he would never spend another night under the same roof as Nigel Holland.

The luminous hands on Joe's wristwatch showed 1am when, to his left, he heard the living room door open, then quickly close. He knew instinctively that it was Lilah. As she approached in the half-light, he could see she was wearing an oversized white t-shirt emblazoned with an image of Snoopy. Her legs were bare and she wore nothing on her feet. She sat down on the edge of the sofa bed and said, 'I couldn't sleep.'

'Me neither,' came the unsurprising reply.

Looking around the dimly lit room, she started to giggle. 'We've had some laughs in here, haven't we? Practising our dance moves for the scout hut. Watching Monty Python and Morecambe & Wise on TV. All those Motown Chartbuster quizzes.'

She turned to face him, 'Remember when I was fifteen and went out with that boy from school, trying to make you jealous?'

'I remember. It worked by the way.'

Looking somewhat pensive, she revealed, 'There were a few boys in Italy,' quickly adding 'Nothing happened though.'

'It's none of my business,' replied Joe, hoping to dissuade her from going any further down that path.

'That's the point. I *want* it to be your business. Are you seeing anyone?'

'No.'

'What about the tall blonde giving me daggers when I walked in with you last night?'

'She works in head office. I hardly know her.'

'So, we're both free agents?'

He nodded. Seemingly in slow motion, she stood up, raised her arms, pulled the t-shirt over her head and dropped it on the floor. She had nothing on underneath. Silhouetted against the light-coloured curtains he could see that her breasts were fuller. She was curvier than he remembered her but all the physical activity in Sorrento had toned her. She looked stunning. His eyes took in her face, breasts, stomach, hips and the neat black triangle between the top of her thighs. Visual stimulation merged with anticipation to make it the most erotic image he'd ever seen. His thoughts were jumbled, but this wasn't a time for thinking, and nature took over. Invitingly, he opened the covers and she slid in beside him, pushing her body against his.

This time her kiss was gladly accepted and reciprocated, as their tongues met. Her hand pulled his briefs down and he kicked them off. Joe nuzzled her neck, smothering it with gentle little kisses. Continuing downwards, his mouth locked on first one nipple, then the other, teasing them until they hardened in his mouth. Testosterone coursed through him and the blood raced to where it was needed most. Stroking his erection, Lilah whispered, 'It was always going to be you, Joe.' They kissed fiercely, then gently and for the next half an hour Joe employed all the tips and skills that Suzanne had shown him in her tutorial on how to please a woman. For that is now what Lilah was.

After they'd explored each other with fingertips, mouths and tongues, she took the lead by hungrily manoeuvring Joe onto his back and positioning herself above him. With both hands on his chest for leverage, she moaned softly as she lowered herself onto him, moving her hips up and down and from side to side. Slowly to start, then faster, before slowing down again and repeating the cycle. Afraid he would finish too soon, Joe retook control and lowered her onto *her* back. Varying his speed, angle and intensity, he knew exactly what he was doing. After ensuring she had climaxed it was now *his* turn. Moving her onto her hands and knees, he knelt behind her, savouring every contour of her. One of his favourite parts of the female body was the gentle curve of the lower back and he ran the tip of his tongue along it, savouring the taste of her warm skin. Finally, holding her hips, he eased himself into her and went hard in pursuit of his own orgasm.

Completely spent, they fell asleep in each other's arms. When Joe opened his eyes, it was 2.45 and he was alone. For a second he wondered if he'd dreamt it, but her scent was on his pillow and on *him*, verifying it was real. Lilah was the twelfth girl he'd had sex with but the first one he'd made love to. The mechanics were the same, but Joe now knew that when your partner was someone you truly cherished, it took the experience to a whole new level. And yet, he had mixed feelings. He should have felt elated, so why didn't he? He couldn't shake the thought that he was tainted. Unworthy of Lilah's love. Something less than he was previously.

Physically, he'd given her everything, but emotionally he had short-changed her. His mindset wasn't right and that bothered him. A girl like her deserved 100% of him, not 75%. It was still wonderful, but it could have been even better. It did dispel any doubts he'd harboured about what he felt for her, though. It was confirmation of what he'd known all along but was too proud, stubborn or scared to admit; he was very much in love with Lilah Massetti.

CHAPTER TWENTY FOUR

TELL IT LIKE IT IS

When the car pulled up outside the Holland house, Paolo could tell that his friend was in no rush to get out. 'You okay?'

'I really don't know. This whole thing is fucked up.'

He banged his fist on the glove compartment and shook his head. Paolo was uncertain what to say but offered, 'Well, at least hear what she's got to say, eh? And remember what *my* mum said.'

He was referring to Ellen's parting words fifteen minutes earlier. 'Nothing is black and white, Joe. Give your mum a chance to explain. But if you can't resolve it, you're welcome here until you sort yourself out.'

What a lovely woman, thought Joe. *No wonder Paolo and Lilah turned out so well.*

Ellen's kind offer had come after a very subdued breakfast at the Massettis'. Joe never could eat anything when he felt anxious, so he just had a mug of tea. He and Lilah exchanged the secretive, knowing looks exclusive to new lovers. Nobody knew quite what to say, until Ellen, being older and wiser than the other three, took the initiative.

The shrill ringing of the telephone startled the already tightly wound house guest. Paolo answered it, informed Joe it was David and passed him the receiver.

'Hello,' he mumbled.

'Joe, please come home,' blurted out the clearly agitated caller. 'Mum's acting really strange.'

'Whoa, slow down. What do you mean, strange?'

'She's just sitting at the kitchen table, staring into space.'

'David, calm down. Where's Nigel?' He almost retched at having to say his name.

'Dad's gone.'

'Gone?' puzzled Joe, 'Gone where?'

'I don't know. He left last night.'

Joe could tell that his little brother was getting more flustered. 'Take a breath and tell me exactly what happened.

'We got home before him last night. As soon as he came through the front door mum attacked him.'

'Attacked him?' Joe couldn't believe what he was hearing.

'Yes, she picked up the umbrella in the hallway and started hitting him with it. When it broke, she carried on with her fists. She pushed him outside and he fell on the doorstep, splitting his lip. All the time she was shouting at him, telling him he'd never set foot in this house again. Then she took her wedding ring off and threw it at him. After removing the front door key, she threw his keys at him too. I froze. I didn't know what to do.'

'I'm really sorry you had to witness all that, David.'

'I've never seen mum like that before. She was going berserk, and it scared me. Last off, she went upstairs, piled some of his stuff in a suitcase and threw it out of the bedroom window. It just missed his head. She didn't go to bed last night. Please come home, Joe.'

'Paolo's driving me home now. I won't be long, twenty minutes tops.'

From hearing half of the telephone conversation, the Massettis figured out most of what had happened and Joe filled them in on the rest. It was hard to believe that his placid, reserved mum had acted in such a way. The worm had not only turned, but it had grown fangs by the sound of it.

Steeling himself, Joe thanked Paolo for the lift, got out of the car and made tracks toward the house. The story that awaited him inside would be harrowing but he needed to hear it. As he walked up the garden path, he spotted something glinting in the flower bed. It was his mother's gold wedding ring. He picked it up, tucked it in his waistcoat pocket and turned his key in the lock. Just as David had described, Mary was sitting at the kitchen table. She looked shell shocked. Utterly defeated. Her eyes were red-rimmed and hollow, and she had on the same dress she'd worn to the party. David sat opposite her, looking desperate and helpless. 'Look Mum, Joe's here,' he offered, trying to galvanise her.

Without looking up, she replied flatly, 'Go up to your room please, David. I need to talk to Joseph alone.'

The teenager looked to his older brother for guidance and Joe nodded, signalling it was for the best. Once David had vacated the kitchen, he occupied the seat opposite Mary. She spoke first. 'Nigel's gone for good. I told him never to show his face around here again.'

'What about David? It *is* his dad.'

'If David wants to go and see him, that's fine. But I never want to set eyes on him again.'

'Where's he gone?'

'I don't know and I don't care. His sister's in Radlett probably.'

'The state of him, I'd be surprised if he got to the end of our road, let alone Radlett.'

'If that's where he went. Can't think who else would have him. Perhaps he parked up somewhere and slept in his car. I really couldn't care less. The things he said last night were awful. Unforgivable.'

'Yes, but were they true?' he ventured, desperate for her to say it was all a pack of lies.

For the first time she made eye contact, and her silence killed any tiny hope he had left. So, it was true. He *was* the result of a rape. Of the myriad of emotions coursing through him, anger was proving the strongest. Then he remembered Ellen Massetti's words. 'Nothing is black and white, Joe. Give your mum a chance to explain.'

'Christ Almighty. Right, I want to know everything, Mum. Chapter and verse,' he demanded. 'Who fathered me? Was he a stranger or did you know him? And who was John Hudson?'

As he spoke the last name, Joe had an epiphany. A real lightbulb moment. Whenever a film starring John Wayne or Rock Hudson showed on TV, his mum would be glued to it. They were her two favourite Hollywood stars when she was a girl. Could it be that she'd merged their names to create John Hudson? He almost asked her but decided it would be counterproductive at that point, settling on, 'What was his name, Mum? I want his name.'

Mary shifted uneasily in her chair, her face a mask of pain. 'You know the circumstances, why do you need his name?'

'Because I have a right to. Yesterday, I was the son of a man who died before I was born. Today, I'm a... question mark.'

She rocked back and forth then shook her head. 'No good can come of this.'

'Look, one way or another, I'm going to find out, so you might as well tell me.'

After mulling it over for around ten seconds, the floodgates opened. 'Northbridge. His name was James Northbridge.'

It sounded like exhuming that name from its burial place in her memory physically hurt.

'And did you know him before?'

'We'd been out a few times. Without my father's knowledge, of course. He was charming. Fun to be with. And he listened to what I had to say. Except when I told him "no", when he wanted to take things further.'

'You don't have to go into detail, Mum.'

'We'd been to see a jazz quartet in town,' she continued 'It was dark when we came out and he offered to walk me home. He said he knew a shortcut through the park. I had no reason to feel concerned, he'd always behaved like a perfect gentleman. In the park he kissed me, which we'd done before, but he started to paw me, making me feel uncomfortable. I told him to stop, but he didn't. He put his hand over my mouth and dragged me into the bushes.'

She wiped away a tear and her son felt terrible for taking her back there. 'What happened to him?' probed Joe, as gently as he could.

'Bizarrely, when it was over, he finished walking me home. I was in a daze and he kept apologising and begging me not to tell anyone. And at first, I didn't.

Not a soul. For my sake, not his. I was scared. Ashamed. Then when I found out you were on the way, it got to the stage where I couldn't hide it, so I told your granddad. When he calmed down, he contacted a bigwig at Merseyside police that he knew and James was arrested and charged. He denied everything but the jury believed me and he was found guilty and sentenced to eight years in prison. That's all I know; I swear to God.'

'So, even in the unlikely event he did the full term, he'd have been released... thirteen years ago.'

'I guess so,' she shrugged. 'We moved down here shortly after he'd been jailed so I don't know. My father said we needed a new start where nobody knew us or our business. You roll your eyes when I talk about how different things were back then, but it's true. For a girl to have a baby out of wedlock brought shame, not just on her, but her whole family. And your grandfather was a well-respected man. A pillar of the community. Not only a GP but a Mason and a member of the Parish Council.'

'Always thinking of others, wasn't he?' came the sarky reply.

His mum chose to ignore the remark and resumed her sorry tale. 'Anyway, he bought this house, we moved in, and you were born two months later. Together we concocted the husband killed in a motorbike crash story. I even changed my name to Hudson by deed poll, so no-one got suspicious.

'John Hudson R.I.P.,' remarked Joe, not quite finished with the sarcasm. 'So, when did Nigel appear on the scene?'

'When you were three, I found myself a part time job at a school. Only three mornings a week. I met him there.'

Joe was familiar with this part of the story. Holland was a teacher at the primary school where Mary fought nit epidemics and stuck band-aids on cut knees.

'Dad had been diagnosed with lung cancer the previous year and was getting worse, so I was looking after a dying man *and* a toddler. It was exhausting. In fairness, I have to say that Nigel was a great help to me. And I know I've said it before, but he really did take a shine to you. Always buying you little dinky toys and taking you to the park. I was never in love with him, but he'd been so good to us that when he asked me to marry him, I said "yes". You were our page boy, in a little sailor suit.'

'I know, I've seen the photos. I look ridiculous.'

'Nigel officially adopted you and David was born on our first wedding anniversary. We were a happy little unit, the four of us. We really were.' A fleeting smile crossed her lips.

'So, the question must be asked: "What the hell happened?"'

Her face clouded over. 'With father gone, Nigel suggested we take his room as ours as it was bigger. We planned to get rid of the old iron bedstead, rip up the carpets and put up brighter wallpaper. Totally refurb it.'

'I think I vaguely remember that. There were tins of emulsion and dust sheets everywhere. You told me off for painting the wheels on David's pram.'

'That's right. You'd have been about five. Any road, the only furniture of Dad's we couldn't move was his solid oak wardrobe. It was Victorian and weighed a ton.

There was no way we could lift it, so Nigel said he'd dismantle it and get rid of it.'

Fascinating as decorating stories are, Joe wondered where this one was leading. He soon had his answer.

'Whilst breaking it up, Nigel discovered the wardrobe had a secret drawer. Not unusual in furniture of that period apparently. Inside, for reasons known only to himself, Dad had kept copies of all the paperwork from James Northbridge's trial. His statement, my witness statement, the judges summing up. Everything. I tried to explain but he wouldn't listen. He just couldn't accept what had happened. As far as he was concerned, I was a liar *and* damaged goods. And you were a constant reminder of my past.

Now, at last, it all made sense to Joe. Why he could never please his stepdad, no matter how hard he tried. It had been mission impossible. He never stood a chance. Resentment welled up in him. 'But you were quite happy to let me spend years trying to win him over, knowing full well I could never do it. How could you put me through that, Mum?'

'I was hoping he might come around. I hated the way he wanted nothing to do with you. Many's the time I thought about divorcing him.'

'But you were afraid he'd reveal your little secret if you did,' he concluded.

'Partly that,' she conceded, 'plus he was a good dad to David.'

'Oh, I know, I witnessed it every day. I was desperate for just a speck of it. But he completely shut me out, and you stood and watched.'

'He shut me out too,' she protested.

'There must have been times when you wished you'd got rid of me before I was born.'

'Never,' she replied adamantly. 'Not even once.'

'It would have made your life a lot easier.'

'You were my precious boy, and you still are. I'm proud of the young man you've become. What can I say except that I'm sorry?'

Rising from his chair, Joe's weary response was, 'I'm tired and I need to sleep.'

'Don't hate me, Joseph. I couldn't bear that.'

'I don't hate you, Mum. And my heart bleeds that such an awful thing happened to you. But to find out the way I did last night, in front of all those people. I'm going to bed.'

'I'll bring you a cup of tea up later, shall I?'

'I just want to sleep.'

He reached into his pocket and placed her wedding ring on the table. 'This is yours, I think.'

She baulked at the sight of it. 'I won't be putting that on again.'

With one last pained look, he sighed, 'Oh Mum, what a mess,' and left the kitchen. She was head in hands weeping before he reached the foot of the stairs.

CHAPTER TWENTY FIVE

BALL OF CONFUSION

Joe stayed in bed for pretty much the next thirty-six hours, only getting up to make himself the odd snack and drink or take a trip to the toilet. He wanted neither to see or talk to anyone. Not his best friend, not the girl he adored, not his little brother, and not his mum. He had to work out where to go from here on his own, with no outside interference, no matter how well meaning. There was no way he could stay working for Edwards & Sons. They'd either pity him or patronise him, and he didn't want either. He'd miss Lenny but they wouldn't have seen as much of each other anyway, now Joe was out of his time. But firms were crying out for qualified electricians, so he wouldn't be unemployed for long.

When he wasn't asleep, he was reliving his party, his mum's disclosures and the all too brief interlude with Lilah. He sought refuge in sleep, not having the energy or inclination to do anything else, but it wasn't restful. Saturday night's ignominy even penetrated his dreams, meaning he had no respite. The most vivid dream saw him back standing on the beer crate, looking out on that sea of shocked faces. So many familiar faces. His family, his work colleagues, his football mates, the crowd from town, Linda, Paolo and Lilah. All awaiting *his* reaction to Nigel's outburst. Then, one by one, all of them started to laugh and point their fingers at him.

Their cruel laughter was deafening, and he covered his ears with his hands – but nothing he could do would mute it. The laughing heads then separated from the bodies and swirled around, as if he was looking at them through a kaleidoscope. That's when he woke up, sweating.

Joe's thoughts leapt around his mind like jumping jacks, but they always led him back to the same conclusion; his old life was finished. From now on people would look at him differently. He even looked at himself differently. His whole genetic code had changed. Well, half of it anyway. What had he inherited from this Northbridge creep? Perhaps a lot more than nose shape or hair colour. Was it possible he'd taken on his sexual behaviour gene, if there was such a thing? The thought of being turned on by hurting and violating women repulsed him. He thought back to each of his full sexual encounters and the handful of near misses. Had he ever been too forceful? Too rough? Overstepped the mark? He was pretty sure he hadn't, but one of Lenny's favourite sayings was 'The apple never falls far from the tree'. Joe hoped in his case he'd fallen as far away as he possibly could.

Early that Sunday evening there was a light tapping on Joe's door. Mary's frail voice enquired, 'Are you awake?' When there was no reply, she entered. He lay with his back to her but didn't acknowledge her presence.

'I've made you some soup, Joseph. Potato and leek.'

'Thanks,' was all he said as he heard her set the tray down. He knew she was suffering too, and he took no pleasure in it, but he was angry with her. Since he turned eighteen, she'd had ample opportunity to take away

Nigel's hold over her by telling him about his conception. Yes, it would have been painful and hard for them both; but a hell of a lot easier than him finding out the way he did on his twenty-first birthday. The fact was that his seemingly charmed life had been cursed from the very beginning. Built on a dark lie with an even darker truth behind it.

What was his mother thinking, inventing John Hudson and presenting him as his dad? What if he'd wanted to search out relatives on the Hudson side of the family? Would she have let him waste his time on a wild goose chase or invent more falsehoods to try and throw him off the trail? Lies, wrapped in more lies, tied together with secrets.

Behind him, Mary tried to make conversation. 'Paolo phoned. And his sister.' She thought mentioning the girl who wrote to him regularly might spark his interest but to her dismay he remained lethargic.

'If they phone again, please tell them I'm fine and I'll call them tomorrow.'

'Are you really fine, Joseph?'

'Just take care of yourself and David,' he advised. 'He needs you. All I need is some time to work through this.'

'I'll be downstairs if you want anything.'

'Thanks for the soup,' he said, still facing away from her. After consuming the warm liquid he retreated back under his duvet, where he felt safe.

Sometime during the night, the dream about the laughing faces revisited. It was exactly the same as before except there was an extra guest standing at the back. At first Joe thought it was Nigel, but he soon located him; his laughter was the loudest of all. He homed in on the mystery face and was alarmed to see it was more like a shop mannequin than a human. It had no discernible features, other than a mouth, its cruel, thin lips laughing along with everyone else and its long waxlike finger pointing at him. Taunting him. This time, before all the heads detached themselves from the necks and began their macabre dance, Joe woke up. Immediately, realisation hit that the faceless apparition was James Northbridge. And he was certain, absolutely positive, that there would be no peace for him until he tracked him down and put a face to that name. It shouldn't be too difficult. A lot easier than finding a Smith or a Jones.

On Monday morning, Mary called him for work and didn't seem too surprised when he told her he wasn't going. She left the house just after David. Poor kid. He was a sensitive boy and the recent upheaval must have been hard for him to deal with. The whole family was fractured and each member somehow had to find a way forward. None more so than Joe. But at least a clearer picture was forming in his head. A plan, of sorts. Still feeling mentally wiped out, he slept the rest of the morning.

His mum arrived home just after 2pm. The two full carrier bags indicated she'd done a food shop. It was evident she was happy that he was up and dressed but Joe knew her mood would soon change when he told her what he intended to do.

'It's good to see you up and about, Joseph,' she remarked as she prepared to put the shopping away.

'Here, let me give you a hand,' he offered, trying to soften the impending blow.

'Waitrose was packed today. Braising steak, mash and peas for dinner. I know that's one of your favourites.'

As he handed her two tins of baked beans, he decided to wade straight in. 'Mum, I've reached a decision about where I go from here. And I don't think you're going to like it.'

Her face froze in horror as she seemed to anticipate what he was about to say. 'Please don't tell me you're going to try and trace him, Joseph.'

'I have to, Mum. I need to.'

She slumped down in the kitchen chair, shaking her head. 'No good can come of it. No good at all.'

'I'm not looking for a relationship with him. I just need to look him in the eyes, once.'

'He's a manipulator. A world class liar. He'll turn you against me,' she lamented, getting even more agitated than he'd envisioned she would. Joe walked across, put a reassuring arm around her shoulders and squeezed.

'That's not going to happen, Mum. You were seventeen and naïve. Nothing that man says could justify his actions.'

With pleading eyes, she implored, 'Please don't meet up with him. He has a superficial charm that takes people in. That's what happened to me. I'm begging you not to contact him, Joseph.'

'As I said, I *need* to, Mum. It feels like half of me is missing. For one thing, he may have medical issues I need to know about that might affect me in the future.'

'Don't use that as an excuse,' she shot back, defiance replacing supplication. 'You're doing this to hurt me. Getting your own back because *I* never told you.'

'Think that if you want, but it's not true. Yes, I'm annoyed that you could have prevented it coming out the way it did, but if I don't do this, I'll drive myself mad thinking about it. I have to take back some control. Sorry if you don't like it, but that's the way it is.'

Their evening meal was eaten in near silence which, apart from there being one fewer plate, wasn't much different from when Nigel was there. Joe and Mary were entrenched in their positions with David stuck in no-man's land. It was with some relief that the teen said, 'I'll get it,' when the doorbell rang.

'I don't want to see anyone,' warned his brother, listening intently as the door was opened and a familiar male voice enquired, 'Is Joe there?'

'It's okay, let him in,' came the shouted instruction.

Paolo appeared in the kitchen doorway with Lilah just behind him. His awkward greeting of 'Hi, Mrs Holland,' was responded to with an even more awkward timid nod of her head. It drove it home to Joe that he wasn't the only one Nigel had humiliated last Saturday. He scraped the remains off his plate into the pedal bin and led his visitors up to his room.

'So, how are you doing?' asked Paolo, once they were inside.

'Not great, but better than yesterday.'

'Good. Did you check if your inheritance money's in the bank?'

His inheritance money! With everything else going on it had completely slipped his mind.

'I'm going into town tomorrow, so I'll pop into the main branch of Lloyds and check. I've got a few things to do.'

'Like what?' asked Paolo, trying to mask his concern.

'Like, buy a ticket to Liverpool.'

'Liverpool?' queried Paolo, 'You going to see a match?'

'No, I'm going looking for the bloke who... (he couldn't say the word 'raped') ...assaulted Mum.'

'To do him over?'

'It's tempting. But no. I've got his name; I just need to put a face to it. Look him in the eye. After that, I don't know. Maybe tell the bastard exactly what I think of him.'

'I think you *should* find him,' chipped in Lilah, 'get it out of your system.'

Joe smiled his thanks to her. 'Apparently, he wasn't a stranger. Mum knew him.'

He then related the story that his mother had told him.

'But how do you know he's still in Liverpool?' queried Paolo.

'I don't, but it's possible. Or maybe he's got family there who can put me in touch with him. Northbridge is not that common a name.'

'Well, good luck, mate,' said Paolo. If you want company, I'll book a holiday day and come with you.'

Joe was grateful but declined. 'Thanks for the offer, but this is something I have to do on my own.'

Tentatively, his friend replied, 'It's a big decision. Have you thought it through?'

Joe nodded, his face the picture of determination.

'Your call. I just wanted to check you were okay. Right, I suppose you two would like a bit of privacy then. Let me know how the trip up north goes, yeah?'

'Will do.'

'I'll be in the car, Lilah.'

Once Paolo had left, Joe mused, 'Privacy? You mean he knows about us?'

'He's not deaf, dumb and blind, Joe. Mum knows too.'

'Everything?' he exclaimed.

She put her arms around his neck. 'Well, not *everything*, otherwise I wouldn't have gone back to my own bed, would I? But they're aware that we're... close.'

'And they're alright with it?'

'Of course. Why wouldn't they be? Mum said she always knew we'd end up together and Paolo couldn't believe it took us so long.'

'Bloody hell,' he exclaimed, thinking of how often he'd fretted over what their reaction might be.

'If you like, I'll come into town with you tomorrow.'

'I'd like that very much. I'm a bit worried I'll bump into someone who witnessed what happened at my party.'

Her brow furrowed. 'You have to stop thinking like that. You've done nothing wrong.' Changing the subject, she said, 'So, ask me what *I* did this afternoon.'

'Lilah, what did you do this afternoon?'

'I'm glad you asked. I went to the family planning clinic and I am now on the pill.'

It was further proof, if any were needed, of how much more mature she was than him. Not once in his sexual history had he given much thought to contraception, assuming that if a girl was willing then she must have some sort of birth control in place. The onus was always on *them*. It was irresponsible, presumptive, and typical of young men of his era.

Joe clung to her. He was still struggling to come to terms with his earth-shattering news, leaving him feeling like his boat had capsized; but Lilah was his branch in the water, stopping him going under.

174

CHAPTER TWENTY SIX

PICK UP THE PIECES

Tuesday morning, Joe and Lilah met outside Watford Central Library, opposite The Horns pub. He'd caught the bus in from Garston but, living a lot closer to the town centre, she'd walked. After a short hug and a quick morning kiss, they set off up Watford High St, first stop Lloyds bank. She linked her arm with his, which always made him feel good. He'd slept a little better too. Not soundly but he'd had no nightmares, so that was something. Whilst not yet back on his feet, at least he was up off his knees. And he had a semblance of a plan.

After Mary had made him aware of the trust fund, she told him to open a bank account as the final sum would be transferred straight from the solicitors on its maturity date. He'd chosen Lloyds for two reasons. Firstly, they had a small branch on Garston Park Parade, near his house, and secondly, he liked their emblem, a black horse rearing up. His initial (and so far only) deposit was ten pounds, five of which was a twentieth birthday present.

At the counter, the bank clerk utilised her well-rehearsed smile and asked how she could help. In turn, Joe told her that he was expecting a payment into his current account and was there to see if it had been made. He gave his account details and she left the counter to check. When she returned, she was accompanied by a tall, bespectacled man wearing an ill-fitting suit and a huge grin. That's when Joe knew the money was in. Lilah squeezed his hand.

'Mr Holland,' gushed the suit. 'I'm Martin Ashton, deputy manager. Miss Layton here tells me you wish to know if a transaction has taken place?'

'Miss Layton is correct,' confirmed Joe.

'Excellent. Well, I'm pleased to inform you that we received a transfer from Markham, Sandford & Welby yesterday morning for the sum of ten thousand, one hundred and twenty pounds and err... fifteen pence. With what you already had in your account; that's a total of...'

'Ten thousand, one hundred and thirty pounds and fifteen pence,' announced the stunned customer.

'Indeed,' confirmed the eager Mr Ashton. 'And may I take this opportunity to thank you for choosing Lloyds to look after your money. You obviously compared us with the other High Street banks and we came out favourably.'

'No. I just liked the black horse,' confessed Joe, invoking sycophantic laughter from the deputy manager and his subordinate. 'Now,' he continued 'I'd like to make a withdrawal. Fifty pounds should suffice.'

Ashton's affable smile turned to an apologetic grimace. 'Sorry Mr Holland, I'm afraid that's not possible.'

'Why not? You've just told me I've got over ten thousand pounds.'

'Yes, but it has to be in your account for five working days before you can access it.'

'But it's there, you just told me.'

'I do apologise but rules are rules.'

'Well, how much can I have then?

'Now, let me see. Ah yes… ten.'

'A tenner? Is that it?

'Yes. That being the amount that's cleared.'

'Right,' sighed Joe, 'I'll take it please.'

'Certainly. Miss Layton, give Mr Holland ten pounds from the drawer, would you? Mr Holland, I'd be happy to discuss high interest savings accounts with you.'

'Tempting, but not today, thank you. I'll make an appointment at a later date.'

'Oh, please do. And I wish both you and your lady friend a good day.'

And with that, Martin Ashton went back into his office, disappointingly not walking backwards with his head bowed. Once outside, Joe and Lilah looked at each other in disbelief and burst out laughing. The first real laugh Joe had enjoyed for three dark days. It was bizarre to think of himself with such an amount of cash. Crazy. Last week, Martin Ashton wouldn't have given him the time of day, now there he was treating him like the king of Siam. As the pubs weren't open yet, he suggested, 'Shall we celebrate with a soft drink?'

'Sounds good to me.'

'Just one thing, Lilah' said a slightly embarrassed Joe, 'Could you pay? I don't know how much the train ticket will be.'

Shaking her head in disbelief, she chided, 'You were more generous when you were poor.'

As they sat on the bench overlooking the pond, drinking their cans of Fanta, Lilah nodded toward the old Top Rank building, now in its new incarnation: **Bailey's Cabaret/Disco.**

'Remember when you and Paolo took me to my first Saturday morning disco there?'

'Yeah, you begged us for months, then when we finally took you, you left early cos you were bored.'

'Confession. I wasn't bored, I left because you danced with another girl and I couldn't stand it.'

'Really?' he chuckled.

Playfully, she cuffed him. 'Don't laugh, it was agony watching you holding her, swaying to the music. The Jackson Five – "I'll Be There". Chartbusters Volume Five. Side two. Track… eight?'

'One point. It was track seven. Anyway, you got your own back with Russell wanky name.'

'Who?'

'The school heart throb who took you to see *Love Story*.'

'Russell wanky name,' she giggled. 'God, he loved himself. He couldn't walk past a shop window without checking his reflection.'

Joe's thoughts were a million miles away from vain schoolboys. 'I hope you understand why I need to find this Northbridge bloke. It might seem odd to some people, but if I don't do it, it will haunt me for the rest of my days.'

'I get it. The decision is yours and yours only.'

'Thanks for supporting me. Mum is dead set against it.'

'I support you because I love you, Joe. And I can see that it's important to you, only…'

'Only what?'

'Don't let it take over, okay?

'What does that mean?'

'No pressure, but if we have a future together, you have to be as committed as I am. No half measures.

Or let's just stop before we start. If you're not all in, then I may as well make a life for myself in Italy. I appreciate you can't think of much else except finding your biological father right now, but I promised to tell Aunt Rosa by June 21st if I'm returning or not. So, you need to let me know before then if you and me are "us".'

Nobody could accuse Lilah of beating about the bush. It was one of the many things that he admired about her. He had around a month to achieve his quest. That should be more than enough time.

'I agree about no half measures. You deserve all of my attention, mind, body and soul. And once I've done what I have to, you'll get it.'

Their kiss was rudely interrupted by the first spots of rain from an increasingly moody sky.

'Come on,' said Lilah, pulling him up by the hand. 'Let's go and get your rail ticket, then I'll give you that free haircut you asked for. Are all rich people tight?'

The expected rain didn't materialise so they took a slow walk down Clarendon Road to Watford Junction. The man in the ticket office told Joe his best option was a cheap day return, then clobbered him for almost eight pounds.

Should be called a bloody expensive day return!

It would have been even dearer if he wasn't coming back on the same day. Oh well, he was good to go. Wednesday, 8.15am, Watford Junction to Liverpool (Lime Street). With Paolo and Ellen both at work, the young couple had the Massetti house to themselves. Joe got his neat trim, but it was quickly messed up when the pair made love again, this time in Lilah's bed. It was broad daylight and felt deliciously naughty.

CHAPTER TWENTY SEVEN

READY OR NOT HERE
I COME

On the train journey, to kill some time, Joe played games with his fellow passengers. Not that they were aware. He invented lives for them, solely by their looks and the auras they gave off. The superior looking gentleman with the pencil moustache sitting across the aisle was definitely ex-military. Army. An officer, but not too high in rank; a captain, or major at best. Caressing his neck was a white silk cravat, tucked into his blue blazer. His trousers were grey flannel with turnups and sharp creases, his brown brogues polished to a high sheen. He was reading the Financial Times and Joe could tell by his demeanour that he considered himself a cut above his fellow travellers. He should really be in First Class but was too mean to pay the extra.

He was undoubtedly a member of his local golf or country club. Perhaps both. Intimate relations with the wife, once a month on a Saturday night: same time, same position. Her pretending he was the builder with the cheeky smile who laid their patio, him pretending she was the girl from accounts with the 36 DD's.

Directly opposite Joe was a lady with a pleasant face. Early fifties. Dowdy cardigan, tweed skirt and sensible shoes. Strands of grey permeated her chestnut brown hair, cut into a practical, short bob. She wore no rings on her left hand, but she'd have had plenty of admirers when she was younger. In fact, Joe imagined her to be quite a beauty before she gave up on herself. She just never met the right person. No, there *was* someone, but he turned out to be the wrong person and ended up breaking her heart. She accepted he was a wastrel, not worthy of her love, so why did she keep all his love letters, neatly tied with red ribbon, in the bottom drawer of her dressing table? Now, she found herself stuck at home looking after her ailing, widowed mother and projecting herself into Mills & Boon novels, like the one currently resting on her lap. There was an unmistakable longing in her eyes and Joe couldn't look at her for long because it made him sad.

He continued the game with a few other passengers before going back to the crossword he'd started in the puzzle book he'd bought at Watford Junction. In just under three hours, he'd be in Liverpool. In a strange way, he was looking forward to being in a busy city where he wouldn't know anybody and, more importantly, nobody would know him.

He imagined that, if any of the people in his carriage were playing the same game as him, it was a fair bet that they never had him pegged as 'illegitimate offspring of a convicted rapist'. *Major Haughty* harrumphed and turned the page of his newspaper as *Miss Lovelorn* gazed wistfully out of the window, as the landscape, like her life, sped by.

Just like her brother, Lilah had offered to accompany Joe, but he politely declined. It wasn't a pleasure trip and she would have proved a distraction, albeit a very pleasant one. Joe had business with James Northbridge. He hadn't worked out exactly what he was going to say, but it was important the man was made aware of the damage he'd caused. Without his depraved behaviour, Mary wouldn't have moved south, which means she'd never have met Nigel Holland and become trapped in a loveless marriage. Northbridge had a lot to answer for. Effectively, he'd ruined her life. As well as sending a wrecking ball through Joe's.

Perhaps he would be remorseful, ashamed of what he'd done. Or maybe, if he's still the liar and manipulator Mary said he used to be, he'd concoct his own version of events. That possibility made the anger rise in Joe, but he knew he had to suppress it – for now. To have any chance of engineering a meeting he'd have to appear calm, presuming he could locate him.

At 7am, as he prepared to leave the house, his mum had handed him a pack of sandwiches, tightly wrapped in tinfoil. 'I still say no good will come of it, but these are for the journey.'

As the train approached Birmingham, Joe felt peckish so peeled back the foil and was surprised to see a small envelope. The note inside read:

Dear Joseph, you know my opinion on what you are doing, but I accept that nothing I do or say can stop you. I'm so sorry that what happened so long ago has resurfaced and knocked your life off track. Just remember, if you do find him, take whatever he says with a pinch of salt. I'll save you a dinner. See you tonight.

Love,

Mum xxx

Joe was pleased. By no means had she given him her blessing, but it seemed she was starting to understand. As he folded and returned the note to its housing, he was equally pleased to find she'd tucked a five-pound note into the corner. It was a welcome boost to his meagre funds and made him even more determined to lavish some of his trust money on her, once it had cleared.

Out of the corner of his eye, Joe noticed 'the Major' shoot a condescending glance at his packed lunch, so with a flamboyant gesture he held the sandwiches out toward him and said, 'Ham and pickle. Would you like one?'

Without making eye contact the older man muttered, 'No, thank you,' and buried his head behind his FT. Miss Lovelorn had the trace of a smile on her lips and Joe imagined she'd relate the story to her mother when she got home. He ate his sandwiches and then must have dozed off. When he awoke, they were pulling into Crewe and the sad-eyed lady opposite was gone. He hoped her real life wasn't as bleak as the one he'd invented for her.

Lime Street station was the Merseyside equivalent of Euston, or any of the other huge termini that serve large cities. A hurly-burly of noise and movement, as people of all shapes and sizes jostle along crowded platforms, some struggling with suitcases, others struggling with life. Businessmen with purposeful walks rubbed shoulders with harassed young mothers, herding sticky fingered, bemused children.

A disembodied voice boomed departure and arrival information from strategically placed tannoys. At the barrier, a weathered British Rail hand tore Joe's ticket and handed him back the return stub before allowing him out onto the concourse. Now to put phase two of his plan into action.

His eyes scanned the huge, hangar-shaped building until he spotted what he was looking for: a row of telephone kiosks. The end one was free so Joe jumped in before anyone else could and closed the folding door. Opening the thick, fixed directory he flicked through the pages until he came to the letter N. He ran his finger down the page. *North* – he was glad he wasn't out to trace one of *them*, there were loads. *Northacre* – four of those. *Northbridge* – just the one. What a result! The initial next to it wasn't a *J* though, it was a *K*. Must be a relation, surely?

Northbridge K. 7 Abercynon St, Toxteth L8.

Furtively, Joe tore out the relevant page and slipped it into his jacket pocket. Thanks to his mum's generosity, he wouldn't have to mess about with buses and instead slid into the backseat of a taxi outside the station, finding himself directly behind a fat red neck with a checked flat cap about eight inches above it. A pair of inquisitive, bespectacled eyes studied him from the rearview mirror. 'Where to, mate?' Joe read the address from the torn-out page.

'No problem lad. First time in the 'Pool, is it?' probed the driver, flicking the meter on.

Without thinking Joe said, 'Yes,' inwardly cursing his naivety, because now he'd just blown his chances of being taken by the shortest route.

'Don't get many first-time visitors going to L8. Normally businesspeople going to conventions or Yanks wanting to see Penny Lane and Strawberry Field. Most don't even know the Welsh Streets exist.'

'Welsh Streets?'

'That's where you're going. The whole area was designed by a Welshman named Richard Owens in the late nineteenth century. All the houses were built for Taffy migrants who moved their families here looking for jobs. Most ended up working on the docks, and all the streets are named after Welsh villages and towns.'

Joe knew a few families of Welsh descent in Watford whose ancestors had relocated there looking for work around that same time period. It seemed that while the Irish and Scots emigrated to every corner of the globe, their Celtic cousins from the valleys preferred to stay closer to home.

'Hope you don't mind me gabbing on. I'm a proud Scouser, you see. Good ear for accents too. What part of London are you from?'

'Not quite a Londoner. I live in a small town just north of it called Watford.'

'I've heard of it. Footie team in the third division?'

'Not anymore. They've just been relegated to division four.'

As the journey progressed to the south of the city, Joe could see more and more signs of urban decay, indicating they were heading into the poorer areas. The back-to-back, tired-looking terraced dwellings looked nothing like the house Mary described growing up in.

'My mum's a Scouser, born and bred in Woolton,' he divulged.

'Oh aye, a step up from Toxteth. Got relations here, have you?'

'Possibly,' was the cryptic answer. He tried a long shot. 'Does the name Northbridge mean anything to you?'

'Don't know of any North bridge. We've got the Silver Jubilee bridge between Runcorn and Widnes.'

Oh well, it was worth a punt. He asked the driver to drop him off at the corner of Abercynon St. His first impression was how much it reminded him of television's Coronation St, with all the bay windows and front doors leading straight onto the pavement. The first house was converted into a newsagent/tobacconist/convenience store. The little kids playing in the street barely gave him a second glance, once they were satisfied he wasn't a truant officer, unlike every adult he passed who, without exception, viewed him with suspicion, intuitively aware that he wasn't 'one of theirs'.

Joe stopped outside number seven, took a deep breath and brought the door knocker down twice. He was starting to think no-one was home when the door half opened and a ruddy face with a woodbine sticking out of it appeared. 'Yeah?'

The caller's attempt at a friendly smile was nullified by the stoney glare. 'Mr Northbridge?'

'Who wants to know?'

'My name is Joe Holland.'

'That's nice for you. What do you want.?'

'I'm trying to trace James Northbridge.'

Indifference turned to hostility. 'Well, if you're a reporter, you can fuck off.'

'I'm not a reporter,' assured Joe 'I'm err…'

'You're err?' mocked the other man. There was no diplomatic way to say it, so Joe bit the bullet. 'I'm his son.'

His statement was met by a look of confusion. 'Bollocks. He hasn't got a son.' Very slowly, the penny started to drop. 'How old are you?'

'Twenty-one last Saturday.'

After doing the maths, realisation registered on the man's face as to who this stranger was. Joe spoke next. 'I just want to meet him. Talk to him.'

The reward for his honesty was an expression of disdain. 'Why? If he did what your mum and grandfather claimed he did, why would you want to see him?'

'I only found out on my birthday. I feel like half of me is missing.'

'Well, he doesn't live on Merseyside anymore, so you've wasted your time,' came the curt reply.

'I'm willing to travel anywhere in the country to meet up with him,' declared Joe.

'Are you now? Even if that country is America?'

He seemed to revel in the young man's surprise and disappointment, his face contorted with resentment. 'After his release he wanted a new start. Said he was finished with Britain. And since I'll never be able to afford to go over there, I won't ever see my brother again. And it's all thanks to *your* family.'

Remembering his inheritance, Joe regained his composure and resolve. 'I'll even go to America if I have to.'

The Scouser studied him closely, his eyes narrowing. 'Why are you so keen? He's not rich, if it's money you're after.'

'It's not like that. I just want to hear his side of the story,' appeased Joe. 'Please, just ask him if he'd be willing to see me. All I want from him is a couple of hours of his time.'

He detected a slight softening of the other man's stance. 'Personally, I don't see any use in it, but I guess the decision should be his. I'll ask him. Give me your phone number. If he's agreeable, I'll call you Sunday morning. If you haven't heard from me by noon he's decided against. If that's the case, then that's the end of it. You don't contact me or show up here again. Clear?'

Joe agreed and wrote his number on the empty cigarette packet he'd been handed. His 'thankyou' went unacknowledged and the front door was unceremoniously closed in his face. There was no way of telling if James Northbridge's brother would even deliver his message, but there was a chance, so maybe his trip north hadn't been entirely fruitless. On Sunday morning he would find out, one way or the other.

The journey home was uneventful, and he was back in his house by 7pm. Over dinner, Joe recounted his doorstep conversation, concluding by revealing that James Northbridge was now living somewhere in the USA. He didn't spoil his mum's obvious relief by stating his intention of flying out there, should the opportunity materialise. There was nothing to be gained by stirring up *that* hornets' nest unless it was definitely on. And in all probability, it wouldn't be.

Later, when David was upstairs doing homework, Joe discovered he wasn't the only one who'd had an eventful day. Mary disclosed that Nigel had picked David up from school and driven him home. It killed two birds with one stone, as it gave him a chance to speak to his son in person and also take his remaining belongings, neatly bagged by prearrangement and waiting for collection on the front path. Mary had watched through the net curtain as David helped his dad load them into his car. An agreement was made that Nigel would see the boy every other weekend, until he found a place of his own. Then it would be David's choice which parent he lived with full time. His younger brother was slap bang in the middle of this almighty mess, and Joe felt sorry for him. The other news was that the DJ had dropped the birthday cards and presents off.

'Oh, and Lenny Coleman phoned saying to ring him, if you want to talk.'

Dear Lenny. For five years he'd been more of a father figure than Nigel Holland ever was. Joe felt too embarrassed to speak to him in person, but he resolved to drop him a line. Which he did, while it was fresh in his mind, thanking him for being a good teacher and a good friend and explaining why he couldn't carry on working at Edwards & Sons. A more formal letter followed, to the company itself, handing in his resignation, citing 'personal reasons'.

What those personal reasons were would have been common knowledge by first break on Monday morning. Next, he phoned Lilah and arranged to call for her the following day at 10am. To end the current day, he lay on his bed wondering if he would get the green light or the red one on Sunday and, if it was the former, how he would break it to his mum. No doubt Lilah wouldn't be too thrilled either. He wasn't in the mood to open his cards or presents so they remained untouched in the corner. In the background, James Brown's horn section were getting a sweat on and he turned the volume up. He would never know how relieved Mary was to once again hear vibrant music coming from his room.

CHAPTER TWENTY EIGHT

STAND BY ME

It was a warm late spring morning so Joe asked Lilah if she fancied a stroll into town. A visit to Cassiobury Park maybe? She readily agreed. As her arm found his, she said excitedly, 'Right, you said on the phone you'd tell me how it went yesterday. So, tell me.'

'I didn't find James Northbridge.'

'Oh, I'm sorry. Bit of a waste of time then?'

'Not completely. I spoke to his brother. He didn't tell me his name, but mum said it's Kevin. No, Kelvin, that's it. Let's say that he didn't exactly roll out the red carpet when he found out who I was, but he took great delight in telling me that James moved abroad when he left prison. America.'

'So, you hit the buffers then?'

'Looks like it.'

'Oh well, you tried. Now you've got to put it behind you.'

Just like with his mum, he didn't see the point of revealing it might not quite be the end of the road and get into a possible altercation over something that might never happen. So, he changed the subject by asking Lilah what she did yesterday. She told him that she cleaned the house from top to bottom in the morning and, after lunch, popped into the salon where she used to be a Saturday girl to see her old work colleagues.

They arrived at the huge park, the jewel in Watford's crown for generations of local children. A one hundred and ninety acre adventure playground. Great expanses of mown grass and towering trees interspersed with asphalt walkways. Both the river Gade and the Grand Union Canal cut through it. There is a miniature railway for the kids to ride on and a manmade paddling pool for them to splash around in on warm days, such as this one. One of Joe's earliest memories, from when he was no more than three, was entering the park through the castellated main entrance, built of orange bricks with tall, wrought iron gates. Originally, in the early 1800's it was the gatehouse entrance leading up to the long-gone Cassiobury House, ancestral home to the Earl of Essex but to countless toddlers it was a castle wall. The council had it demolished in 1970 in a road widening scheme. Proof that some vandals wear suits and ties and destroy things with pens.

Joe bought two lollies and they sat under the shade of an ancient oak tree to eat them. The infectious shrieks and laughter of the tiny children in the paddling pool caused them both to smile. It was impossible not to. Some had bathing costumes on, some vests and pants, and one or two were completely in the buff, but all were having a great time. Not a care in the world. Nothing was said but Joe and Lilah were both thinking the same thing; perhaps one day they'd be watching their own kids laughing and playing. They lay next to each other on a grass verge, held hands and let the sun warm their upturned faces. After an hour they made the decision to go and get some lunch in town.

As they ambled along in their lovers' bubble Joe was perturbed when Lilah returned to the topic he'd previously steered her away from.

'I think you should take a couple of weeks off, gather your thoughts then see what jobs are going. As you say, qualified electricians are always in demand. As are good hairdressers. I don't need to wait until June 21st, I'm phoning Aunt Rosa tonight to tell her I'm staying here.'

His reaction was the polar opposite to the one she'd expected. 'No.'

She stopped walking and faced him. 'What?'

'Stick to the original plan, eh?'

'Why? You've already said your biological dad lives in America now.'

He took both her hands in his. 'He does but there's a possibility he'll meet up with me. Nothing definite.'

'He's coming back to England?'

Steeling himself he revealed, 'No. I'd be flying out there.'

It was time to come clean, so he told her about Sunday's impending phone call. Her mouth pursed as she replied, 'Bloody hell, Joe, this is becoming an obsession.'

'You said you supported me in trying to locate him.'

'I didn't know you'd be chasing him halfway around the world!'

'What am I supposed to do? Forget about him? Just close the book on it?'

'Why not? The past is dead, it's the future that matters.'

'If you don't understand why I have to see this through, then you don't really know me.'

Pulling her hands from his, she unexpectedly agreed. 'Maybe you're right. I thought I did, but I'm starting to wonder. What if you get to America and he's buggered off to, I don't know – Australia? Is that your next stop? Where does it end, Joe?'

'It ends when I'm sitting across from him in a room, making him face the consequences of his actions.'

'Your trust fund money can give you the start most young people can only dream of. Don't waste it.'

'It's *my* money, Lilah. I've earmarked a thousand for the trip. That still leaves me with over nine thousand pounds.'

She'd heard enough. 'You do what you want. As you said, it's your money. If you think the answers you want are in America, then go find them. But get this business sorted by June 21st or I'm back off to Sorrento. I've grown up, Joe. I'm not the besotted little girl anymore. I do love you and I do want to be with you, but I won't play second fiddle to a shadow.'

'Okay,' he soothed, 'my gut tells me he won't want to meet me anyway, so we're arguing for nothing.'

'No Joe, we're arguing for *everything*.'

Lilah left him standing there and walked off toward the park exit. Suddenly, the prospect of them one day watching their own children laughing and playing seemed like a million to one shot. He hurried and caught her up. 'Let's not fight, Lilah. It took us so long to get to this point.'

'Don't take me for granted then.'

'I don't. Believe me.'

He slipped his arm around her waist and kissed her hair, but he could feel she was tense. Deep inside, he accepted that she was right. Finding his biological father *had* become an obsession. The most sensible course of action would be to end his pursuit of a man he'd never even heard of seven days ago and commit there and then to the girl he'd loved for years. He wanted to. Truly he did. But the need to find the man who made him burned fiercely. And a need always trumps a want.

Lilah chose not to see him for the next few days, opting to catch up with old friends she hadn't seen since her return to England. Joe knew she was punishing him but didn't make an issue of it. He was aware he was walking a tightrope; he was recklessly risking losing her to Italy, not just for two years but forever. They agreed he should phone her on Sunday after midday, when he knew what his next step was. Part of him hoped James Northbridge wanted nothing to do with him. That would take the decision out of his hands.

Excluding a bout of flu two years earlier, it was the first whole weekend Joe had stayed in since he started work. Paolo tried to tempt him out for a beer, and it was hard not to succumb, but he wasn't ready to socialise after the debacle of the previous Saturday. Only Lilah stood a chance of changing his mind, and she was giving him the cold(ish) shoulder. So, on Friday night he stayed home playing his music, alone, with his mind working overtime. He wondered what Lilah was doing. Was she out on the town with friends? Were any of them male? She was bound to get chatted up.

Enough. Just pack it in. It's you she loves.

Right, let's take it somewhere else. How did James Northbridge gain access to live and work in the U.S. with a criminal record? Maybe he was there illegally, flying under the radar and earning a living through the black economy. Or perhaps he had a contact in the immigration department. There are always ways to beat the system, if you know the right people and grease the right palms. Prison would have been the perfect environment to make useful connections; a fake passport wouldn't be a difficult job for a skilled forger.

On Saturday, more out of boredom than excitement, he opened his birthday cards and presents. There were a lot more in the bag than he realised. The cards were opened first. More than a few people had written slight variations of the same sentiment. '*Hope your 21st is a birthday to remember.*' Well, that would certainly be a safe bet. It was unlikely anyone there would ever forget it.

Next came the presents. He unwrapped a couple of dozen gift cards for clothes shops and numerous record vouchers, for W.H. Smith mostly. They had a large record department but didn't diverge much from mainstream chart stuff. He'd never find any hidden gems there but never mind; it's the thought that counts. He recognised Paolo's handwriting on the gift tag of what felt like another voucher but was in fact two tickets to see The Detroit Emeralds in seven days' time – May 31st at the California Ballroom, Dunstable. Joe almost phoned to thank his friend but quickly realised it was 8.15pm on a Saturday, so he'd be out. Everyone under thirty in the entire world was out. Except him.

The next gift he opened contained a Swiss-made wristwatch with *Happy 21st, Love Mum* engraved on the back. It had a black leather strap and came in a smart presentation box. Joe loved it. His hackles raised slightly when he read the accompanying card which said, '*From Mum, Nigel and David xx*,' but as it was written before the drama ensued, he understood. The boys from his football team had (hopefully) jokingly bought him a Buck Ram Stimulus Kit – *'for the gentleman who needs a little help to please his lady.'*

Cheeky sods. It was typical dressing room humour, and it made him grin. He saved Lilah's present until last. He'd remembered the fancy green wrapping paper from when she handed it to him outside the leisure centre. As he unveiled it, he thought the small rectangular box looked like it might contain aftershave. He was right, but it wasn't one he'd heard of. The writing introduced it as Acqua di Genova. She'd bought him a 100ml bottle of Italian eau de toilette. Inside was an elegantly shaped glass bottle with a spray top, like women have on their perfumes. He sprayed one squirt on the back of his hand and inhaled. It was pleasant; a clean, fresh scent consisting of Amalfi lemon, orange, lavender and sandalwood. A stark contrast to the unsubtle Brut he was used to splashing on.

If Joe had kept a diary, the entry for Saturday May 24th, 1975 would have read:

'Stayed in for seventh night running. Bored shitless. Finally opened cards and presents. Nice watch from mum and genuine Italian aftershave from Lilah. Watched a bit of Saturday night telly for the first time in years. Nothing's changed. Still game shows where people are happy to be patronised in exchange for a fondue set. Couldn't take more than ten minutes of it so went and sorted my albums into alphabetical order. Told you I was bored shitless. Trying not to think about tomorrow but can't help it. Got into bed at eleven and

read the latest Blues & Soul *for the third time. Did I mention I was bored shitless?'*

His last conscious thought before sleep arrived was to wonder if Kelvin Northbridge had even informed his brother of Joe's visit. He was certainly a bitter individual and more than capable of stringing him along as a cruel joke.

Sunday morning saw Joe up and dressed just after dawn. He planned to be no further than ten feet away from the telephone until noon. The hours dragged slowly by, made bearable by endless cups of tea. He had all but given up when, at one minute to twelve, the trimphone started to purr. He grabbed up the receiver immediately, 'Hello.'

'Is that Joe?' asked a brusque Scouse voice.

'Speaking.'

'Right. I spoke to me brother and he says, if you go over there, he'll meet up with you.'

'Great.'

'Shut up and listen. He said to choose somewhere public in Manhattan, anytime on a weekend or after six in the evening, Monday to Friday. Write to him with the time and place and he'll be there.'

'Okay. I've got a pen. What's his address?'

'You don't get his address. You send your letter to a P.O Box and he'll pick it up from there. And he won't be replying.'

'How do I know he'll turn up then?' queried Joe.

'Cos he said he will. Are you ready? J. Northbridge, P.O Box 4722, New York City, New York State 11217.'

'Got it. Thank you.'

'Don't thank me lad. I think it's a fucking terrible idea. Oh, he's not listed and there's nearly eight million people living in that city, so don't waste your time trying to find out his home address. Bye.'

The whole call lasted around thirty seconds. Kelvin Northbridge wasn't a man to waste words. Joe replaced the handset and stared at the address on the pad in front of him. It took a few seconds to sink in. 'Jesus, it's on,' he muttered to himself. 'I'm going to New York City.'

For some reason his first thought was of a record store in Harlem called "Grooves" that he'd read about in Blues & Soul. How cool would it be to present Paolo and Lilah with a bunch of albums not available in the U.K.

It was with some trepidation that he dialled The Massettis number at 12.30pm to break the news. Paolo answered. 'Hello mate,' said Joe. 'Thanks for the Detroit Emeralds tickets. Why did you put yours in the card, though?'

'It's not for me, you dope; it's for my sister. Sort yourselves out. She's been moping around for days, and I don't even have to ask if you have.'

'It's her I wanted to speak to really. Is she around?'

'Hold on.' He heard the sound of the receiver being placed on the small unit their phone sat on and then Paolo walking away. A muffled, 'Lilah, Joe's on the phone,' was followed by distant footsteps hurrying down the stairs.

'Hi Joe, did he call?' Straight to the point. No messing.

'Yes, he did. Kept me waiting until the last minute.'

'And?'

'James Northbridge is living in New York. He's agreed to meet me if I go over there.'

An ominous silence followed until she broke it with, 'Right. Well, I've been doing a lot of thinking since I last saw you...'

Oh no. His heart almost stopped. She was going to finish with him. He'd blown it.

'...and I've come to the conclusion...'

He closed his eyes and waited for the axe to fall.

'...that this must be really, really important to you and it would be unfair of me to ask you not to do it. I think you need to bring this to an end before you and I get serious.'

Joe asked himself how was it possible for anyone of eighteen to be so wise? It was scary. Surely, she must have lived before. With a mixture of relief, admiration and respect he told her, 'God, I love you. Can I come over? I need to kiss you.'

'Sure. Just give me half an hour to get rid of Russell wanky name,' she giggled. What a lovely sound. What a lovely girl.

CHAPTER TWENTY NINE

GET READY

'Ladies and Gentlemen, please give a warm California Ballroom welcome to The Detroit Emeralds.'

Joe and Lilah clapped and cheered as loudly as everyone else, grateful to anyone willing to bring to these shores in person the music they loved. The three smiling black singers in front of them were still riding the wave of their 1973 top ten hit. "Feel the Need in Me." And why not? The young couple went on to enjoy a memorable evening, and an even more memorable night, staying at an olde worlde hotel that had once been a coach house. It was their first full night together and they made the most of it.

The previous Monday, Joe had booked his return flight to New York, a five-day trip, flying out on Sunday, June 15th and home on Thursday the 19th. If he thought the £8 train fare to Lime Street was steep, the £475 he paid to fly the Atlantic and back almost caused him to faint. For somebody not used to having money, it seemed astronomical. Luckily, he already had a passport, purchased the previous year for a lads' holiday which never materialised, due to his lack of cash. There was no lack of cash now, though. And that would take some getting used to.

That same evening, he wrote to James Northbridge via his P.O Box that he'd be at Big Dino's Diner on Wednesday, June 18th at 7pm. The meeting place had been chosen from the *Guide to New York* that he'd purchased from W.H. Smith, selected for no other reason than he thought the name sounded cool. He imagined Big Dino to be a large, blue-chinned, wisecracking Italian/American, tossing hamburgers onto the grill whilst telling anyone willing to listen why he fancied the Yankees to win the World Series.

Feeling guilty at spending what he saw as an obscene amount with British Airways, Joe decided to find his own accommodation when he arrived in the Big Apple (he'd seen it called that in the guidebook). Nothing fancy. He didn't need The Waldorf or the Plaza, just somewhere to lay his head. The plan was to do a little sightseeing on Monday and Tuesday-Liberty, Empire State Building, Times Square etc. On Wednesday check out the soul L.P's in the music store in Harlem, then meet with Northbridge in the evening. A little more sightseeing on Thursday, then get the overnight flight back to Heathrow on Thursday. For some reason, Lilah was still insisting that he confirm the episode was done and dusted on his return then she could phone her aunt, as planned, on the 21st stating her future was in England. Joe saw no reason why she couldn't make the call before he left, but she was adamant that he couldn't know how his trip would affect him until he'd experienced it, so she would hang fire. Once again, he marvelled at her maturity.

It was a huge relief to have Lilah comprehend what he was doing and why, especially as his mum had taken his decision so badly. When he broke it to her as he helped her lay the cutlery for dinner, all the colour drained from her face and she had to hold onto the table to steady herself. She'd thought his unfruitful visit to

Liverpool was the end of the matter, so this latest development hit her hard. When she eventually spoke, it was in little more than a whisper, 'Is this to get back at me for not telling you myself?'

'Get back at you? For what? Mum, this isn't about you, it's about me. I just want to see him, one time. It won't develop into a relationship if that's what's worrying you.'

She shook her head. 'He's clever. He'll twist everything.'

'I'm ready for him. I won't allow that to happen.'

'No, you'll underestimate him. He'll get inside your mind. Joseph, please don't go.'

'Stop it, Mum. The flights are booked and I'm going.'

'I know it's not been easy for you, but I've always tried to be a good mother.'

'You have been. You still are. But I've got to face this chapter of my life head on before I close it and go onto the next one.'

'No good will come of this. Mark my words.'

Joe hated seeing his mum so distressed and a part of him wanted to do as she urged and call the whole thing off. But even her obvious despair wasn't enough to make him change his mind. Mary was an intelligent woman, so why couldn't she work it out, as Lilah had done, that if he didn't scratch this itch now it would never go away? If he turned down this opportunity to challenge the man who had inflicted such misery upon his family, it would torment him for the rest of his days.

Though he wouldn't be swayed, her reaction did concern him. Her disapproval had been anticipated but the magnitude of it had surprised him. It seemed to go beyond apprehension and border on fear. But then, she had slowly come around to the idea of him travelling to Liverpool, so he figured she'd eventually come around to this. After all, it was the same scenario, but on a larger scale. But he soon learned that he'd miscalculated. Whilst she didn't quite give him the silent treatment, it was unquestionably the quiet treatment. For almost a fortnight, it went on until, on the eve of his departure, the dam broke. Joe was packing when she entered his room and sobbed openly in front of him. Huge, gasping for air sobs accompanied by floods of tears. It was pitiful to witness her literally beg him not to get on that plane and repeat what had become a mantra. 'No good can come of this.'

Any son would have had to be made of stone not to waiver, but he knew there was no turning back now. He held her in the same comforting way that she'd held him when he was upset as a child and assured, 'Mum, it's just five days. Then I'll never mention his name again. I promise.'

CHAPTER THIRTY

KEEP ON PUSHING

Just after 11am a car horn sounded outside Joe's house. 'That's my lift, Mum. I'll call to let you know I arrived safely. See you soon.'

This trip there was no packed lunch with a note from her or even any parting words, just a sullen, deflated look. Joe gave her an unrequited hug, picked up his holdall and left. Parked up, engine running, was Paolo's latest project: a Mk 2 Cortina that he'd equipped with a Lotus engine. Lilah was in the backseat and Joe joined her, his hand immediately finding hers. The conversation was light, but his heart was heavy. His mother's aloofness since he told her his intentions nearly a fortnight ago hadn't worn off one iota, and it disturbed him. The sooner all this was over and they could revert to some sort of normality the better.

At Heathrow, excitement took over. He'd never flown before and a transatlantic crossing was a hell of a way to start. In a Boeing 747, with the first and only stop being JFK airport, New York City. The Massetti siblings stayed with him until he checked in and then the three said their farewells. Joe shook Paolo's hand warmly and thanked him for the ride, then the latter walked discreetly away. After a kiss and a cuddle, Lilah whispered, 'Call me on Friday when you get back. And don't forget, whatever happens out there, I love you.'

'Love you too. I just want to see for myself that I'm nothing like him.'

After sharing one last kiss, he walked through to departures. At the barrier he glanced back. Lilah hadn't moved an inch. She slowly waved and smiled. A smile can convey many things. This one was definitely saying, 'Get this done and come back to me.'

Up close, the 747 was huge. No wonder it was referred to as a Jumbo jet. It wasn't just the size that was impressive, it was a beautiful machine. The bottom half was painted dark blue, the top half white, with two cavernous jet engines on each of its elegant silver wings. The tailfin proudly displayed the red & white BA logo and Joe instinctively knew he couldn't be in safer hands. In no time, along with around three hundred and fifty strangers, he was welcomed aboard by a smiling blue uniformed stewardess, strapped in and ready to go. Off to an unfamiliar land where he wouldn't know a single soul, not even the person he was going there to meet.

Joe found the sudden surge as the plane started its take off run and the steep climb towards the heavens exhilarating. Ten times more thrilling than any fairground ride he'd ever experienced. Having a window seat, he had the perfect view as everything earthbound become a miniature of itself. How did something that size even get off the ground? It was a modern miracle. And still the gigantic metal bird soared until it levelled out at 37,000 ft, way above the clouds, which looked like great swathes of white candyfloss. But after the initial thrill subsided, he found it wasn't much different to riding a bus. A very large, extremely fast, seven miles above ground level bus. He worked his lower jaw until his ears popped and he could hear properly again.

For the following eight hours, he read magazines, dozed a little, walked the aisle occasionally, chatted politely with nearby fellow passengers and partook in the hospitality of the attentive cabin crew. But mostly, he questioned himself. Was he doing the right thing? Why did he feel it necessary to meet James Northbridge? Would he regret it? All he could offer by way of explanation was that he felt compelled to do it, as if being drawn by some giant, invisible magnet.

At JFK airport a stocky individual wearing grey sweatpants and a tight t-shirt pressed a pamphlet into his hand. Joe noticed others doing the same, making sure every new arrival had one. He surmised it to be a list of popular attractions and entertainment in the city but was shocked by the front cover – an illustration of a hooded deaths head.

WELCOME TO FEAR CITY

A SURVIVOR'S GUIDE FOR VISITORS TO THE CITY OF NEW YORK

The newcomer found a vacant seat in Arrivals and flicked through the pages. The introduction alone made him feel like he was about to go swimming with alligators: *In the four-month period up to April 30th, 1975 robberies in New York went up by 21%. To solve the budget problem the mayor has cut the number of firefighters and law enforcement officers. This emboldens the criminals as they have less chance of being caught. The best advice is to avoid this city if you can.*

Christ almighty, if this was the work of the NYC tourist board, they were doing a really bad job.

The final sentence of the introduction revealed the organisations behind the publication: *However, if you do come to New York City, the following guidelines have been drawn up by firefighters and law officers to help you to stay safe during your stay.* What followed were nine 'do's and don'ts' you should adhere to if you wanted to make it through your stay. Namely:

1/ STAY OFF THE STREETS AFTER 6 PM.
2/ DO NOT WALK ANYWHERE.
3/ AVOID PUBLIC TRANSPORT.
4/ REMAIN IN MANHATTAN.
5/ PROTECT YOUR PROPERTY.
6/ SAFEGUARD YOUR HANDBAGS.
7/ KEEP PROPERTY CONCEALED IN AUTOMOBILES.
8/ DO NOT LEAVE VALUABLES IN YOUR HOTEL ROOM OR HOTEL SAFE.
9/ BE AWARE OF FIRE HAZARDS.

The shocked young Englishman decided to read the paragraphs under each heading in the safety of his hotel room. Had Joe caught the wrong flight and ended up in Beirut? No, there was the sign – John Fitzgerald Kennedy Airport. Tentatively, he ventured outside, clutching his holdall tight in case someone tried to snatch it. The taxi queue was long but there were plenty of yellow cabs and soon it was Joe's turn. From the front seat, the Hispanic driver asked in broken English, 'Where to please? Thankyou.'

Joe guessed he was Cuban, or possibly Puerto Rican. Rosary beads and a crucifix dangled from the rearview mirror and the small identity plate revealed the man behind the wheel to be Manito Perez.

'Manhattan,' replied Joe.

The shrug of the shoulders and outstretched hands indicated that the driver wanted something more specific.

'Hotel?' he said, with undisguised irritation.

'No Waldorf. No Plaza. No grand hotel. Something modesto. Cheapo,' explained the passenger, pointing his thumb downwards to try to get his message across. Amazingly, it seemed to work.

'Ah, barato? Economico?'

Joe had no idea what barato meant but economico was self-explanatory and he seized upon it.

'Sí. Trés economico.'

Trés? That's French, you prick.

Oh, shut up, I'm doing my best.

'Liberty Belle,' offered the cabbie 'mucho economico.'

'Sí,' repeated Joe, relaxing into his seat. 'Mucho thanks.'

Liberty Belle. That sounded just the job. With the language barrier, making conversation was impossible so the journey from Queens to Midtown Manhattan was made with a soundtrack of non-stop, high-volume Salsa. This suited both parties. Manito could enjoy his music and Joe could take in the sights made so familiar by films and imported cop shows like Kojak and McCloud. His first impression of NYC was its sheer scale. Everything was bigger than back home. The buildings, the roads, the cars and the trucks. The latter were highly polished impressive beasts with their vertical chrome exhaust pipes, airhorns mounted on the cab roofs and multiple wheels. It was clear that their proud drivers personalised them, as no two looked the same.

When the sign for the Midtown Tunnel appeared, he knew they were getting close. His guidebook had told him that the one and a half mile long tunnel went under the East River and up into central Manhattan. The traffic was now getting denser and every third vehicle seemed to be a yellow cab. How did they all make a living?

Within five minutes of exiting the tunnel, he was standing outside The Liberty Belle in West 32nd Street. The tired-looking exterior didn't inspire much confidence. The paint was flaking and the windows were so filthy there was no point in having them. Perhaps it would be nicer inside – it wasn't. The cramped reception area was too dingy to see straight away and it took Joe's eyes a few seconds to adjust. Behind the reception counter sat a podgy, middle aged man watching baseball highlights on a small black and white portable TV. He wore a striped unbuttoned bowling shirt over a vest that was once white. Perched on the back of his head was a brown pork pie hat and a slim cigarillo protruded through the hole in his four-day-old stubble. If he was going for the *Fistful of Dollars* look, he'd missed the target. A fistful of doughnuts would be more apt.

As the stranger advanced, the cigar chomping man's eyes didn't leave the flickering screen. 'Jesus Christ, my grandmother could have hit that, and she's been in a coma for six months!'

With a cursory glance up he asked, 'Yeah? What can I do for ya?'

'I'd like to rent a room please.'

Now he had the clerk's full attention. 'It's six dollars a night, first two nights payable upfront.'

As Joe's details were taken, he was asked, 'How did you hear about us?'

'The cab driver who brought me in from JFK. Manito... Perez?'

'Ah, Manito. He stayed here when he first shipped in from Cuba. Then he got all la-di-da and found himself a cardboard box in Central Park.'

When he saw that his newest guest didn't know if he was joking or not, he explained, 'I'm yanking your chain. I know we're kinda low end, but the beds are clean and we're good value for six bucks a night.'

Joe's next sentence escaped before he could stop it. 'Do you have a safe?'

You idiot. Why would anyone staying here need a safe?

Rubbing his whiskery chin the manager replied, 'I can honestly say that's the first time I've ever been asked that question. Let me consult the concierge, he's been here longer than me. Hey George, do we have a safe?'

It was then that Joe noticed the semi-comatose figure sat at a small table just inside the door. He was slumped forward with his head resting on his arms. Next to his elbow was a three quarters empty bottle of Jim Beam and a smeared glass. At the sound of his name the inebriant's reply was to raise the middle finger of his right hand.

'He says he thinks not, sir. But if you have any valuables or cash I can personally look after them for you.'

Quickly back peddling, the young Englishman deflected, 'It's okay. It's only my wristwatch and it's not worth much anyway.'

He thought it prudent not to mention he had close to a thousand dollars on his person. As Joe handed over a twenty dollar bill and pocketed his eight dollars change, the sleazeball handed him a key off the hook. 'Room 22. We call it the Burton Suite. Richard and Liz insist on it whenever they're in town. Second floor. The john is last door on the right.'

Joe grinned, bypassed the out of order lift and walked toward the stairs. The voice from behind the reception desk stopped him, 'Oh, we do have a policy about women being in your room after midnight. If you haven't got one let me know and I'll make a few calls.'

'I'll bear it in mind. Thanks.'

'But make sure she's not a screamer. The old guy in 23 is a paranoid schizophrenic. He hates noise and he keeps an axe under his bed.'

The Liberty Belle's latest guest laughed. The receptionist didn't. Unsurprisingly, room 22 was more 'Gone for a Burton Suite' than 'Burton Suite'. The wash basin tap dripped constantly, the carpet was threadbare and the curtains looked like they'd disintegrate if touched. On one wall, hanging on a nail was a framed ariel photo of the New York skyline, circa 1930; probably put up when the room was last decorated. With trepidation, Joe approached the bed, like Van Helsing approaching the sleeping Dracula's coffin. To his astonishment, the sheets and pillowcase looked freshly laundered, as did the towel hanging under the sink. Looking around what would be his abode for the next four nights Joe guessed that 'barata' must be Spanish for 'shithole'.

Had the bed not been clean, he couldn't have stayed, and the room was basic to say the least, but it was for a relatively short time, so it would do. Also, as well as a lock, the door had a sturdy chain, always conducive to a good night's sleep when the person in the next room may be 'unpredictable'.

Joe looked around for somewhere to hide the bulk of his cash. No way did he want to take more than fifty dollars out onto the streets. There was a rickety old chest of drawers and a cramped closet, but they were too obvious. He was certain that the moment he left the hotel, the sleazeball would be up here to nose around. It was then that he spotted the double electrical socket by the bed. If he could remove the screws from the faceplate there would be plenty of room inside to fit a wad of rolled up dollars. Rescrew the front into place and no-one would dream of looking there. Short of a fire, his money would be safe. One snag; he didn't have a screwdriver.

And so he found himself back downstairs. Reception man had returned to watching TV and the 'concierge' remained on Jupiter, or whatever planet he was currently visiting. Joe coughed to make his presence known. 'Do you have a screwdriver? The mirror above the sink needs tightening.'

The desk clerk fixed his weasel eyes on him. 'A screwdriver, you say. Let me ask our maintenance division. Hey George, do you have your utility belt with you, perchance?'

'Who do ya think I am, fucking Batman?' came the slurred response.

'He says no, unfortunately his tools are elsewhere on this occasion... Hey wait, I did have to tighten something or other recently. Let me check my drawer.'

With that he opened the crammed desk drawer and started rummaging around inside, taking out paperclips, a ball of string, a girlie magazine and a box of matches before triumphantly holding up a small red screwdriver. 'There you go,' he imparted, handing the tool over the counter. Joe saw that it was a crosshead. Perfect.

'Thankyou.'

'No problem. Our guests having a pleasant stay is always uppermost in our minds. Ain't that right, George?'

George's non-verbal reply was a long, rasping fart that sent Joe scurrying back to the Burton Suite before it caught up with him. From the top of the stairs he heard a voice below shout, 'He says, "Absolutely".'

With the bulk of his money concealed inside the electrical socket, he sat down on the bed and took the FEAR CITY pamphlet from his pocket. It was plain that its purpose was to scare the hell out of tourists and, for this particular tourist, it was doing a fine job. The gist of it was not to walk the streets alone after dark, don't use buses or the subway, don't think you're safe anywhere except Manhattan (and even there you stand a fair chance of being mugged or murdered), and hope the building you're in doesn't catch fire because the mayor has laid off numerous firefighters. Surely it was just sour grapes. Clearly the people distributing this had an axe to grind. Hopefully, the old guy in room 23 didn't. Surely the city couldn't be *that* dangerous. His watch read 10pm. Remembering that New York is five hours behind GMT, he wound the hands back to 5pm and decided to find somewhere to eat. If possible, he intended to stay awake for five more hours, sleep for ten hours straight and hope his body clock would reset itself.

Joe determined that his first stop should be Big Dino's Diner where, in four nights time, he'd rendezvous with James Northbridge - if the snake had the guts to show up. After spending half an hour familiarising himself with the street map in his guidebook, he finally felt ready to venture out. Unlike British cities, the vast majority of Manhattan's streets had numbers instead of names. It was a rectangular grid system. Avenues ran the length of the Island, north to south and streets intersected them east to west, with Fifth Avenue being the central dividing line.

It's not impossible to get lost but if you do it's fairly easy to get back on track. For example, if you set off on foot from West 32nd Street wanting to go to West 56th Street and the first street you come to is West 31st, you would immediately realise that you're going in the wrong direction and turn around. For a visitor it's a lot easier than navigating your way around Los Angeles, Chicago or Washington.

In the lobby of The Liberty Belle, Joe debated whether he should wipe his feet on the way out so as not to dirty the pavement: sorry, sidewalk. As the new arrival passed the reception desk, the clerk nodded toward the drunk and confided in a hushed tone, 'He doesn't really work here, he just comes in out of the rain sometimes.'

'It's not raining,' pointed out Joe.

'Yeah, but *he* don't know that!'

CHAPTER THIRTY ONE
NEW YORK CITY LIFE

It soon became apparent to Joe that his pre-conceived idea of a typical male New Yorker being white and heavily built was well wide of the mark. Walking alongside him and toward him on the crowded, bustling streets he encountered black men, Hispanics, Asians, and even a smattering of Hasidic Jews, with their distinctive black hats and side curls. There were sharply attired businesspeople, hard-hatted construction workers and casually dressed teens. A true melting pot. Plainly, there was no such thing as a typical New Yorker. Before he'd walked even a hundred yards the visitor was aware that this was the strangest, most unique place he'd ever been. It had its own vibe, an energy that was inherent to it. As if this city was a living, breathing thing. And whilst the different cultures didn't exactly revel in each other's company, they tolerated each other, showing that it could be done.

Thanks to the grid system he found Dino's without any problem and went in. It was everything he hoped it would be. A perfect replica of a 1950's diner. As you entered, the grill was directly opposite the street door. There were nine fixed chrome stools around the lunch counter and four-seater leatherette booths lining both sides of the room. At the far end a brightly lit Wurlitzer jukebox took pride of place. On the wall above it were framed photographs of James Dean, Elvis Presley,

Chuck Berry, Little Richard and Marlon Brando (a still from *The Wild One*, wearing his peaked leather motorcycle cap).

There were around twenty other patrons and, above the sound of chatter and sizzling burgers, Buddy Holly proclaimed his love for Peggy Sue. Joe chose a booth near the impressive record machine and gazed out of the window. An unenthusiastic nasal voice enquired, 'So, what can I get you?'

Looking up, he saw a bleached blonde waitress, pencil and pad at the ready. Her name badge revealed her as Donna. She'd been pretty once but, although still probably just the right side of thirty, her features were beginning to harden.

'Do you have any tea?'

'Nah. We got Coca Cola, Cherry Cola, Dr Pepper, Lemonade, black coffee, white coffee and cappuccino.'

'What's that last one?'

'Frothy coffee.'

'Okay, I'll have one of those.'

'Are you eating?'

'Um, yes. Hamburger with onions and fries, please'

'Please? You can tell you're not from around here.'

'England,' he smiled. 'First day.'

Suddenly she was his best friend. She tore off his order and slipped it in her apron pocket. 'I love the English. I saw The Beatles at Shea Stadium in '65. I didn't *hear* them, but I did *see* them. The screaming. It was like a jet plane taking off. And I was as loud as any of them. Paul McCartney – oh my God – those eyes! One of these days he's gonna dump Linda, come in here and whisk me away.'

'Stranger things have happened,' replied Joe, fully realising that they really, really hadn't.

An impatient voice from the other end of the diner skewered her daydream. 'Hey Donna, get your tush over here; we got other customers to serve.'

'Alright, already,' she fired back, 'keep what's left of your hair on.'

With a roll of her eyes she muttered, 'Paul, where are ya?' and headed for the service counter, leaving Joe to take in his surroundings. So, this was it. The place where he would come face to face with the elusive James Northbridge. He wondered which booth their meeting would take place in. How long would it last? This was all presuming that he turned up of course. If he was a no-show there would be no attempt to contact him again. That missing chunk of his identity would have to stay that way. Just as the order arrived, Elvis sang about checking in to Heartbreak Hotel.

If you thought that place was depressing mate, you should try The Liberty Belle, thought Joe.

He enjoyed his first American meal and his 'frawthy cawfee' and Donna suggested that, as well as hitting all the usual tourist spots, he should consider a visit to the Museum of Natural History on Central Park West.

In turn, he informed her of the Fear City pamphlet and she confirmed what he suspected – it was compiled by disgruntled cops and firefighters, bitter at the Mayor for cutting their numbers. Worryingly, she confided that New York was bankrupt; debt ridden; financially on its knees. And central government was loathe to bail it out. Joe couldn't believe it. How could a vibrant city crammed full of people and businesses be skint? But his waitress lived and worked here, so she should know.

It was 8pm when he left Dino's, pleased with his choice of venue. It was compact and intimate without feeling cramped. Realisation hit that he hadn't called home to say he'd arrived safely. Shit. It would now be 1am in Watford and his mum was always in bed before 11pm. He'd have to phone her tomorrow and hope she wasn't worrying too much. His eyes felt heavy and he really wanted to go to bed himself, but he was determined to hold out until 10pm. Perhaps have a couple of drinks to help him sleep then crash out and start afresh tomorrow. Where to go? The guidebook stated that Times Square was lively and it wasn't too far from his digs, so he decided to check it out.

Heading south up 7th Ave, Joe noticed the change at around the intersection with W50 St. Dotted among the usual shops were the first signs of things to come: adults only bookstores. By the time he'd reached 43rd St every other building seemed to be sex orientated. Peep shows, burlesques, topless bars and picture houses showing classics like *Snow White and The Seven Perves*. Joe had never seen anything like it. As the street numbers got lower so did the number of female pedestrians. Nearly all the sightseers were male, with sporadic couples arm in arm.

Broadway was an exception to the city's grid pattern as it already existed before the system was designed. It ran diagonally and the point where it met 7th Ave near 42nd St seemed to be the epicentre of the flesh trade. Joe had presumed that Times Square would be an actual square, like Trafalgar or Leicester Square in London and was surprised that it was a generic term to describe an entire district, nine streets long and three avenues wide. Over thirty blocks in all. Numerous cinemas all showed XXX skin flicks, and bar signs promised LIVE NUDE GIRLS!

'Always preferable to *dead* nude girls,' he muttered to himself. The neon screens and signs that weren't promoting sex advertised Coca Cola, Gordon's Gin, Canadian Club whiskey and Winston's cigarettes. All good healthy stuff. Yet this modern-day Gomorrah obviously held a fascination for thousands of people. Everyone seemed to be either seeking or selling sex. Pornographic bookstores vied with strip joints and even live sex shows to separate the punters from their dollars. Micro skirted working girls went through their patter as Joe walked by. 'Hi handsome, want your dick sucked?'

'Over here, sugar. Whatever floats your boat, I'll do it.'

'Five bucks. Best fuck you'll ever have.'

An afro-wigged black transvestite in yellow leather hotpants boasted, 'I've got something for you none of these other ladies have. How about it, cupcake?'

It was a carnival of lust. Add in the drug dealers, hawkers and hustlers and it was clear that this slice of the Big Apple was full of worms. Joe only saw two cops and they seemed more interested in eating their hotdogs than making any arrests. He was as red blooded as any twenty something male, but he didn't find it enticing or sensual at all. It was seedy and degrading, with a palpable air of danger. In just half an hour Joe witnessed three fist fights break out and a man grab one of the prostitutes by her hair and slap her, warning, 'You hold out on me again, bitch, and I'll cut your nose off.'

The Englishman wanted to step in but the handle of a large knife protruding from the pimp's waistband stopped him. Most pitiful of all was when a girl who couldn't have been more than fifteen whispered nervously from a shadowy doorway, 'Hi, want to go somewhere private?'

She was wafer thin, had an elfin face and wore an orange mini dress and white ankle socks. What Joe really wanted to do was buy her a meal and put her on a Greyhound bus back to wherever she'd run away from. But he guessed that she'd return in a few days, weeks or months. Whoever, or whatever, had lured her here wouldn't let her go *that* easily. His gaze met hers for an instant and she smiled. Only with her mouth though. Her eyes, like every sex worker he'd seen that evening were lifeless. Like dolls' eyes. This had to be one of the most depraved places on planet earth. Soulless. During the next twenty minutes he was offered every sex act he could imagine; and a fair few he couldn't.

But it was the buyers not the sellers who were most disturbing. People willing to do literally anything for money will always attract certain dangerous individuals. Characters drawn to the dark side of the human psyche who get their kicks doling out pain and sometimes even death.

A crowd of people were gathered outside a wide plate glass window covered by thick black drapes. A hand painted sign promising LIVE SEX sat on an easel outside. All eyes were on the window and Joe stopped as his curiosity got the better of him. What were they all staring at? His answer came swiftly when the drapes parted and there in the shop window was a young woman dressed as a nun performing oral sex on a Charlie Chaplin lookalike, complete with bowler hat, toothbrush moustache and thin cane, with which he tapped his co-star's wimple, by way of encouragement. It was easily the most bizarre, surreal thing Joe had ever seen, and he got a few irritated glares when he couldn't suppress an involuntary laugh. If the real Chaplin had an appendage the size of his impersonator's it would explain why he always wore baggy trousers.

After thirty seconds the drapes closed, much to the crowd's disappointment. It had been a taster, in more ways than one. The club barker promised that two dollars would gain you entry for the entire show; first drink free. Within seconds a long line of eager punters formed as Joe's brain began to process what his eyes had just seen. He concluded that if the female performer was a genuine Catholic, her next confession would be a classic.

'Bless me father for I have sinned.'

'What did you do, my child?'

'For monetary gain I fellated a man who was dressed as Charlie Chaplin in Times Square.'

'I see. Well, I absolve you of your sin. Say a prayer of repentance, three Hail Marys, have a good gargle with holy water and don't do it again.'

Joe really needed to sleep and made for The Liberty Belle. Stretched out on the bed in his poky room, he contemplated what he'd seen and heard in the last two hours. Every perversion was catered for. He was certain that if he'd requested a threesome with an albino Egyptian girl and a goat in a bath filled with jam, the only question would have been, 'What flavour jam?'

London had its seedier side and Soho wasn't short of strip clubs or ladies of the night, but it was like a church fete compared to what he'd just witnessed. In that condensed section of Midtown Manhattan sex was a commodity. No different to selling NYC t-shirts or cheap plastic models of the statue of liberty. And Joe was slightly surprised to find he found nothing appealing about it. To turn sex into a business transaction was to rob it of its intimacy. It diminished it into a sordid, animalistic short-term fix. It certainly didn't bear comparison to discovering the wants and desires of someone you had a deep emotional connection with. Someone like Lilah. Making love with her and falling asleep holding her was beautiful.

The guidebook description of Times Square as 'lively' must be the biggest understatement ever printed. But then they couldn't really say 'pervert's paradise' could they? Even if they had described it thus, nothing could have prepared him for the unbridled brazenness of it. As he drifted into unconsciousness it was the hollow eyes of the young girl in the orange dress that haunted him.

CHAPTER THIRTY TWO

TROUBLE MAN

Monday, June 16th. Being awake for eighteen hours straight had the desired effect. Joe slept soundly for the following ten and woke refreshed. He'd earmarked today for some sightseeing, making a mental note to telephone his mum at noon, which would be 5pm in Watford, so even if she shopped after work, she'd be home by then. Also, he'd need to find a hardware store to purchase a screwdriver, the one he'd borrowed having disappeared from the sink top where he'd left it. That, along with the cigar ash on the floor was confirmation that the sleazeball had been in his room whilst he was out. At a nearby Deli on E34th St, he ate a light breakfast consisting of freshly squeezed orange juice and French toast with eggs, which he asked for 'over easy', purely because he'd heard it said in so many American films. It sounded good but all it equated to was lightly fried eggs flipped and cooked on both sides.

It was shaping up to be a mild morning so, after consulting his guidebook, Joe decided it was the ideal weather for a boat ride. He hailed a yellow cab to Whitehall St, the terminal for the Staten Island Ferry. Donna had told him that, for just 10 cents, it would take him out into the harbour and close enough to Liberty Island to give him good views of both the green lady with the torch and the Manhattan skyline, before docking at St George, Staten Island. Then he could sail straight back. The round trip would take less than an hour.

As the large orange boat sailed adjacent to Lady Liberty, Joe wished he had a camera with him. The morning sun lit up her crown, making it look like a halo. Including her pedestal, she was 305ft tall, the equivalent of a 22-storey building. To the shiploads of European immigrants in the late nineteenth and early twentieth century she must have looked like one of the wonders of the world. She was still an impressive sight but now, to her left, many of the original low buildings had been replaced by man-made monoliths of concrete, steel and glass stretching skyward and dwarfing her. None more so than the neighbouring twin columns known as the World Trade Centre, which dominated the skyline at 110 storeys high. These giants had reduced Liberty's impact in scale but not in importance. She was known throughout the world as a symbol of freedom and hope, and it was inspiring to see her in person.

By 11am, Joe had travelled to Staten Island and back to Manhattan. The weather was too nice not to be outside, so upon disembarking the ferry, he walked to nearby Battery Park on the southernmost tip of the island, buying a bag of pretzels from a street vendor to see what they tasted like. 'Salty cream crackers' was his answer. Very salty. Which was a good move by the seller as the buyer would inevitably also end up buying a cold drink to quench their sudden thirst.

Finding an empty bench, the visitor enjoyed the view of the harbour waters with the side silhouette of Liberty in the distance. As ever, the warmth of the hazy sun felt good on his skin. With his eyes closed and head tilted up toward the sky, he didn't see the old man with the young dog approach.

'Beautiful day.'

'Certainly is,' agreed Joe.

'Mind if I sit down?'

'No. Please do.'

The white-haired gentleman let out an involuntary groan as he took the weight off his feet. Looking out over the water, he shared, 'Before Ellis Island took over in 1892, this stretch we're sitting on was where thousands of immigrants first set foot on American soil.'

Joe tried to imagine all those steamships, full of all nationalities, leaving their homelands, desperate for a better life.

'Been a few since then.'

'Millions. Each one with dreams and aspirations. Including my Irish grandparents. My Grandpa helped build the Brooklyn Bridge,' he added proudly. 'Nigh on a century ago.'

'Wow,' was all the young Englishman could manage. He noticed that the dog hadn't taken its eyes off the paper bag on his lap since its master sat down. 'Is he allowed a pretzel?'

'Sure.'

As the mongrel pup hungrily accepted the treat, Joe tickled his ear and asked, 'What's his name?'

'Gerald,' said the old man, 'after our esteemed President Ford.'

'You're a fan then?'

'Hell no, that yoyo is so dumb he couldn't find his ass with both hands and a compass. The dog's not very bright either, so me and the wife thought the name was a good fit.'

Joe chuckled, delighting in this unexpected conversation.

'You're obviously a limey,' continued the American. 'Where's home in merry old England?'

'London. Well, just north of it.'

'Anywhere near St Albans?'

'Right next door,' came the astonished reply.

'I've seen photos of the Cathedral. I love old religious buildings. Especially European ones. All that history. I was hoping to be posted to England in the war, but I drew the short straw. It was the Pacific for this boy. Always wanted to visit London, though.'

'It's never too late.'

'It is for me, son. These creaky old bones won't be leaving the U.S again.'

Joe didn't know what to say to that so held out the paper bag. 'Where's my manners? Would you care for a pretzel?'

'No, thanks. That much salt plays havoc with my blood pressure. I'd best be getting along, if I'm late home my other half has me lying in a ditch somewhere. Nice talking to you. Enjoy your stay in our city.'

'It's been a pleasure,' replied Joe, before adding as an afterthought, 'Oh, could you tell me where the nearest public telephone is?'

He was told there were phone kiosks just outside the northern entrance to the park. As he watched the elderly man shuffle off, with Gerald sniffing in front of him, Joe thought what good company he'd been – one of those interesting characters who floats all too briefly into your life and is gone before you know it. His watch read 11.50am, time to find a phone. So, he walked purposefully past the statues of people he didn't recognise and out of

Battery Park. Sure enough, there stood a line of three public payphones.

Thinking ahead, at the Deli earlier he'd obtained five dollars' worth of quarters from the cashier, thinking that would be ample. He didn't anticipate a long conversation, just a chance to say he'd arrived in one piece. Most American public phones weren't housed in solid four-sided booths like the red ones back home, meaning the user was exposed to the elements and the traffic noise. It had been an enjoyable morning and he was upbeat. Now to see if his mum's mood had mellowed.

The operator confirmed that a two minute international call to England would be $2.50c a minute. How many minutes would he like?

'Two,' he replied, wishing all maths was as simple as that. The detached voice instructed him to put the coins into the appropriate slot. (There were three slots, one each for nickels, dimes, and quarters.) Once that was done, she would connect him. If he wished to extend the call, he should put more money in when the beeps sounded or the call would be terminated. Joe fed the metal box twelve quarters and waited. And waited. It was a good two minutes until a faint but familiar voice said, 'Hello.'

'Hi David, it's me. Just wanted to let you and Mum know I arrived safe and sound. Is she there?'

There was a pause before his brother revealed, 'She's in hospital, Joe.'

The caller was shocked and immediately felt helpless, being so far away. 'Why? What happened?'

'I got home from Dad's yesterday afternoon around five and found her sitting at the kitchen table, like she was the morning after your party. Except this time there was a bottle of pills in front of her.'

Joe's blood ran cold. 'Please don't tell me she's taken an overdose?'

'No, the bottle was unopened, but she was like a zombie. She wouldn't speak to me and I didn't know what to do, so I phoned Dad and he called an ambulance. They took her to Watford General to check her over. I went too. The doctor said she hadn't taken anything, but they were worried about her mental state and were keeping her in for observation.'

'Dear God. You did the right thing, David. Well done. Listen, flush the pills down the toilet. I'll find out when the next flight home is.'

His brother's reply continued the surprises. 'There's no point, Joe. You can't do anything. I went to see her this afternoon and I'm going again this evening. I can handle it.'

'You're sixteen, you shouldn't have to deal with this shit.'

'Neither should you. Just do what you went there for. Mum knew what time I was due home. She had loads of time to take those pills if she really wanted to.'

What a dilemma. He had to make a quick decision but needed more information.

'What did the hospital say?'

'That once they're sure that she's not a risk to herself she can come home. There was some talk of putting her on anti-depressants. I'll be going to see her every day until she's out.'

'Okay. I'll be back early on Friday morning. Tell her I phoned and give her my love. If it all gets too much, stay at your dads. Are you sure you don't want me to fly back?

'I'm sure.'

The beeps started, indicating the call was coming to an end. 'I'm proud of you, David. Take care of yourself.'

'You too.'

The line went dead. As Joe placed the handset on its cradle, he felt numb. Stunned. He knew Mary was feeling low, but he hadn't seen *this* coming. Not in a million years. Slowly, the numbness subsided and a white-hot rage surpassing any anger he'd ever felt rose in him. It solidified into a hatred so intense it consumed him. That excuse for a man, who hurt his mother so badly twenty one years ago, still continued to hurt her. In all that time there probably hadn't been a single day that she hadn't thought of him. Like a spectre casting its constant, evil shadow over her. Refusing to release her from his grip.

Filth like him leave a trail of destruction in their wake, destroying lives without a second thought. The world would be a better place without him. That's when all became clear to Joe. He would later describe it as 'like someone flicking a switch in my head.'

Destiny hadn't brought him across continents to merely confront James Northbridge; it had brought him here to kill him. This animal had destroyed Mary's life and now he was destroying Joe's. Causing him to be crushingly humiliated in front of all his friends. Making him feel terrible shame for something he didn't do but was the product of.

Just like at Paolo's house after his party, Joe was retreating into himself, but this time he went deeper.

To a dark place within that he didn't know existed. His post twenty-first birthday life had finally caved in on him, trapping him in the rubble. However, this time there was no Lilah to pull him out. The only answer was to eliminate the architect of all this pain and misery, otherwise it would never stop. James Northbridge was a cancerous tumour. And you don't reason with a tumour, you cut it out.

CHAPTER THIRTY THREE

I SHALL BE RELEASED

The next thing Joe knew, it was getting dark and the city was beginning to light up. He had walked all afternoon and into the early evening but if asked where he'd been he wouldn't have been able to say. It was as if he was outside his own body, watching himself aimlessly traipse around the city. They were just anonymous streets to him. Buildings, people, traffic, walk/don't walk signs. Awareness temporarily pushed its way to the surface when he saw a hardware store and purchased a screwdriver. Without that he couldn't get to his money. Without his money he couldn't purchase a gun. And without a gun he couldn't shoot James Northbridge dead.

After careful consideration he decided shooting him to be the best option. Other possibilities were mulled over and discarded. He first thought he would suggest the pair take a stroll after meeting at Dino's, then push him under a moving vehicle, but the traffic only crawled along in Manhattan so that was out.

A knife would be easier to get hold of, but it would be incredibly messy with no guarantee of success. Anyway, Joe knew he couldn't go through with something so savage.

Strangulation would take too long and he'd likely be hauled off before completing the task. No, shooting would be quick, efficient, with the highest chance of success. If the first bullet didn't finish him then he'd put a few more into him. Job done.

There was an article a while back in Lenny's newspaper stating that figures suggested that there was one firearm per two people in the U.S.A. If that statistic was true, it meant there were close to four million guns in New York City alone. And Joe only wanted one. How difficult could it be?

The smell of hamburgers made him recognise his hunger and he ambled into a busy bar/bistro on E39th St. As he sat at the bar waiting for a table an obvious working girl sidled up to him.

'Hi there. Wanna buy me a drink?'

His curt, one word answer of 'no', elicited five in return. 'Fuck you then, ya faggot.'

The meal was a lot more agreeable than the girl. No doubt better value too. All that walking had made him ravenous. Steak, boiled potatoes and spinach, followed by apple pie and ice cream, washed down with two bottles of Rolling Rock lager. By 9.30pm he was back at the Liberty Belle. Sleazeball was on his usual perch behind the counter, glued to his TV, so Joe sensed an opportunity. 'Hi,' he beamed.

'Hi yourself,' returned the clerk, engrossed in an old James Cagney movie. *Angels With Dirty Faces*, unless Joe was mistaken.

'I was wondering if you can tell me where I can find a gun shop?'

Aware his unusual request had aroused some suspicion, the guest elaborated, 'My kid brother is fascinated by guns, and since we don't have them in my country, I was going to take a few photos for him.'

Immediately realising that, having been through his things, 'Sleaze' would know he didn't have a camera, he quickly added, 'After I've bought a camera, of course. Got my eye on a nice Polaroid.'

Seemingly satisfied, the American revealed that his personal favourite was John Jovino's in Little Italy, which also happened to be the oldest gun dealer in the city. He scribbled down the address, slipped it to Joe and turned his attention back to Cagney.

In room 22, Joe locked the door and unscrewed the faceplate from the double socket. His wad of notes was rolled up inside, just as he'd left it. He peeled off four fifty dollar bills, three twenties and four tens. With no clue how much a handgun would cost he figured three hundred would cover it. After replacing the front of the socket he lay on his bed, tired but far too stimulated to sleep. In his head he went over the telephone conversation with David and concluded that his younger brother was correct – if Mary had been serious about ending it all she had six hours to do it between him leaving for Heathrow at 11am and David arriving home at 5pm. There was no doubt, though, that she was in a dark, dismal place and it strengthened Joe's resolve.

You slimy fucker, Northbridge. You instigated this. But you'll pay. I'll make you pay!

CHAPTER THIRTY FOUR

TIME IS TIGHT

Tuesday, June 17th. At 10am Joe's cab pulled up outside John Jovino's gun shop in Grand St, Little Italy, on the Lower East side. It was founded by Jovino, an Italian immigrant, in 1911 and was not only the oldest firearms supplier in New York but reputedly the entire U.S.A. It had changed ownership but kept its original name. The young Englishman was glad he'd taken a cab because the area below 14th St all had named streets, as they'd been established before the grid system was devised, making it harder for strangers to find their way around. The cabbie informed him that Little Italy was the area from Canal St to the south, Bleecker St to the north, the Bowery to the east and Lafayette St to the west, with Mulberry St at its centre. He said it was almost like a Sicilian/ Southern Italian township had been lifted from Europe and dropped into NYC.

The first thing you noticed as you approached Jovino's store front was that hanging above the sign was a huge, outwardly pointing wooden revolver, resembling the type Clint Eastwood used to settle arguments in those spaghetti westerns. The second thing you noticed was the sign itself.

JOHN JOVINO

FIREARMS-POLICE EQUIPMENT

The word 'police' made Joe uneasy, and he hoped that none of New York's finest were inside. The interior was smaller than he'd expected, but it was an Aladdin's cave of all things gun related. Adorning the walls were pistols, automatics and rifles of various shapes and sizes as well as shoulder holsters and bulletproof vests. Inside the glass display cabinets were even more guns and ammunition. Joe was relieved to see that, apart from himself, there was just the salesman and one other customer, receiving his change and goods. The tourist made out he was browsing, until he and the clerk were alone, then gingerly approached him.

'Good morning, I'm after a handgun.'

The storekeeper smiled amiably, 'Well, you've come to the right place. We have everything from Smith & Wesson's down to .22's.'

None of that meant anything to Joe, so he just tried to look impressed, 'Great.'

'I couldn't help noticing your accent, sir. Are you a resident of the state of New York?'

'Err, no. I'm from England,' answered Joe, wrongfooted.

'Then I'm sorry, I can't sell you a firearm. And even if you *were* a resident, you'd need a licence.'

This was unexpected. Naively, Joe had thought that, in this gun-obsessed country, purchasing a pistol would be as easy as buying a bagel. Maybe it was just the policy of this particular shop.

'So, where might I get one then?'

'No reputable gun dealer will accommodate you without the necessary paperwork.'

'What about the unreputable ones?' ventured Joe.

The clerk's features hardened. 'If you leave now, sir, I'll forget that you said that.'

Bravo idiot. How to draw attention to yourself!

'I understand. Just kidding,' lied the potential buyer and hurriedly left the shop.

Right Einstein, what now?'

He had around thirty-three hours to get hold of a gun and no idea how to do so. On a whim he decided to have a stroll around Little Italy while he tried to come up with a Plan B. The cabbie was spot on, if you didn't know better, you'd swear you were in an Italian town and not a great, sprawling Metropolis. There were no skyscrapers or honking lines of stationary cars. It seemed to be a self-contained little community where everyone knew and looked out for one another. He must have stood out like a sore thumb, but the atmosphere was genial and he never felt threatened. The few wary looks he received were to be expected.

Within a few blocks, he saw four barber's shops, two Italian leather goods wholesalers and various discount clothes retailers, but the majority of the businesses were food related. Greengrocers, pizzerias, cafes, bakeries, olive oil suppliers and numerous dairy stores specialising in Italian cheeses like Mozzarella and Burrata. Naturally, the predominant colours were red, white and green and in some places the Italian flag and Stars and Stripes flew side by side, indicating that these third and fourth generation Italian/Americans were equally as proud of their roots as they were of their ancestors adopted country. The sounds and smells would have been no different in Giovanni Massetti's pre-war Positano than they were in present day Lower East Manhattan. Some of the streets, tenements and store fronts looked familiar to Joe and he was sure they may have featured in one of his favourite films, *The Godfather*.

Wait a minute… The Godfather=Mafia=Gangsters. This neighbourhood must have real mob connections and that meant plenty of guns.

Yes, but why would they sell one to you? They're a tight-knit organisation and you're not even Italian or Sicilian.

Alright, clever clogs. Got any better ideas?

Central Park came into his head. In all likelihood there would be some shady characters there. Perhaps one of them would sell him a gun if he paid over the odds. With limited options and the clock ticking, it had to be worth a try.

Joe's cab dropped him off at W72nd St where he entered the sprawling 843 acre green oasis via the ornate Bethesda Terrace steps. At the bottom, in the middle of the lower terrace, stood the magnificent Bethesda Fountain, with the bronze angel statue at its middle. Wings outstretched; it presided over the central column with four cherubs in attendance beneath.

At twenty-six feet high by ninety-six wide the fountain was imposing yet lacking something that other great fountains like the Trevi in Rome had. Oh yes – water. It was bone dry. Another casualty of a city with no money. Standing next to the fountain, facing the grand steps and strumming an acoustic guitar, stood the man whose real name Joe would never learn. It was clear from first sight that he was a one off.

The busker wore an army issue jacket with two stripes and under his left arm was a wooden crutch to compensate for his missing left leg, amputated just below the knee. His dark, wavy hair was long and he sported a full beard. Perched on his head was a black top hat with a long white feather in the band and on his remaining foot was a scuffed, off-white tennis shoe. Two chains hung from his neck, one with dog tags and one with a peace sign. On the ground his guitar case lay open for donations. Joe was mesmerised by him. If this was Watford High Street, the residents would think he'd landed from outer space.

The U.S. involvement in Vietnam had only officially ended in ignominy two years earlier, with many Americans viewing their returning soldiers with indifference and even embarrassment. It had been a very unpopular war. For their part, a lot of the combatants felt abandoned by their countrymen as they tried to pick up the pieces of their lives. But it seemed this individual, whose guitar looked in much better shape than he did, either had no resentment or hid it very well.

To Joe's untrained ear his playing sounded good and he soon learned the veteran, who he guessed was in his late twenties, had a strong, clear singing voice to go with it. For the next thirty minutes the young Englishman watched in fascination as this strange-looking fellow tailored his songs to what he thought the various passers-by might like to hear, thereby increasing his chance of reward. When the 'straights' approached he'd play "God Bless America" or "New York, New York". The younger set would get varied contemporary numbers. There was no doubting his versatility. He was quick witted and self-deprecating too. A teenage girl dropped some coins into his case, and he stopped halfway through "Blowing in the Wind" and launched into Roy Orbison's "Pretty Woman". As the girl walked off giggling with her friend, the busker shouted, 'If you need someone to take you to the School Hop, who better than me?'

When a middle-aged woman asked him, 'Do you know "I Left My Heart In San Francisco?"' his immediate response was, 'No, do *you* know I left my leg in Mekong Delta?'

It started to form in Joe's head that this man could be the key to him getting hold of a gun. Being ex-military he might have smuggled one back from Vietnam or at least know people who had. He wanted to engage with him but wasn't sure how to go about it. The offer of refreshment might ingratiate him. After a couple more songs, Joe made his move.

'Hi. Would you like a cold drink?'

The ex-soldier stopped, looked up, studied the stranger in front of him and replied in a southern drawl, 'Are you after my ass?'

Joe was horrified. 'No. I just thought you might like a drink.'

'Hey, I ain't judging. Throw in a chilli dog and I'll consider us engaged. You Australian?'

'English.'

The disabled busker scooped the meagre amount of cash out of his case, lovingly placed his guitar inside and swung it over his shoulder. Clamping a second crutch under his right arm he tipped his hat. 'I could use a Pepsi. Thank you kindly.'

'My name's Joe.' They shook hands.

'Everyone calls me Memphis.'

'Because that's where you're from?'

The vet pursed his lips and sucked in air, 'You're sharp as a tack boy. I can see I'm gonna have to watch you.'

Joe smiled weakly but inwardly cursed himself for stating the obvious. At the nearby hot dog cart,

Memphis addressed the vendor. 'Morning Ramone, this here is Joe, my biggest fan. Came all the way from Europe to see me play and buy me a chilli dog and a Pepsi.'

Joe told Ramone that he'd have the same. While their order was being prepared, Memphis noticed his benefactor looking across the terrace at the fountain's centrepiece.

'She's called The Angel of the Waters,' he explained 'Supposed to have healing powers but that's bullshit. Back when the fountain was full, I got drunk one night and bathed my stump. Well, it's still a stump.'

'You shouldn't test God, my friend,' admonished Ramone, handing over the sodas and snacks.

'Why not? He's sure as hell tested *me*.'

The duo sat on the outer perimeter of the fountain with their drinks and food. Memphis got straight to the point. 'So, what's your angle, Joe?'

'What do you mean?'

'Everybody has an angle. No-one does anything unless it benefits them in some shape or form. So, what is it you think I can do for you?'

Such candour was disarming, but a direct question deserves a direct answer. It was time to come clean.

'I'm after a gun,' declared Joe.

Without batting an eyelid the vet returned, 'Now what would a nice English boy like you want with a gun?'

'To take it home as a souvenir.'

'Really? T-shirt or a key ring not good enough for you, eh? Let me try and educate you, Joe. A gun is the devil's right hand, my friend. I've seen close up what they can do. If I had my way every firearm in this fucked up world would be melted down and made into something actually useful.'

'I'll give you thirty dollars to point me in the right direction.'

Exasperated, Memphis replied, 'Hello! Did you even hear what I just said? I feel strongly about this and you try to buy my principles for thirty bucks?'

'Fifty.'

'Deal. I'll have to set it up, though, so meet me here at eleven tomorrow morning. And don't judge me; a man's gotta eat. Give me half the money now and half tomorrow.'

'I'll give you ten now and forty tomorrow.'

'You ain't as dumb as you look,' grinned the older man, wiping mustard from his beard. He took out a packet of tic-tacs and swallowed two. 'Word to the wise. Out on the streets, don't flash the cash around. You'll wake up with a sore head and empty pockets. Or maybe you won't wake up at all.'

'Thanks for the tip.'

'And don't walk through The Ramble,' he further advised, pointing to a wooded area in the distance. 'Stick to the open spaces and be careful who you talk to.'

With that the busker went back to work and the tourist set off to explore. The park was far too large to see in its entirety, so Joe determined to wander around for a couple of hours and see what he came across. Right next to the fountain was a boating lake, and as well as a dozen or so row boats, Joe spotted a young couple in a bright yellow paddle boat, their knees rising and falling as they propelled the craft along. On the far shore a protective line of trees in full leaf shielded the lake from the giant buildings looking down on it. Sadly, the discarded polystyrene cups, tin cans and plastic bottles bobbing on the murky water's surface did nothing to enhance it.

Near the bow bridge that crossed the lake was a stall selling brightly coloured balloon animals. It was manned by a well-built, shaven headed black gentleman wearing shades. A female assistant accompanied him. The man was a dead ringer for singer Isaac Hayes, but Joe was reasonably confident that the "Theme from Shaft" composer had never sold an inflatable red giraffe in his life.

Wandering on, he was startled when two teens on bikes sped past him, one either side. He was tempted to take a stroll through The Ramble, an urban nature reserve, when he locked eyes with a raccoon, just outside the entrance. The creature darted inside the woods as if daring him to follow. Remembering Memphis's warning, the challenge went unaccepted. From where he stood, Joe could see a winding pathway, flanked by flora, fauna and canopies of trees. It was a perfect habitat for various species of birds and other wildlife, as well as muggers and other lowlife.

Continuing his exploring, Joe spotted a distant building sitting on higher ground and headed for a closer look. As he got nearer, an intermittent rattling sound puzzled him. At the top of the hill was a folly in the Gothic design, built of grey rock and granite, like a mini castle in appearance with a conical roofed turret as its highest point. The rattling sound ceased when the two teenage boys spotted him, put their aerosol cans away and sped off on their bicycles.

He'd stumbled upon Belvedere Castle, a quaint feature that had adorned the park for over a century, built like a scaled down version of one of Germany's castles on the Rhine. Back in the 1860's it must have looked splendid but in 1975 it was dilapidated, graffiti strewn and had weeds growing through it's cracked masonry. Reading the freshly painted slogans on the wall, Joe sighed. Couldn't *Billy from The Bronx* express himself some other way? And if *Otis* really was *4 Carla* why didn't he just tell her or send her a card? What little he'd seen of Central Park must have looked lovely when it opened but in 1975 it was sad, tired and neglected. Like the story of Cinderella in reverse. It had started out adorned in elegance and refinery but was now in rags.

City Hall had to shoulder the bulk of the blame for decades of underinvestment and neglect. A fountain without water isn't really a fountain, is it? But some native New Yorkers should also take a long, hard look at themselves. They were the ones tossing trash into boating lakes and daubing slogans on picturesque old landmarks. As Lenny Coleman put it, 'Only a fool shits on their own doorstep.'

But that's exactly what they were doing. Then again, Joe couldn't get too self-righteous. Tomorrow evening, he was going to commit an act far worse than littering or spray painting a public space. But that was different; it was for the greater good.

Back at The Liberty Belle he prepared to go out to eat by having a strip wash in his room. There was a shared shower in the bathroom/toilet, but he wasn't risking *that*. And not simply because an axe might appear through the door. God alone knew what resided behind that plastic shower curtain. Or even *on* it.

So, every day he limited himself to washing his hair and body in the lukewarm water of his sink.

He'd decided on the walk back from Central Park that tonight would be his penultimate visit to Big Dino's, to case the joint properly. Planning was the key to success. After taking fifty dollars plus coins from his pocket he concealed the remaining notes in the plug socket.

Arriving at 6.30, Joe chose a seat on the juke box side of the diner, first booth down from the grill. There were a few more patrons in than on his previous visit but it was far from packed. He could hear the grill chef holding court with the regular crew seated around his station. Was he Big Dino? If so, he was nothing like he'd imagined him. Small in stature and balding. Perhaps Big Dino was an ironic nickname. Tonight's deep philosophical discussion was-who would win in a fight between Superman and Batman.

Superman, obviously, decided Joe, though he could see where the guy was coming from who stated, 'Neither. They don't fuckin' exist.'

'Well, hello again,' smiled Donna 'what can I get you?'

Guessing prison food was going to leave a lot to be desired, Joe went all in. 'I'd like a 16oz steak, with fries and mushrooms please.'

'Anything to drink?'

'Dr Pepper.'

'And how do you like your steak?'

'Medium.'

'Onions?'

'No. Thank you.'

'Thank you,' she echoed, scribbling the order on her pad, 'something else I don't hear much around here. So, what have you been up to?'

'I saw Liberty from the Staten Island Ferry, like you suggested. Today I spent the morning in Little Italy and the afternoon in Central Park.'

She looked sad at the mention of his last destination. 'It breaks my heart to see what that place has become. When I was a kid, my parents would regularly take me and my baby brother there for picnics. These days families are too scared. There's always talk of cleaning it up, but nothing ever gets done.'

Before Joe could reply, the Everly Brothers butted in to tell Little Susie that she needed to wake up and Donna got distracted by a customer who broke a glass and went to check that they were okay. If possible, tomorrow he would choose a booth further down the diner on the opposite side. That would provide a clear view of the street and place him further away from the grill, so if any of the locals tried to intervene it would take them longer to reach him. After the deed, though, he wasn't going to put up a struggle or even attempt to escape. He didn't want anyone other than Northbridge to get hurt.

Once it was done, he intended to hand over his gun and wait for the cops to arrive. Even if it took more than one bullet the whole thing should be over in ten seconds. He surmised that the people from his previous life would be shocked when they heard the news. But why should they? Is it so surprising that the rapist's son should also turn out to be a bad seed? But hopefully one day they would understand that he'd rid the world of a malevolent soul.

CHAPTER THIRTY FIVE

WALK IN THE NIGHT

Wednesday, June 18th. Joe arrived at the Bethesda Fountain ten minutes early but there was no sign of Memphis. At the appointed hour he was still a no show, causing some concern. No Memphis meant no gun. No gun meant the whole plan was scuppered. At 11.10am the alarm bells really started to ring. What did he actually know about this eccentric Vietnam vet in the top hat? Maybe he too was only passing through and right now was heading back to Tennessee.

And that's when he saw him, skilfully propelling himself forward between his crutches as he emerged from the arched walkway that linked the terrace to The Mall.

'Sorry I'm late, English. Got into a poker game with the guys last night, drank one beer too many and slept in.'

'I was getting a bit worried,' admitted Joe.

'Why? We shook hands on it, didn't we?'

Peeling the guitar from his shoulder he set it down and asked, 'Do you have my forty?'

He accepted the two twenties and stuffed them in his breast pocket. 'Alright, you see the balloon seller by the bridge?'

'The big black guy.'

'That's him. Tell him you want to make a purchase and that Memphis sent you.'

'I thought *you'd* be supplying the gun.'

'Not me. I told you – devil's right hand. Whatever he instructs you to do, do it. You can trust him.'

With little choice, Joe did as he was told, proceeded to the stall by the bridge and announced to the black guy, 'I want to make a purchase.'

'Take your pick, buddy; we got swans, dogs, giraffes and snakes, in red, white, blue, yellow and green.'

'No, I don't want to buy a balloon.'

'Well, that could prove a sticking point cos that's what I'm selling.'

Realising he hadn't verbalised the second part of his introduction, the prospective buyer remedied it. 'Memphis sent me.'

The balloon seller looked over his sunshades at the slight figure in front of him.

'You won't mind if I check then.'

With that he set off toward the fountain just as a mother and her toddler son stopped and looked at the sign on the stall that read: BALLOONS 30c EACH OR TWO FOR 50c. The little boy pointed at the dog and asked for a blue one. Whilst inflating it, the young female assistant asked, 'Are you sure you don't want two, ma'am?'

'I've only got one child so why would I want two balloons?'

'Sometimes their little hands lose their grip and whoosh... their new pet ends up in Coney Island. I've seen it happen a thousand times. An extra 20c can save a lot of tears.'

'Okay, we'll take a red dog as well.'

'Very wise. You're a good mother.'

And you are a good saleswoman, thought one impressed Englishman.

Within five minutes, 'Isaac Hayes' was back, having received confirmation that Joe was legit. Reaching inside his jacket he produced a pair of sunshades not unlike his own and ordered, 'Put these on. And don't take them off until I tell you.'

Joe did as he was told only to discover the lens of the glasses had been coated with thick black paint. He couldn't see six inches in front of him.

'Don't be alarmed, it's only a precaution. Just do as I say.'

Grabbing the totally sightless young man by the elbow, he led him away from the stall. To passers-by it appeared to be a blind person being guided by a friend. Joe Holland had never felt so vulnerable, helpless and alone. A stranger in a strange land; and it was getting stranger by the minute. It soon became apparent that 'balloon man' wasn't big on conversation. All he said was 'Stairs up' and 'Stairs down' or 'last step' when the stairs were ending. Without his sight to rely on, Joe's other senses picked up the slack. Smell, touch and hearing were all heightened, although, taste didn't really help much.

It would be hard enough to put your life in the hands of someone you knew and trusted, so to do so with somebody you'd only just met bordered on insanity. But this man had something Joe needed and so held all the aces. Besides, for some peculiar reason, Joe was confident that Memphis wouldn't put him in harm's way. The guy was off the chart eccentric, but there was an honesty about him. No denying it was a massive gamble though.

After five minutes walking, the guide's voice warned, 'Stairs down,' and the pair started to descend. Joe could hear that they were somewhere busy and he was jostled once or twice by people ascending. Currents of warm air came and went. Twenty steps down he realised that they were entering a subway station and fear gripped him. Not only was he breaking Fear City guideline number three, he was doing it blind. Common sense screamed at him to take the glasses off and get out of there, but he resisted, knowing the deal would be off if he went into flight mode.

Terrifying thoughts attacked from every angle. It would be so simple for his escort to rob him and throw him under a train. There were, irrefutably, people in this city, perhaps even in this station, who would commit murder for a fraction of the three hundred dollars he was carrying. His silent prayer was that one of them wasn't currently holding his elbow.

'Last step.'

They were now on the platform, but Joe had no idea how close to the edge they were. His nose told him that someone to his left was eating something with onions on it and a youthful voice behind him said, 'Hey, watch it, man. There's a blind guy in front.'

It did nothing to calm his nerves. A rush of air and the rumble of an approaching train elevated his fear level. Beneath the blacked out lenses his eyes were shut tight, half expecting a push in the back followed by oblivion. It didn't come and it was with great relief that he heard the train brake, the doors slide open and the words, 'One step, up.'

Inside, as they shuffled along, his olfactory receptors were blitzed with different smells. The most prominent was ammonia, not quite eclipsing the urine it had been used to neutralise. He got a waft of a lady's perfume. Hot chocolate. Body odour. The seats felt like hard-moulded plastic. Easier to clean than fabric. A couple of youngsters were laughing. Were they the ones behind him on the platform? He'd never know. Mostly, nobody spoke though. Around quarter of an hour and six stops later, Joe felt a tug on his sleeve. 'This is us.'

He didn't have a clue where he was, but it felt good to be above ground level and out in the fresh air again. Well, as fresh as the air in a big city can be. They walked for about ten minutes, crossing four roads (another scary thing to do blind). Eventually, he was steered left through the doorway of a building. Cigarette smoke hit him and the odour of spilled beer that hadn't been cleaned up properly. The clicking of snooker balls hitting each other came next. No, this side of the pond it was more likely to be pool. His best guess was that he was in some seedy bar/pool hall. Where in the city, he knew not.

'Isaac' led him to a private room at the back of the bar and lowered him into a chair. 'Tilt your head downward and take the glasses off. Keep your eyes on the table and do not look up. Clear?'

Joe nodded and obeyed the instructions. His eyes welcomed the light, but he had to blink a few times until they reacclimatised to it. On the table in front of him was a small handgun. *Really* small. Next to it was a clip of six bullets. Opposite him a pair of hands adorned with numerous gold and silver rings rested on the tabletop. The fingers were long and slender. Female hands with bright red nail polish. Joe sensed that there were others present but didn't dare check. The woman kicked off the conversation. 'I'm told you want a gun as a souvenir. Maybe you do, maybe you don't. That's your affair. But before we do the deal, here are some facts to consider. Just being in possession of this firearm puts you on the wrong side of the law. Understand?'

Eyes fixed on the weapon, Joe replied, 'Yes.'

'And if the cops ask you where you got the gun and you mention Memphis, the balloon seller or this little gathering, that puts you on the wrong side of *us*. Which is a place you really don't wanna be. Do you understand?'

'If anyone asks, I found it in an alley.'

'Good. Okay, let's do business. What you are looking at is a Raven MP-25 semi-automatic.'

The weapon looked tiny. No more than five inches long by three and a quarter wide. To Joe it resembled a toy, or one of those novelty cigarette lighters.

'Pick it up if you like.'

He complied and was amazed how light it was. It crossed his mind that perhaps it *was* a toy and he was being stiffed.

'The MP-25, among other makes of a similar size, is what's known as a Saturday Night Special. Being so small, light, and easy to conceal makes them the perfect choice for every stick-up merchant in the city. Have you ever fired a gun?'

'Once,' replied Joe, fascinated by the compact object in his hand, 'when the funfair came to town. I won a coconut.'

The guffaws from the other side of the table confirmed the presence of at least two others. His cheeks blanched at how pathetic his last sentence must have sounded.

Won a coconut? Jesus. Why don't you tell them how you won a goldfish on the tombola too?

'Sounds like we got a regular John Dillinger,' mocked a raspy, gruff voice.

Once the laughs had subsided, the female talked Joe through the pistol's features and the correct way to handle it. How the magazine clipped into the grip. To make sure he heard a click, meaning it was in properly. Revealing it was made of zinc-alloy, which is why, even fully loaded, it weighed under 14oz. She went on to show him how to work the safety/fire slider with his thumb. If the safety was 'on' the gun wouldn't shoot. In conclusion, she warned him never to have the safety off when the gun was loaded unless he intended to use it, and to get as near as possible to his target because it was designed for close quarters firing. It was obvious she wasn't buying his 'want it for a souvenir' line.

'Are you happy with all that?'

'It's perfect,' he affirmed, loathe to put it down.

'Then let's talk money. The gun is one hundred dollars and a clip of six bullets is fifty, making one hundred and fifty dollars.'

He could tell by her tone that she expected him to haggle and that she was asking for way over the going rate, but it was actually less than he'd expected.

'Fine. I'll take the gun and the clip.

Before she could reply, gruff voice butted in. 'I'd say Mr Dillinger here would be willing to up it to two hundred.'

He was absolutely right; Joe would have done. But the woman, who appeared to be in charge, wasn't as greedy as her subordinate. 'No. I gave him the price and he accepted it. One hundred and fifty dollars it is.'

As the money changed hands it was apparent that her underling had taken a dislike to Joe. 'You seem pretty flush. What do you do for a job in Limeyland?'

Recalling his past life, Joe proudly stated, 'I'm a qualified electrician.'

'Oh yeah? Well, over here you're a qualified fucking moron.'

'Now, now, don't insult our guest,' reprimanded the boss.

'Come on. What else would you call someone with a pocketful of cash who lets a stranger lead him blind to a bunch of *other* strangers in a city he doesn't know?'

Put like that, the Englishman had to agree it did sound pretty moronic. Addressing Joe, his detractor warned, 'This is a dog-eat-dog city friend, and you are a fucking chihuahua.'

Slipping the MP-25 and clip into his jacket pocket Joe replied, 'Perhaps, but now I'm a chihuahua with a gun. That should make the rottweilers think twice.'

The remark earned a ripple of amusement across the table and he felt pleased with himself. Trade completed, balloon guy told him to put the glasses back on and they made the return journey to Central Park. But even with the deal done, Joe couldn't relax, fearing that his burly minder might yet relieve him of the gun and shove him under a train. Then his friends would have his hundred and fifty dollars *and* their weapon back. He was discovering that being led blindfold around a dangerous city to have dealings with criminals can make you somewhat paranoid.

On the upper terrace, at the top of the Bethesda steps, Joe was relieved of the borrowed eye wear, which his guide consigned to a nearby trash can. Without a word, balloon guy descended the steps and headed back to his pitch by the lake. As he passed Memphis, he tossed something into his guitar case. His cut, probably.

With six hours to wait until the fateful meeting, he opted to go for a stroll along the famous Fifth Avenue. Leaving the park by its south-east exit the first thing he saw was New York's answer to London's The Ritz. Only bigger. After all, this was the USA, where size really did matter. The Plaza hotel: eighteen stories high and built in the style of a French château. Definitely somewhere that *would* serve tea. Likely in china cups and saucers served on a silver tray. Opulence from a bygone age.

The next familiar name to jump out at him was Tiffany & Co. Looking in the window, Joe noticed that none of the pieces of jewellery on show had price tags. Obviously if you were concerned by cost then you really didn't belong in there. To the smartly dressed clientele going in and out, the likes of him were invisible. A snooty looking elderly lady wearing a fox fur stole and carrying a white Pekingese exited the store. Even the dog gave him a condescending look. And not a sign of Audrey Hepburn

It seemed that almost every establishment he passed was a flagship of some elite brand, including Rolex, Cartier and Gucci. A window displayed a wristwatch retailing at an eye watering $3,750. It was an impressive piece but one made of plastic with Mickey Mouse's face on the dial did exactly the same job – they both told you what time it was. But it wasn't about function, it was about status. 'Look at me. I can afford this.'

Out of the blue a weird thought came to him. He could enter any of these fancy shops, clip the magazine into the MP-25, point it at the assistant and they would give him anything he asked for, including the money from the cash register. He'd never do so, of course, but just knowing he could if he wanted to was intoxicating. At his fingertips he had the means to take any man down, regardless of their size or strength. He was starting to understand America's love affair with the gun. It was exhilarating... and somewhat alarming.

Between 51st and 50th St, looking completely out of place, was St Patrick's Cathedral. Light cream in colour and of a neo-Gothic design, its twin front spires reached for the heavens and its beautiful, ornate carvings appeared totally at odds with the straight-lined steel and glass of its overbearing neighbours. It was as if some giant hand had plucked this holy building from a more suitable, tranquil rural setting and placed it as a joke in the middle of the thoroughfare that was the very definition of consumerism. Being overshadowed on all sides by towering Lego blocks didn't detract from its beauty though. The contrast actually enhanced it. A reminder of what human beings are capable of with a little imagination.

Joe was certain the old guy he'd met in Battery Park would have been here countless times. He was tempted to enter to see if the interior was as beautiful as the outside, but he didn't think he'd be welcome in God's house. Not today.

His verdict on the Fifth Avenue clientele he'd observed? Shallow people with deep pockets. It wasn't their fault, though. They'd been conditioned and we're all products of our upbringing.

His perfectly adequate, moderately priced Swiss watch revealed it was nearly 2pm. Five hours to go.

He had no appetite to speak of but decided to grab a coffee somewhere then head back to his room to get properly acquainted with the Raven MP-25.

With his door locked he familiarised himself with the feel of the grip, his index finger poised on the trigger. His thumb joined the action. Safety on/safety off. He repeated this half a dozen times, then half a dozen more without looking. Ensuring the safety was on, he pushed the clip of bullets up into the grip until it clicked into place. Then he released it, took it out and did it again. Raising the gun to eye level, he targeted the door handle of the closet, aligning the rear sight with the one on the barrel. Accuracy wasn't really an issue as he intended to be no more than a foot away from Northbridge. A headshot.

He retrieved his remaining cash from its hiding place and counted it: $636:50c. A ten and two ones were separated and put on the bedside table to settle his bill with Sleazeball, the rest was rolled up and pushed into the front pocket of his jeans. He was hoping that when he was arrested the money might be sent back to England, but he didn't know the law on that one. Closing his eyes, he napped for half an hour so as to be alert and focused later. A wash, a shave and another hour of getting accustomed to handling the gun and he was ready.

6.p.m. The walk to W56[th] St should take around twenty-five minutes. That would give him approximately half an hour to mentally prepare himself once he arrived at Dino's. Ensuring the clip was in properly and the safety was on, he secreted the weapon in his jacket pocket and left The Liberty Belle for the last time.

CHAPTER THIRTY SIX

NOWHERE TO RUN

Wednesday June 18th. At 6.57pm the diner door opened and a muscular guy in a black t-shirt and blue jeans stepped in. Joe's pulse quickened. Early forties, six-one, broad shoulders, cropped hair; there was an air of menace about him. Not a man to take no for an answer. This might take more than one bullet. He appeared to look straight at Joe before sinking onto a stool at the counter and joining in with the banter between the cook and the regulars. False alarm. Damn.

Not one minute later, another man entered. Around the same age as the previous one, but that's where the similarities ended. This one was five foot nine, tops, and slim. His dark hair was swept back off his forehead and behind his ears. Small ears, like Joe's. The newcomer spoke to Donna, who smiled and gestured toward the serious looking young Englishman in the end booth by the window. Surely this couldn't be the predator that had taken advantage of his mother. Everything about him was... ordinary. Average height-average build. Blue zip up jacket, corduroy jeans and plain brown shoes. A very unremarkable man. Somewhat warily, the stranger approached.

'Are you Joe?'

The younger man nodded.

'I'm James Northbridge,' he affirmed, his scouse accent much more diluted than his brother's. 'May I sit down?'

The request was met by another nod and the man sat directly opposite. Joe was taken aback at how unexceptional in the flesh this figure that had loomed so large in his family's life was. Donna arrived and placed a cup of black coffee on the table.

'My oh my. You two just have to be related. Like two peas in a pod,' she declared, causing both men to look embarrassed. Apart from the ears, Joe couldn't see it. Perhaps he didn't want to.

'Just holler if you need anything,' the waitress concluded and went about her business. Cautiously, Northbridge kicked things off. 'Look, I know this must be even harder for you than it is for me, and I thank you for coming all this way.'

Joe found his tongue. 'Don't flatter yourself. It's mostly out of curiosity.'

'Well, I thank you anyway. I thought maybe I could speak first, answer any questions you have, then you say your piece. Is that alright with you?'

'I guess so.'

'Let me start by saying that I really did love Mary.'

What? For fucks sake. Shoot him now, the lying piece of shit.

'And I believe she loved me. We met at a jazz club called The Blue Note. I was a shy lad, and she was shy too; we sort of gravitated towards each other. We found we could open up to each other.'

What are you waiting for? Put one in his twisted brain.

'Mostly we'd go to the pictures or jazz clubs, but I had a motorbike in those days so sometimes we'd take a ride out to New Brighton or find a quiet spot for a picnic. All in secret of course.'

Not going to mention hauling her into the bushes in the park?

'If the weather wasn't good, which was often, we'd stay in my bedsit, listening to Miles Davies or Charlie Parker and sharing tea and toast. Getting to know one another.'

Mum was right, he's a world class liar.

One day she phoned and said she didn't want to see me anymore. I was devastated. There'd been no arguments or falling outs. The first I knew about her being pregnant was three months later when I was arrested.'

There was a look of regret in his eyes. He truly was a master actor, that was undeniable.

'When they told me the charge was rape, I was gobsmacked. She and I both knew that wasn't the case. All that stuff about pulling her into the bushes was complete rubbish. No evidence was presented, but who were the jury going to believe, the son of a docker or the daughter of a doctor? A doctor with friends in high places.'

Joe could hear his mother's voice, 'He's clever. A manipulator. He'll twist everything.'

Unable to contain himself he snarled, 'If she stitched you up like you say, then how come you don't condemn her? Or are you some latter-day saint?'

'No, I'm no saint but I'm no rapist either. The good thing about prison – the only good thing – is that you get plenty of time to think. Six years, in my case. Don't get me wrong, for the first two years I hated her for helping put me in there.'

'Don't tell me,' sneered Joe, 'you found Jesus.'

'Not quite. One of his troops: the prison chaplain. Eventually, he convinced me that if you hold a grudge, the grudge will hold you. Prevent you from moving forward. It will squeeze the life out of you if you let it. So, I tried to look at it from Mary's point of view. Seventeen is so young. I was only twenty-one myself. She must have been terrified, what with a baby on the way and her domineering father pushing her to say I'd forced myself on her.'

He's lying. Do it!

'I'm certain that *he* convinced her. Tell a lie enough times and it becomes your truth. The alternative was that she'd consented and people would think he'd raised a 'bad girl'. Whereas, if it was sexual assault she'd be absolved of all blame, his reputation would be intact and she'd still be a 'good girl'. Had she confided in me when she found out, I'd have asked her to marry me and got her away from him. But his hold over her was too strong.'

Joe had heard enough. He'd badly underestimated how convincing and believable this weasel was. Lying came as naturally as breathing to him. It was time. His hand found the grip, his thumb slipped the safety off and he raised the gun upwards from its hiding place. When the shot rang out it was hard to gauge who was more startled, Joe or the man sitting opposite.

Northbridge probably, as he was the one slumped forward with blood spurting out of his neck.

What the hell just happened? Joe was preparing to fire, but he hadn't. The MP-25 wasn't even clear of his pocket. Maybe it had discharged accidentally? There was no exit hole through his jacket pocket so he could rule that out. And the gun barrel wasn't warm. Instinctively he grabbed a napkin from the table, held it against the wound and watched it go from white to crimson in seconds. He saw that real blood is nothing like the fake blood in films or on TV. It's a brighter shade of red and thinner in consistency. With both hands he pushed the cloth into Northbridge's neck as hard as he could which seemed to help stem the flow. There was a commotion at the far end of the room, near the counter. Screaming – shouting – panic. The big guy in the black t-shirt was punching someone and wrestling them to the ground. Donna bellowed, 'Is everyone okay?'

'No,' shouted Joe, 'phone an ambulance. Now!'

The victim was trying to speak but his aide shushed him and assured, 'Help is on the way.'

The ambulance crew were there in seven minutes, which seemed like seven hours. Joe didn't ease the pressure on the napkin for a second and was relieved when a paramedic told him,

'Okay sir, we'll take over now.'

Two of them laid the semi-conscious patient on a gurney whilst a third pushed what looked like a giant tampon into the wound. Joe followed them out. As he passed Donna he felt her squeeze his arm. A cop was cuffing and dragging up the man being subdued on the floor, while his partner carefully deposited a gun similar to his own in a plastic evidence bag. So, it was *him* that fired the shot.

Outside, the gurney was loaded into the back of the waiting ambulance. When Joe went to step in, a member of the medical team stopped him, 'Only family members allowed. Are you related?'

'Yes, he's... he's my dad.'

It was the first time he'd referred to James Northbridge that way. Joe was ushered aboard, the doors closed and the sirens soundtracked their short journey to the Roosevelt Hospital on W59th St. Once there, the first responders rushed the gurney into the emergency room and through some swing doors. Joe was told he couldn't go any further and a nurse with a kind face showed him into a side room, promising a doctor would be along to see him as soon as they had any news. It was a narrow little room; six chairs placed around the walls and a low coffee table adorned with magazines in the middle. The nurse left him alone, only to reappear a few minutes later with a paper cup full of water and an oatmeal bar. He thanked her and she went back to her duties.

His adrenalin level was off the scale, and he paced around the cramped space like a caged tiger. The sound of the gunshot had acted like a hypnotist snapping their fingers to bring someone 'back in the room' and the sight of all that gushing blood had repulsed him. Would he really have gone through with it? Pulled the trigger? The possibility now made him feel nauseous and he thought he might vomit. A swig of water helped keep his stomach contents where they were.

After twenty minutes, the door opened but it wasn't a doctor, it was a uniformed cop. Shit, Joe still had the MP-25 in his pocket. Would a trained eye recognise the outline? The cop was stone-faced, stocky too. Did New York have an assembly line that churned them out?

'Hi, I'm Sgt Tauber. If you're up to it, I'd like to ask you a few questions about the shooting. It won't take long.'

'Of course.'

The officer flipped open his notebook, took out a pencil and wrote down all the information Joe could give on the patient, which, other than his name and age, wasn't much.

Home address: 'Don't know.'

Place of work: 'Don't know.'

Next of kin: 'Don't know.'

The cop gave him a quizzical look. 'I was led to believe that you're his son.'

'That's correct. But I live in England. He and my mum split up and he emigrated. Tonight is the first time I met him.'

'I see. Tough break. The paramedic said he had a wallet on him, so I'll get the information from there. Now, tell me everything you remember about the shooting.'

Joe racked his brain, trying to rewind an hour. 'We were just talking. Sitting facing each other. I heard a sharp crack and a split-second later Mr Northbridge – my father – had blood pumping out of the left side of his neck.'

Dutifully, his words were copied down.

'What exactly happened?' asked Joe.

'Well, as far as we can tell it was a botched robbery and your dad was very unlucky. A junkie pulled out a firearm, demanding cash from the register. An off-duty cop grabbed his arm and, during the tussle, the gun went off.'

'I just want him to be okay.'

'The trauma team here are second to none. And from what I hear, you did pretty well too.'

Joe smiled weakly. If the dice had landed differently, this might have been the very cop who would have handcuffed him and read him his rights.

Putting his notebook away, the lawman said, 'We may need to speak to you again. Where are you staying?'

'The Liberty Belle on...'

'Oh, I know where it is,' came the raised eyebrowed response. 'Take it easy. He's in good hands.'

Joe appreciated the officer's reassuring words, but he knew that '*We may need to speak to you again,*' meant, if the case becomes a homicide. An hour and a half went by and Joe was almost climbing the walls with frustration. Why was no-one telling him anything? Ten more slow minutes passed until the door opened and this time a doctor wearing green scrubs entered. He was middle-aged, paunchy, and wore horn rimmed glasses. Like an accountant going to a fancy-dress party.

'Hello, I'm Dr Schaffer, the vascular surgeon who attended your father.'

'How is he?'

'Weak. The bullet partially severed his left carotid artery and he lost a lot of blood. But we managed to clamp and repair it and his vital signs are stable.'

Joe breathed a sigh of relief and silently thanked God.

'Have you phoned your mother?'

Putting the young man's look of confusion down to shock, he continued, 'His wife.'

'Oh sorry. Crossed wires. I'm his son from a previous relationship. I don't know his wife. Didn't even know he was married. Tonight was our first face-to-face meeting.'

'Some first meeting, eh? Don't worry, most people carry I.D. in their wallets. The police will inform her.'

'Thanks for saving him doctor.'

'You did your part. Without your quick thinking, he'd have bled out before the ambulance got there.'

All this praise made Joe feel like a fraud. To set out with the worst of intentions and end up being hailed as a hero was uncomfortable as well as undeserving. 'I didn't know what I was doing,' he admitted, 'it was pure luck.'

'Luck or not, you did well. Listen, we gave your father some strong sedatives, so he'll be sleeping like a baby for the next ten hours. There's no point in you hanging around here so get some rest yourself and come back in the morning.'

Walking out of Roosevelt into the cool night air, Joe was struck by the irony of the situation. He'd ended up saving the life of the man he'd set out to kill. Knowing it would be futile to try and sleep, he started walking, with no idea where he was heading and caring even less. If there was any doubt that he was suffering from shock, the tremor in his right hand confirmed it. He walked and walked. Processing. Trying to make sense of what had possessed him for the past four days. Oblivious, he made left or right turns as the mood took him, the night's events churning in his head.

At the mention of The Blue Note jazz club, and the motorbike, he'd known deep down that the man talking was on the level; he just refused to acknowledge it. If the stranger across the table was telling the truth, then that made his mum the liar. A fantasist. And that was tough to accept. It was basically the story she'd told Joe when he was seventeen. Only the names and the endings were different. The mythical John Hudson had smashed his motorbike into the telegraph pole, whereas the very real James Northbridge had been thrown under the bus. Sacrificed to maintain his grandfather's reputation. What a despicable, evil thing to do to someone. And, unpalatable as it was, Joe had to concede that although his grandfather had driven the deception, his mother had been a willing passenger.

Finding himself outside a topless bar on the corner of 42nd St and 9th Ave, he decided a couple of drinks might combat the trauma. His shirt was streaked with blood but, as these places weren't big on dress code, he didn't think it would be enough to deny him admittance. Even so he buttoned up his jacket, which covered most of it. The woman sitting in the kiosk at the door looked up from her knitting long enough to take his 25c and he entered the dimly lit club. A spotlight lit up a Chinese girl wearing only a G-string and a fake smile. On a makeshift stage she gyrated, high kicked and did the splits for the salivating front row.

Seating himself at the bar, with his back to the action, Joe ordered a double brandy and downed it in one. Then he ordered another and did the same. With all his heart he hoped his dad would make a full recovery. He seemed like a thoroughly decent human being. Predictably, a seen-better-days hostess wearing too much make up was on him within a minute. 'Want some female company, handsome?'

'Yes, but she's three thousand miles away.'

'Well, *I'm* here. Are you going to buy me a drink?'

'Okay. As long as you don't talk to me.'

'It's your dollar, sugar.'

Unsurprisingly, she chose the most expensive drink on offer at an exorbitant price. He didn't mind, though; it was nice to sit with another human being while he took his time over his third double, even if they didn't speak. When he stood up to leave, he handed the hostess a ten dollar bill and asked, 'Would you give me a hug? I could really do with a hug.'

She took the money, hugged him and patted him lightly on the back. He thanked her and hit the streets again. At the very least, the alcohol had relaxed him enough to stop his hand shaking. It was pointless going back to his room while he was so tightly wound, so once again he walked aimlessly until he found himself staring into the inky black waters of a wide river. It had to be either The East River or The Hudson but he didn't know which. The night sky was cloudy which gave this dilapidated section of shore an even eerier feel. The deserted waterfront was lined with old warehouses and a few rundown businesses like 'Jake Myers-Discount Tires'. An arrow painted on a wooden signpost pointed the way to Pier 91.

Deciding that he hadn't ended up here by accident, Joe knew what he'd been guided here to do. The MP-25 made a plopping sound as it pierced the water's surface and disappeared. Hopefully, that particular sinew of the devil's right hand would never see the light of day again. The night was taking on a chill and the brandies were wearing off, so he turned his jacket collar up and headed off to look for a street sign. Once he was back on the grid system he could get his bearings. Movement caught his eye. From the shadows of the warehouse in front of him emerged three ominous figures. They were human but their features were obscured by the darkness. Joe turned to walk the other way but there were three more. He had nowhere to go except into the river, but that wasn't really an option as he was a weak swimmer so would almost certainly drown.

With close to six hundred dollars on him, these faceless thugs were about to hit the jackpot. He knew he was in for a severe beating, or worse, and his only bargaining chip was on its way to the riverbed. Bizarrely, dread soon turned to calm acceptance. He deserved everything coming his way after the terrible thing he'd almost done. Paolo and Lilah came to the forefront of his mind. He'd locked them in a room deep in the inner sanctum of his brain when he made the decision to kill James Northbridge. Imprisoned and isolated them, as he knew they'd try and talk him out of it. Now he had set them free but they couldn't help him. No one could.

Oh Lilah, I've really fucked everything up, haven't I?

The Strawberry Moon peeped through the clouds and glinted off a metal pipe one of the figures was holding. A Hunter's Moon would have been more fitting; with Joe as the prey. This was going to be bad. If they were going to kill him, he hoped it would be quick. Then, from around the corner, the beam from a car's headlights illuminated the tarmac. In this urban desert it could only mean more gang members had turned up. But in fact, what had arrived was the cavalry, in the wonderful form of a blue and white police cruiser. The sinister figures melted back into the shadows as quickly and silently as they'd appeared. The squad car glided over to the solitary pedestrian and stopped. The passenger side window rolled down and a torch shone in his face, blinding him.

'May I ask what you're doing here, sir?'

'I couldn't sleep,' explained Joe, 'so I thought I'd take a walk.'

'Along the Hell's Kitchen stretch of the Hudson in the early hours of the morning? Are you fucking nuts?'

Not anymore, thought Joe, although he actually said, 'I just wanted to clear my head.'

'Walking alone in this part of the city, you're more likely to get a cracked head than a clear one.'

He was relieved when the light left his face and travelled down his body until the cop's voice took on a new urgency. 'Is that blood on your shirt?'

'Yes.'

'Is it yours?'

'No, it's my dad's.' It still felt weird to say the word.

The passenger door opened and the officer slowly stepped out, with one hand holding the flashlight on the young man and the other hovering over his holster. 'Keep your hands where I can see them,' he commanded. Joe obeyed, holding both hands palms out in front of him.

'What happened to your father?'

'He was shot earlier in Big Dino's Diner on West 56th Street. I was with him.'

Joe noticed the cop nod to the driver, who got straight on the radio mic.

'Okay, tell me what happened at Dino's.'

'An attempted robbery they say. The robber scuffled with an off-duty cop, the gun went off and a bullet hit my dad in the neck. He's at Roosevelt hospital. That's why I couldn't sleep.'

'What his name?'

'James Northbridge.'

Turning to the open car window the inquisitor asked his partner, 'Did you get all that?'

With his attention back on Joe he ordered, 'Don't make any sudden moves and keep your hands where they are. My colleague is just checking what you've told me is true. Meantime, I'm just gonna pat you down before asking you to turn out your pockets, so stay calm.'

Relief flooded over Joe that he'd got rid of the gun. The search proved fruitless but when the young tourist pulled out his wad of cash the policeman's eyes widened.

'How much do you have there?'

'Around six hundred dollars.'

Shaking his head in disbelief, the officer muttered, 'On the waterfront in Hell's Kitchen, after midnight, carrying six hundred bucks. Next to the word "stupid" in the dictionary should be a mugshot of *you*.'

After a tense couple of minutes, a voice from the car's interior said, 'Checks out.'

Satisfied, his partner's hand moved away from the holster and he visibly relaxed.

'Is that an English accent?'

'Yes sir, I'm on a five-day trip.'

'Weren't you given a pamphlet at JFK?'

'Yes. Fear City.'

'"Fear City", son. The clue is in the name. Did you not think it applied to you?'

'I just wasn't thinking straight.'

'Ain't that the truth. Where are you staying?'

'The Liberty Belle,' revealed Joe, correctly guessing what the reaction would be.

'High roller, eh?' mocked the driver, before adding, 'Get in, we'll give you a ride back.'

The grateful young man didn't need asking twice. In the safe haven of the back seat he realised that this was the latest in the litany of ironies this night had thrown up. He'd been certain that the day would end with him in police custody but, instead of carting him off to a cell, they were dropping him off at his digs – not that there was much difference. His transport pulled up outside The Liberty Belle and the passenger cop let him out. The driver shouted to his partner, 'Do you realise, this is the first time we've been to this dump without making an arrest?'

Joe shook both their hands warmly and thanked them for coming to his rescue.

'Go to bed, kid. Lock your door and sleep with one hand on your bankroll. Hope your old man recovers well.'

'Thanks again,' repeated the young Englishman, fully aware what a lucky escape he'd had.

CHAPTER THIRTY SEVEN

REFLECTIONS

When Joe opened his eyes, he was lying on the bed with his jacket over him, fully clothed apart from the blood-stained shirt, which he'd thrown in the waste bin under the sink. Sleep was intermittent but at least he'd had some, of sorts. His watch read 9am. Wanting to be at the hospital between 10 and 10.30, he washed, cleaned his teeth and pulled on fresh underwear, t-shirt and jeans. Everything else he tossed in his holdall, checking that his passport and airline ticket were still in the separate zipped pocket.

When he checked out, as well as settling his bill and handing over the key to 'The Burton Suite', he stunned Sleazeball by giving him a ten dollar tip. His expression indicated that he'd never been tipped before, and probably never would be again, but Joe felt like a death row prisoner who'd got a last-minute reprieve and felt goodwill to all men. Even this one. As the departing guest neared the door he heard, 'I hope you'll recommend us to your friends in England.'

'If I did, they wouldn't be my friends for long,' came the cheery answer, just before Joe stepped out into the fresh, morning air. His rumbling stomach verified how hungry he was, having not eaten the previous day (One oatmeal bar doesn't count). Ducking into the first delicatessen he chanced upon, he ate two bacon baguettes and half a dozen pancakes covered in maple syrup, washed down with a large cappuccino.

The yellow cab dropped him outside the hospital at 10.35 and the receptionist gave him directions to his father's room. The door was open and he was pleasantly surprised to see James sitting up in bed. Even more unexpected was the sight of the dark-haired woman sitting with a miniature version of herself by his side. Standing in the doorway he hesitated, not wanting to intrude, but the woman spotted him and waved him in. His father smiled weakly. He was wired up to various monitors and looked groggy, drawn and pale. Who wouldn't in the circumstances? White surgical gauze was taped over his wound. Now, looking through unbiased eyes, Joe could see glimpses of himself in his father. Slim build, dark hair, similar face shape, identical ears. Unsure what to say, the newest visitor was pleased when James croaked, 'Chrissie, this is Joe.'

The woman, who looked in her late thirties, walked over to the reticent young man and threw her arms around him. 'Thank you, so, so much.'

'She knows all about you,' said his dad. 'Everything.'

Not quite everything, thought Joe, once more feeling like an impostor.

Walking him over to the bed, Chrissie said to the curious seven-year-old child holding her dad's hand, 'Leanne, meet your brother, Joe.'

Her wide, innocent eyes lit up. 'I have a brother?' she enthused. As she studied the stranger, her brow knitted. 'But he's a grown up.'

Everyone was amused, which caused her to pout until her mother assured her, 'I'll explain later.'

However, her daughter needed more information. 'Is he going to live with us?'

'No honey, his home is in England, where daddy used to live.'

'New England?' asked the girl.

'No. Old England,' smiled Joe, 'a long way away.'

'He can always come visit, though. If he wants to,' offered her mum.

Joe felt sick to the stomach that he was a twitch of his index finger away from robbing this delightful pair of a husband and father they clearly both adored. Turning his attention to the fragile looking patient, he asked, 'How are you feeling?'

'Like I've been shot,' came the honest reply. 'Listen, don't be too hard on your mother. It was a different time.'

Joe was humbled by such magnanimity. This man, who had every reason to be filled with hatred and bitterness chose not to be, and he was proud that they shared the same bloodline.

'I never got a chance to ask; what is it you do for a living?' enquired James.

'I'm an electrician.'

'No way,' he exclaimed, 'me too!'

'He learned while he was in Strangeways,' chipped in Chrissie, who was plainly in possession of all the facts regarding her husband's back story. How lovely that he could be so honest with her.

An apologetic nurse poked her head in and announced, 'Sorry folks but he's been through a lot and he needs to rest now. You can come back between six and eight this evening.'

I can't, I'll be somewhere over The Atlantic, thought Joe.

His final words, for now, to his father were, 'You've got my address and phone number. Keep me in the picture. I want to stay in touch.'

'You bet. I lost you once, I won't let it happen again.'

Crouching down, Joe pulled a fifty dollar bill from his pocket and held it out to Leanne.

'Get yourself something from me.'

The girl looked to her mum for permission to accept it and a little nod told her she could.

'Wow! Fifty dollars. I'm rich. Thank you, Joe.'

'You're welcome. That's what big brothers are for.'

Standing up, once again he accepted Chrissie's outstretched arms and, as they shared a farewell hug, she whispered, 'You have no idea what finally meeting you means to him.'

'It means a lot to me too.'

As he left the room he turned his head and filed away the image of the three of them huddled together. He was certain this wasn't the last time he'd see them. On the ground floor he came across a payphone. A digital wall clock showed the time to be 11.05am. That would be just after 4pm in Watford.

'David, it's me. How is she?'

'Hi Joe. A little better. She came home yesterday. They're now thinking she had some sort of nervous breakdown. I made her egg on toast for lunch and she ate most of it.'

'That's good. You've been a real star. Sorry I haven't been around to help.'

'Oh, one thing; she said if you phoned to tell you she's sorry.'

Joe felt a lump in his throat as he replied, 'You tell her that I met with James Northbridge and everything is fine. Absolutely fine. You tell her. And give her my love.'

'I will. Be good to see you. When are you home?'

'Early hours of tomorrow, UK time. Everything is going to be alright, David. I promise.'

He said his goodbyes, hung up and wiped the moisture from his eyes. On a whim he decided he wanted to see Memphis one more time so used his last dime to phone a cab whose card was pinned on the wall above the phone.

From the other side of the Bethesda Fountain, Joe could hear Memphis singing the Joni Mitchell song, "Both Sides Now". He stopped, closed his eyes and just listened. It was lovely. Sometimes all you need is a voice and a guitar. Like everything else good in his life, Joe's love of music had got lost in the darkness that had descended on him. But it was back now. *He* was back. He waited until the song finished before making himself known.

'Hi. Are you due a break?'

'I'll ask.'

Turning his eyes to the heavens, the busker pleaded, 'Well Lord, are you ever gonna give me a break?'

Along with the dozen or so people in earshot, Joe laughed. Memphis gratefully accepted the can of soda from him and asked, 'Are you sure you ain't after my ass?'

He took a swig and said, 'Let's go for a walk, I need to stretch my leg.'

Guitar and crutches in place, they followed one of the winding paths that leads deeper into the park.

'When are you flying out?'

'Soon as I leave here.'

Gesturing at the holdall Joe was carrying, his companion asked, 'And is your 'souvenir' in there?'

'No. I changed my mind. It's at the bottom of The Hudson.'

'Best place for it. Goddamn things.'

An attractive blonde in her early twenties walked toward them, wearing a flowery summer dress and sandals. 'Good morning, Memphis,' she beamed.

'Morning sweetness. You look beautiful today. Like you stepped out of a Monet painting.'

'You southern charmer,' she chuckled.

'Guilty as charged,' he replied, his theatrical bow causing his top hat to fall off and roll onto the grass. Quickly retrieving it he observed, 'Well, *that* never happens in the movies.'

She was still laughing as she neared the bend in the path, the mid-day sun lighting up her long, golden hair. As the duo watched, the American sighed and posed a rhetorical question. 'Is there anything finer in this whole, wide world than a pretty girl on a sunny day?'

'Not that I can think of,' was Joe's truthful answer.

'You got a girl back home, English?'

'I hope so. It's complicated.'

'In matters of the heart, it always is, my friend. It always is.'

'What about you, do you have anyone?'

'Not any *one*, no. But there are several ladies that are happy to welcome me into their boudoirs, on occasion.'

Joe could see that the incline of the path, together with the heat, was affecting Memphis, confirmed when the American suggested, 'Let's sit awhile.'

They utilised a nearby bench. Joe could only imagine the effort it took to get around on crutches. Memphis took out the tiny transparent box of tic-tacs, flipped the lid and necked a few.

'I'd offer you a couple but they're actually painkillers. Another legacy of my trip to the land of the blue dragon.'

Cautiously, Joe ventured, 'Wouldn't an artificial limb make life easier for you?'

'Without a doubt. I tried one but I couldn't get on with it.'

'What a about a wheelchair?'

'No sir,' bristled the Tennessean, 'I ain't spending the rest of my life in no Goddamn chair.'

Joe said nothing. What could he say?'

Two black girls in school uniform passed by. They looked mid-teens. Both sported impressive afros, the taller one wearing glasses. 'Hi Memphis,' greeted the girl without the glasses.

'Good day, ladies. Study hard now. Knowledge is king. Oh, and Elvis of course.'

They giggled and ambled on, enjoying the sunshine; their happy young faces in stark contrast to the girl he'd seen in Times Square on his first day. A desperate look he hoped never to see again. He decided to share the memory with Memphis. 'When I first arrived here, I went for a walk to try and stay awake. Ended up in Times Square.'

'Ah, Disneyland for degenerates.'

'There was this girl,' continued Joe, 'Tiny girl. Looked even younger than those two.'

'A hooker?'

Joe had seen enough American cop shows to be familiar with the term. He nodded. 'She looked terrified.

Like a deer caught in headlights. And I remember thinking, "What is she doing here?" I mean, I knew what she was *doing*, but why? What attracted her to New York?'

'Same thing that attracts all of us, I guess. It's exciting. It's alive. It's a monster. Blink and it'll fucking eat ya.'

It was kind of an explanation, but not one the Englishman could truly comprehend. After the dangers he'd faced, admittedly mostly self-inflicted, safe and sedate seemed a much more appealing choice. Somewhere like... well, sleepy old Watford, Herts. His watch told him it was time to leave this free spirit whose company he'd enjoyed so much and think about getting to the airport. How the hell would he explain Memphis to the folks back home and do him justice?

'I have to go. Check in will be open soon.'

They made their way back to Bethesda Terrace and it's dried up fountain. Joe watched the singer prepare for his next set, getting himself comfortable and adjusting the tuning on his cherished Gibson J-106.

'It's been great to meet you, Memphis.'

'Well, it was good to meet you too, English. Go get that girl.'

'I'll try. Maybe our paths will cross again someday.'

'I doubt it. But that's fine. They crossed once.'

As Joe walked away, Memphis performed Paul Simon's "Homeward Bound", and he knew it was for him.

As his 747 prepared to take to the skies, he reflected on his crazy, surreal New York adventure. Events dictated that he never did get to visit "Grooves" in Harlem. Sometimes things just don't pan out the way you plan them. And thank God for that. A shudder went through him as, once again, he dwelt on how close he'd come to taking an innocent man's life and ruining many others, including his own. What was he thinking? Well, truth be told he *wasn't* thinking. Blind hatred had suppressed all reason. Negated rational thought. He could only describe it as 'temporary madness', and not another living soul need know about it. It was too shameful. Life had dealt him some good cards and he'd almost thrown his hand in. Incredibly, in the shape of a stray bullet from a stranger's gun, fate had gifted him a second chance and he wasn't going to waste it.

The captain's voice asked that all passengers fasten their seat belts.

With that wiseness beyond her years, Lilah was absolutely right when she had said it's not important who it is that makes you, it's what you make of yourself. Yet Joe couldn't help being pleased that he had been created out of love, not violence. Naive, doomed love, but love all the same. Nigel too had been partially right; his stepson wasn't Joe Hudson, nor Joe Holland, but he wasn't Joe Rapeseed either. He was Joe Northbridge, and that was the surname he'd be proudly using from now on.

Back in England there were friendships to be rekindled, as well as finding a job. There was also a difficult conversation to be had with his mother. But that is what it would be, a conversation *not* a confrontation. As gently as he could, he'd tell her that he knew the truth; he understood, James forgave her, and she could finally lay down that burden of guilt that must have been like carrying a rucksack full of bricks around for all those years.

The cabin lights dimmed.

He was looking forward to sleeping in his own bed. Before taking him home though, his cab from Heathrow would have a short detour to make, to the Massetti house. Joe had a postcard to slip through the letterbox. It was addressed to Miss Lilah Massetti. On the front was a close up of the Statue of Liberty. And on the back he had written:

I'm home. My turn. Chartbusters Volume Five. Side two. Track one.

I love you,

Joe xx

Then he would leave it to Stevie Wonder to give her his message – "Signed, Sealed, Delivered (I'm Yours)".

CHAPTER DISCOGRAPHY

1. "UNFINISHED BUSINESS": THE BLACKBYRDS
2. "MOVE ON UP": CURTIS MAYFIELD
3. "RESPECT YOURSELF": THE STAPLE SINGERS
4. "YESTER-ME, YESTER-YOU, YESTERDAY": STEVIE WONDER
5. "BE YOUNG, BE FOOLISH, BE HAPPY": THE TAMS
6. "SWEET SOUL MUSIC": ARTHUR CONLEY
7. "IT'S ALL IN THE GAME": THE FOUR TOPS
8. "A CHANGE IS GONNA COME": SAM COOKE
9. "YOU CAN'T HIDE FROM YOURSELF": TEDDY PENDERGRASS
10. "LOVE CHILD": DIANA ROSS & THE SUPREMES
11. "HELP ME MAKE IT THROUGH THE NIGHT": GLADYS KNIGHT & THE PIPS
12. "SHOP AROUND": THE MIRACLES
13. "SOUL SISTER, BROWN SUGAR": SAM & DAVE
14. "BEHIND A PAINTED SMILE": THE ISLEY BROTHERS
15. "LET THE GOOD TIMES ROLL": RUFUS THOMAS
16. "IF IT FEELS GOOD, DO IT": DELLA REECE
17. "THIN LINE BETWEEN LOVE AND HATE": THE PERSUADERS
18. "LOVE IS HERE AND NOW YOU'RE GONE": THE SUPREMES
19. "I'M IN A DIFFERENT WORLD": THE FOUR TOPS
20. "LOVE THE ONE YOU'RE WITH": THE ISLEY BROTHERS

21. "MONEY (THAT'S WHAT I WANT)": BARRETT STRONG
22. "THE IN CROWD": DOBIE GRAY
23. "FAMILY AFFAIR": SLY & THE FAMILY STONE
24. "TELL IT LIKE IT IS": AARON NEVILLE
25. "BALL OF CONFUSION": THE TEMPTATIONS
26. "PICK UP THE PIECES": AVERAGE WHITE BAND
27. "READY OR NOT HERE I COME": THE DELFONICS
28. "STAND BY ME": BEN E. KING
29. "MAMA TOLD ME NOT TO COME": WILSON PICKETT
30. "KEEP ON PUSHING": THE IMPRESSIONS
31. "NEW YORK CITY LIFE": TONY WILSON
32. "TROUBLE MAN": MARVIN GAYE
33. "I SHALL BE RELEASED": NINA SIMONE
34. "TIME IS TIGHT": BOOKER T & THE MG'S
35. "WALK IN THE NIGHT": JR WALKER & THE ALL STARS
36. "NOWHERE TO RUN": MARTHA AND THE VANDELLAS
37. "REFLECTIONS": DIANA ROSS & THE SUPREMES

www.ingramcontent.com/pod-product-compliance
Ingram Content Group UK Ltd.
Pitfield, Milton Keynes, MK11 3LW, UK
UKHW011301280725
7110UKWH00029B/190

9 781836 152538